Death Runs in the Family

Heather Haven

The Wives of Bath Press

www.heatherhavenstories@gmail.com

Death Runs in the Family © 2012 by Heather Haven

The Wives of Bath Press
5512 Cribari Bend
San Jose, Ca 95135

http:// www.heatherhavenstories@gmail.com

Print ISBN 978-0988408609 (The Wives of Bath Press)
eBook ISBN 978-1-77127-069-4 (MuseItUp Publishing)
First eBook edition May 31, 2012

Praise For The Series

♥ "Heather Haven makes a stellar debut in *Murder is a Family Business*. With an engaging protagonist and a colorful cast, Haven provides a fresh voice in a crowded genre. We will be hearing more from this talented newcomer. Highly recommended." **Sheldon Siegel. New York Times Best Selling Author of** *Perfect Alibi.*

♥ *A Wedding to Die For* "Wonderfully fresh and funny!" **- Meg Waite Clayton, Author of** *The Race For Paris*

♥"I Just finished *Death Runs in the Family* and I loved it! This has turned out to be one of my favorite series and I sure hope there will be another installment in the near future!" **Becky Carbone, Director Global Ebook Awards**

♥ *DEAD....If Only* "There is so much action packed into this book. The characters are terrific. I loved all of them. I will definitely be going back to start at the beginning!" **Linda Strong, Mystery Readers Book Club**

♥ *The CEO Came DOA* "This is a strong work in the genre of the mystery/thriller!" **San Francisco Book Review**

♥ *The Culinary Art of Murder* "This latest installment of Haven's murder mystery series offers a twisty whodunit laced with a healthy dose of suspense. A solidly entertaining mystery." **Kirkus Reviews**

Acknowledgments

I would like to thank Baird Lloyd for her help with the dos and don'ts of footraces and Charlotte (Charly) Taylor for her Spanish language expertise. Both these women not only make me look better, but help me to write a more accurate book for the reader. I am grateful.

Dedication

This book is dedicated to my mother, Mary Lee; husband, Norman Meister; and families everywhere, every type. To love and be loved is to be part of a family in the best sense of the word. This book is also dedicated to my writing buddies, in particular, Baird Nuckolls, whose expertise in all things holds me in good stead. Further, it is dedicated to my friends, bother writers and nonwriting friends, who help me write to the best of my ability, be truthful, and entertaining.
I love you all.

Death Runs in the Family

Book Three

in

The Alvarez Family

Murder Mystery Series

Heather Haven

Table of Contents

Chapter One

Another Mrs. Papadopoulos?

I threw back the covers and staggered to my front door, commanded by the insistent ringing of the doorbell. Ordinarily, after the night I'd had and it being eight o'clock in the morning, on a Sunday no less, I would have just let it ring, hoping whoever it was would go away or fall into a sinkhole. But this ringer wouldn't stop, and the bell sounded more and more like an air-raid siren to my hungover eardrums.

My name is Liana Alvarez. Everyone calls me Lee except my mother, and the less said about that the better. My email reads Lee.Alvarez.PI@DI.com, but I don't always respond in a timely fashion, especially when I'm in the middle of a case. DI stands for Discretionary Inquiries, the family-owned investigative service, and everybody knows what a PI is. I'm thirty-four years old, five foot eight, 135 pounds on a good day, with thick, brown-black hair. The love of my life, the gorgeous Gurn Hanson, says my eyes remind him of deep blue sea. At the moment, however, they resembled a beady-eyed hippo's.

The previous night, Lila Hamilton-Alvarez, mother and CEO, fobbed off a last-minute job on me, one not so good for my California lifestyle. Due to our close relationship, my designer-clad mom knows she can do this.

So instead of being at home playing with my cat and sucking down a mango-orange-guava yogurt shake, I was imbibing huge amounts of tequila slammers.

This slamming was in an effort to get the tipsy girlfriend of a software thief to reveal where he'd gotten to. Said girlfriend dished, but my liver will never be the same.

Me being about as hard-boiled as a two-minute egg, the following morning found me sleep deprived, alcohol poisoned, and feeling enormously sorry for myself. But I still remembered to look out the peephole instead of throwing open the door because LH Alvarez did not raise a stupid child. Not seeing anyone, I leaned against the framework in a hangover-induced quandary. Was someone there or not?

But the ringing continued, so shrill and loud that it had to be an affirmative unless my front door's electrical system had gone wiggy. I squinted into the little round circle of glass again, strained my eyeball downward, and spied what looked like the back of a curly, platinum blonde, female head. I left the chain on when I opened the door because my mother did not raise… never mind.

Facing away from me, the blonde female continued to lean into my doorbell for all she was worth, oblivious to my presence. A serious shrimp, she wore a pair of fire-engine red spike heels and still didn't clear much over five foot two. Looking pretty harmless unless she came at me with one of those six-inch spikes, I undid the chain and opened the door.

"All right, all right. I'm here. Get off the bell."

Startled, red stilettos wheeled around and faced me. "Hi," she said in a voice with no bottom to it, reminiscent of Marilyn Monroe, but not nearly as sexy. "I was beginning to think you weren't here."

As self-confident as her body language had been earlier, she seemed to become unsure of herself, shy almost.

Although how anyone could pull off shyness in that getup I'll never know. The killer heels were a perfect complement to the red satin miniskirt, scanter than a Dallas cheerleader's costume, and the plunging neckline of the yellow-and-green floral blouse emphasized cleavage aplenty. A thin, black polyester sweater, way too small, was buttoned haphazardly below her breasts.

Clanking gewgaws hung from her ears, neck, wrists, and fingers. She looked like a walking display case of gaudy jewelry. Before me, stood a young lady who could send any self-respecting fashionista screaming into the night.

"You're Lee, right?" she said in a barely audible voice.

"That's me," I croaked and tried to clear my throat, which didn't do much good. "And you are?"

"Why, I'm Kelli, with an 'i.'" The name was pronounced as if it should mean something to me.

She waited a beat, expectantly.

I was clueless.

"Kelli with an 'i'?" Although in my condition, it came out more like "Kawawaya?"

"Yes, Kelli. With an 'i.'"

There was the pause again.

She stared at me as if me not knowing who she was made me too stupid to live. I stared back in complete agreement. I think I hiccupped.

"Nick's wife," she said, in a manner reserved for the slow of mind.

"Nick's wife?" I stuttered.

I only knew one Nick, and that was a Nick I'd divorced four years prior with joy in my heart and a gun in my hand. "When you say, 'Nick's wife,' you don't mean, Nick Papadopoulos, as in my Nick or rather my ex-Nick, by way of being my ex-husband, Nick? You're talking about someone else, right? Another Nick I can't quite place…"

My voice trailed off because she was nodding in the affirmative every time I said his name.

"You're Nick's wife?"

She nodded again just as Tugger, my adolescent orange-and-white cat, came out of the bedroom and trotted down the hallway followed by my boyfriend's gray-and-white Persian mix, Baba Ganoush, named for the eggplant dish. My boyfriend, Gurn, was in Washington DC, and I was cat sitting this darling little green-eyed girl until his return.

Baba entered quietly, but Tugger caterwauled the entire time, obviously complaining about being awoken at such an ungodly hour of the morning. He sauntered over, sat down in front of me, stared up at this Kewpie doll of an intruder, and gave a long, wide-mouthed yawn. My sentiments exactly.

Kelli looked down. "What a beautiful cat," she exclaimed, not seeing Baba who was hiding discreetly behind my legs. Then the girl/woman extended both arms out to Tugger.

Without further ado, my traitorous feline leapt into her open arms, snuggled in, and began to purr almost as loudly as he yowls. There was nothing left for me to do. I opened the door wider and stood aside.

"All rightie. You'd better come in, Kelli, and bring the cat with you. He's not allowed outside." I bent down and picked up Baba, who rewarded me with her own yawn.

"What's his name?"

"Rum Tum Tugger, but we call him Tugger. This one is Baba. She's a friend's cat."

"What a darling cat," she cooed, walking over the threshold and into my home. "And I just love your name, Tugger," she said, rubbing noses with my little guy.

"Go straight down the hallway and turn to the right. That's the kitchen."

"What an awesome place. Who would have thought such a hot apartment would be over a garage?" Kelli tottered down the hall chatting away, while I bent over to pick up the morning paper. Barely able to straighten up, I set Baba down, afraid I'd drop her. I needed coffee bad.

"And whose house is in front? Or should I say, mansion?"

"My mother and uncle live there. Back in the thirties, this apartment was for the chauffeur. I've done it over."

"Lucky you."

"Yup, lucky me."

With a throbbing head, I traipsed behind Kelli, my eyes riveted on her foot action in those heels. It was nothing short of remarkable. Even Baba seemed impressed.

"I like your kitchen." Continuing the review of my two-bedroom, one-bath digs, she scrutinized the backsplash. "Those tiles French? I know they use a lot of yellow and blue in France. I read it once in a book."

I wasn't going to touch that statement with a ten-foot pole. "No, Talavera from Mexico. I hauled them back on one of my trips to Dolores Hidalgo."

"Neat," she murmured, now looking up at my ceiling. "What's that?" Kelli slowly spun in place studying the large inverse teacup-shaped dome set in the center of the terracotta ceiling.

"It's called a cupola."

"What's it for?"

"See the series of small glass windows at the top? Not only do you get extra light, but you can open them with this pole for fresh air." I pointed to an eight-foot pole languishing in a nearby corner, while I wondered which kitchen cabinet held the aspirin.

"Cool." Kelli focused again on Tugger, rocking him back and forth in her arms and cooing in a bilious tone of voice.

With the *House & Garden* tour over, I slipped around her, threw the paper on the counter, and reached for the coffeepot with a not-too-steady hand. I poured water into it and counted out scoops, suddenly aware the cooing had changed to sobs.

I turned, scoop in hand, and saw Kelli crying into Tugger's lustrous fur, something I've been known to do myself. Tugger reached out and caressed her face with a soft paw, purring his head off. A true gentleman my Tugger. Even Baba sat at Kelli's feet looking up, emerald eyes large with concern.

I clicked the coffeepot on and let it do its thing while I did mine.

"Sit down, Kelli, and tell me what's wrong." I put my arm around a shoulder and guided her to one of the cobalt-blue chairs gathered around my kitchen table.

Kelli snuffled and wiped at her runny nose with the hand that wasn't wrapped around a cat.

I slapped a paper napkin from the holder into said hand and chucked Tugger under the chin. He was a good boy.

Kelli blew her nose and started talking. I couldn't hear or understand a word.

"Kelli, you'll have to speak up and not just a little."

Whether she was embarrassed, or something else was on her mind, she started playing with Tugger's tail, something he can't stand, so I took her hand, shook it, and made her look up at me.

"What is it?"

Kelli snuffled again, and a large tear ran down a painted cheek. "He told me if I was in trouble, and he wasn't around, I was to come to you."

"Who told you that?"

"Nick."

"Nick said that?"

She nodded. I was shocked but tried not to show it. This was the ex-marine who started cheating on me soon after the honeymoon and who beat me up when I finally confronted him. He was the main reason I got a black belt in karate, to protect myself from his unwanted attentions before and after the divorce. When I flattened him one day, he got the message and left me alone. But I still breathed a sigh of relief when I found out he'd moved to Las Vegas and married someone else, someone currently sitting in my kitchen blowing her nose into one of my paper napkins.

"So where is Nick?"

Her voice nearly gave out on this one. "I don't know." She cleared her throat and began to speak louder. "He's been missing for a week. That's why I'm here."

"Forgive me, Kelli. I'm not quite getting this." I smelled the coffee, got up, poured some into a mug, and took a good, scalding gulp before I turned back to her.

"Coffee?" I offered. She shook her head and wiped another tear away. "If he's missing in Las Vegas, why are you here in Palo Alto?" I started opening cabinet doors, searching for the errant bottle of aspirin.

"Because last night I found this on the doorstep." She reached inside her blouse — I didn't think anything else could fit in there — and pulled out a crumpled envelope. "I got into the car and drove most of the night to get here. I've been waiting in your driveway since around five thirty this morning." She thrust the packet at me.

I stopped my search for aspirin, sat down, took the small, square-shaped envelope, and looked inside. A man's gold wedding ring looked back at me. My PI mind kicked in, albeit if only on one-and-a-half cylinders.

"Is this Nick's?"

She nodded, pursing her lips together.

"Was he wearing it the last time you saw him?"

She nodded again.

"Was there anything else inside the envelope?"

This time she shook her head. I could see this was going to be more or less a one-sided conversation.

"Have you been to the police?"

She looked at me as if I'd suggested we eat the cat she cuddled in her arms.

"I can't go to the cops." This time her voice was loud and clear.

"Why not? It's what they're there for, among other things. We pay them to find missing people. I don't mean to sound like a poster child but I am a big believer in using natural resources."

"You don't understand." Her voice became small and childlike again.

"Then enlighten me."

"Nick has been... we've been... there have been some money problems ever since he had to close the office..." She stopped speaking, sobbed, and buried her head again in Tugger. Looking a little soggy and cramped, my boy had apparently had enough and pushed free of her grasp. He hopped down from her lap and sauntered off toward the bedroom with a careless flip of his long, graceful tail. Baba followed, giving a toss of her luxuriant tail for good measure.

Maybe if I'd had a tail, I'd have done the same thing. But I didn't, so I stayed put.

In that instant, I reevaluated Kelli's persona. Once you got past a face looking like it had been drawn upon by the more colorful contents of a crayon box, she was quite pretty, with a gorgeous kind of coloring that takes your breath away. I'd put her hair down to Clairol's finest but reconsidered. It was a natural pale blonde. Her eyes, huge and round, were the bluest blue I've seen outside a Paul Newman movie, even when red-rimmed and surrounded by running black mascara. Barely out of her teens, there was a residual sweetness to her that bad taste had yet to tarnish.

Still, she was absolutely everything my classy, conservative, and well-bred mother would find appalling. Lila Hamilton-Alvarez's idea of bad taste hovers around the lines of an art gallery showcasing Andy Warhol's work. I just had to get Mom and Kelli together one of these days. Then stand back and watch.

"So tell me about Nick," I said, getting up for a second cup of coffee. "He's a real estate agent or something?" I noticed I could move my eyebrows again. Things were looking up.

"He's what they call a broker. And he was good. We had lots of money, even after the recession. He bought me a new Mercedes convertible for my birthday. Yellow. But something happened, and he had to close the office. And oh, I don't know, everything fell apart about six weeks ago."

"How so?" I said, resuming my search for aspirin.

"Bills were piling up. We got behind in our mortgage payments. We had to sell my car." She shook her head. "He wouldn't let me go back to work either. I offered, but Nick said no."

"What type of work did you do?" Bingo! I found the aspirin bottle hiding behind the sugar.

"I was a blackjack dealer at the Royal Flush Casino. That's how I met Nick." A fleeting smile crossed her lips for the first time: I guess at the memory.

"You don't look old enough." I crammed three pills in my mouth, took a slug of coffee, and sat back down.

"I'm twenty-two. I'll be twenty-three in a couple of months." I realized I was the same age when I married Nick. Glad to see I was part of a pattern here.

"Then he went to work for a bank as a courier or something, I could never figure out what, but when I asked him…"

Her voice faded out. Maybe she was talking; maybe she wasn't. I couldn't tell. I waited. She reached out a hand and touched one of mine. Still looking down at the floor, she began to pour her heart out, loud and clear.

"Nick told me you were the best thing that ever happened to him."

I blanched. *What kind of man makes a statement like that to a current wife about his ex?*

"Nick said if anything happened to him, I was to come to you. He said you're the only person in the world he trusts."

I froze. *What is the matter with the man?*

"He also said you were the most beautiful woman he'd ever seen."

Okay, it's official. The man's a bozo.

She looked up at me with appraisal in her eyes. "I guess I can see why he'd think that," she said, her baby voice riddled with doubt.

"Now wait a minute." I checked out my reflection in the stainless steel toaster and ran fast fingers through hair looking like it had been combed with an eggbeater. "I usually look a little better," I said with a feckless laugh that sounded like the death rattle of a soot-clogged moped. "I've had a tough night. I was up until two thirty knocking back margaritas and tequila shooters with the girlfriend of a missing-in-action software designer, hoping to get her to tell me where the MIA was."

Kelli nodded a little too enthusiastically as if she were the unwilling caretaker of the town drunk.

"And she must have had a hollow leg," I went on, "or me a hollow head, because at last count, four shooters and three margaritas passed her lips and consequently mine before she uttered the magic words, 'Bruce, South Dakota,' and slid under the table."

Out came another feeble laugh. This one sounded like the sucking noise made by a water buffalo's leg when he pulls it out of a mudhole.

"You see?"

She nodded sagely. "You like to drink."

"No, no! Last night's bout was business. I had to get this 3D program, this little computer gizmo back, understand? It was vital to my client."

"Is it like the 3D they do in the movies, like in the cartoons and stuff?"

She was finally with me. "Yes! But this 3D is on a computer. And being worth about fifteen mil, the client wanted it back *pronto.*"

Kelli inhaled a sharp breath at the amount. Money she understood.

"But let's move on," I said, feeling somewhat vindicated even though I needed to work on my laugh. "What exactly do you want from me?"

"I want you to find Nick."

I must have rolled my eyes or something because she grabbed at my hand this time. "Please, Lee. He once said you were the nicest, smartest person he ever knew."

I'll kill him.

Kelli let go of my hand and looked down at short, black fingernails. Hers, not mine. I don't do nail polish. "Please help me. I don't have anybody but Nick. My family disowned me after... after... Then I moved to Las Vegas, but I don't have any friends, not real friends. None that could or would help." She put those black fingernailed hands up to her face and started blubbering into them.

"Did you two have a fight or words?" She shook her head. "Did he seem unhappy or preoccupied about something?" Another shake.

"He has a cell, doesn't he?" She nodded but continued to blubber. "What happens when you call it?"

A muffled voice spoke through her fingers. "Nothing, it goes into voice mail. I must have left fifty messages, and he's never called back."

"What about friends? Has he been in contact with any?" She gave her head another sad shake. "Credit cards? Have any been used during the time he's been gone?"

"The only one not maxed out is in the bureau drawer. I got the statement yesterday, and there aren't any new charges. None of his clothes are missing, and he didn't take the car. I've got it; it's right outside. But he's got to be hiding somewhere."

"Why do you say that?"

She shrunk into herself. "Oh, maybe he isn't. Maybe he's..." She broke off and suddenly leaned into me with such force, I spilled half my coffee in my lap. "I've been reading the papers looking for unclaimed dead bodies. I even called the morgue once."

"Oh, I'm sure he's not dead." *Only the good die young, sweetie.*

I set the dripping cup down on the table and reached for several paper napkins to blot up the mess.

"And I've been calling the hospitals every day too." She went back to blubbering. I patted one of her shoulders with a limp, coffee-drenched hand, while the other dabbed at my wet, stained robe.

"Maybe he rented a car, took a bus, or a plane. There are other ways of getting out of town."

"No, he's around. I can feel." She wiped her eyes with her soggy, makeup-stained napkin. I gave her a fresh one, noting to buy more at the rate we were going through them. She blew her nose into it and handed it back to me.

Gee, thanks.

Then Kelli looked up at me and smiled. It was a rather glorious, angelic smile and made you want to like her. Oh God. I did like her.

I'm doomed.

"Sometimes I think he's watching me," she reflected. "Or somebody's watching me." She actually started to swoon at this point. I thought she was going to pass out and grabbed to steady her.

"When was the last time you slept? Or ate?" She shrugged her shoulders and shook her head in a dismissive manner. "Where are you staying?" She raised the shoulders again, this time dropping them in a sad, waiflike gesture.

"I don't know. The car, I guess. I don't have much money left, only enough for gas, about twenty or thirty dollars. I spent the night in your driveway because I can't afford a motel room. There was four thousand dollars in our savings last week, and it's gone. All his stuff is still in the condo, but the money's gone! All I have left is the car and Lady Gaga."

"Beg pardon?"

14

"Lady Gaga's my goldfish. She's in her tank in the car. I can't leave her out there when the sun comes up; it'll get too hot. I had to keep the heater running in the car last night, so she wouldn't get too cold. They're delicate," she explained, looking into my bloodshot eyes with the sincerity of a true animal lover. "They need a constant temperate temperature in order to maintain optimal health," she said as if reading from a manual.

She looked at me.

I looked at her.

"All rightie." I stood, resigned to my fate as the world's biggest chump. "Go get Gaga. We'll find somewhere in the apartment where the cats can't get at her. Then we're going to feed you. I can only make scrambled eggs, so if you want something else, you're out of luck. You can crash on the couch for a day or two until I make some phone calls and see what's going on. I'm not promising anything, but I'll do the best I can."

Kelli snatched at my hand and held it to her cheek in an act of gratitude and supplication. If I'd been wearing a ring, I think she might have kissed it. If this is what the pope goes through on a daily basis, you can have it. Wait a minute. It was more like the godfather.

I opened my mouth to speak when the landline rang. Pulling away from Kelli, I grabbed the phone after the first ring. Few people know this number, and each person who does means a lot to me. I'd turned off my cell and given the hour, I knew the call had to be important. I looked at the incoming number. Richard, my brother. He knew better than anybody what I'd been doing the previous night.

"What's wrong?" I said, leaving the kitchen and crossing into the living room for privacy.

He paused and gulped. "I'm on my way over to the Big House. I'll be there in about five minutes. Meet me there."

Since we were kids, the Big House is what he and I have called the large two-story family home, an ode to the American success story, Palo Alto style.

"Where are you now?" I asked.

"DI. I just left the office."

"On a Sunday morning? What were you doing there?" Silence. "Richard? What's wrong?"

"Lee, there's some… some news. Vicki just told me it's in this morning's *Chronicle*." Vicki and he have been married less than a year, but she is the finest addition to a family any one could ask for. I adore her. My brother's voice cracked as he went on.

"That's why I'm calling you. Mom didn't want to wake you after the night you had. But I don't want you to find out from the papers. I'll be there in five minutes."

"Find out what? Jesus, Richard, you're scaring me. Just tell me." More silence.

"Richard! The paper's in the kitchen. Should I go read it, or are you going to tell me right now?"

He let out air in a whoosh, then said, "It's Stephen. It's about Stephen." He hesitated. "It's bad."

"Stephen?" I tried to flip my mind around from Kelli's mess to Mom's only living relative, outside of us. My heart began to pound. Something happened to Stephen. Stephen, my older second cousin, who taught me how to ride a bike, play Scrabble, who'd stolen my Easter candy when he thought I wasn't looking, who tipped over our canoe on a disastrous but fun river ride — wonderful, gregarious, sweet natured, joke-telling Stephen. Although he'd moved to Phoenix thirteen years ago, he was still a much-loved, integral part of the family. I tried to steel myself.

"When you say 'bad,' how bad is bad?"

His voice broke. "The worst. There's no other way to say it. He's dead, Lee. He's dead." Richard became lost in sobs.

I gasped, drawing air into my lungs so fast, it physically hurt. Then I half stumbled, half sank into a nearby wingback chair, glad it was there, glad it caught me.

"*Dios mio!*" I whispered.

Richard gulped. "Sorry, Lee. I didn't mean to break it to you like that. But I didn't know… I couldn't think of any other way to say it. I'm sorry."

"But he was only forty-three," I said, faltering over the words.

"I know."

"Maybe there's a mistake." My voice had an anguished yet angry tone. "Maybe—"

"No mistake, Lee," Richard interrupted me, his voice low and hoarse. "The medical examiner's off-the-record comment was it probably was a heart attack. He was dead before he hit the ground."

My kid brother began to cry full out, while I listened on the other end of the line. I sat still, trying not to breathe, trying not to move, warding off the inevitable rogue waves of emotion heading in my direction. I knew them only too well. They would be like the ones pounding at me when our father died.

They would strike again and again, endlessly and without mercy. My mind fought off the oncoming onslaught and hid behind numbness and denial.

"Richard, this can't be. I don't understand. Stephen was in such good health. He had a physical every year. How could this…?"

"I'm searching for the answer to that question myself. Meanwhile, you need to come."

"Of course I'll come." My voice broke. "Where are you?"

"About two blocks from home. Meet me in the driveway."

"Why there? Why not inside the house?" More silence. "There's something else. Something you're not saying." Fear grabbed me. I didn't know why at the time. Call it premonition or something in Richard's voice.

He took a deep breath, exhaling it in a rush but hesitating over the words. "It might be a lack of sleep, Lee, or shock; I don't know—" He interrupted himself. "No, it's not any of those things. I'd thought, I'd hoped, but facts don't lie. I've been up all night, checking stats, looking into this."

"Looking into what?" I demanded. But the other end of the line went stony silent again. "Richard, are you still there?"

"I'm here," he said. His voice was filled with grief, but there was something else besides the sorrow — something that reached out and clamped down on me as if it were a steel vise. For a moment, all I could hear was my brother's staccato breathing and the sound of my own heart thudding in my ears.

"Oh God, Richard, you don't think his death was accidental or from natural causes."

"No."

"You think Stephen was murdered."

"Yes."

Chapter Two

Grief Knocks at the Door

After a hasty, vague explanation to a wide-eyed Kelli, I left her to sort out Lady Gaga, while I threw on some clean sweats and dashed out of the apartment. I took the stairs two at a time and ran along the circular asphalt driveway separating my garage apartment from the white colonial, two-story house, its pool, and hot tub. I sprinted to where the driveway meets the street. Richard's new green Prius was pulling in, his salute to the environment.

Richard flung open the car door and jumped out, his slim frame sheathed in the worn, faded T-shirt and jeans of the classic computer nerd. Barely half an inch taller than me, he seemed even slighter than usual, more vulnerable, as if this tragedy had taken something primal out of him. He looked at me. All the grief and shock I was feeling was mirrored in my brother's light-blue eyes, a color garnered from our mother. Yet, unlike Mom, Richard's were lit from behind with the same burning intensity as our Latino father.

From somewhere within I summoned up the strength to be the strong one. I tried to keep my stance tall and unyielding.

"We'll get through this, Richard. I don't know how, but we will."

Shaking his head, my kid brother walked into my arms. "I can't believe it. We were going to run a 12K next week. I can't believe it." His stifled sobs shook both our bodies.

"I know," I whispered. "I talked to him just the other day about getting together for his birthday."

I broke free and searched his strained face. "What happened, Richard? Tell me what you know." I leaned against the car, feeling the warmth of the metal against my hip.

Richard looked away and into a sky still shrouded in its nightly gray cloud cover. Soon the sun would break through, and we would have another sunny California day, cool and delicious. But Stephen would still be dead.

"He was running the Arizona Road Race and dropped to the ground, dead, right before the finish line. It was in front of hundreds of people. I've seen the video. It was a light race, not even a tough one. He does them all the time." Richard corrected himself. "Did them all the time." He leaned next to me against the car. I put my head on his shoulder and felt his arm go around me. I glanced over at his profile, set with a tension and strain I rarely see.

"Tell me why you said what you said, Richard. Why do you think it wasn't natural causes?"

His face took on an analytical look. I could see him mentally and emotionally pulling away into his world of statistics.

"I think you know I've been paying attention to anything on the internet about road races ever since I took up running about six months ago. Last night around midnight, I remembered reading several articles online recently about four runners dying right before crossing the finish line."

"But that can happen."

"In less than three months? One was a thirty-seven-year-old woman in Arkansas. Another was a thirty-five-year-old man in Upstate New York. Both dropped dead right before the finish line of heart attacks. No previous history of heart problems."

I fought back. "But it could be a coincidence. Why should anyone want to kill Stephen? He was a corporate lawyer for God's sake." I broke off not knowing what else to say. I stared at Richard, who shook his head.

"There's more, Lee. I'm onto a gambling cartel. Big. But let's not get into it now. I shouldn't have said anything until I was one hundred percent sure."

"Richard," I said, with no small part of exasperation.

He merely shook his head. My brother can be the most stubborn person I know. When he puts his figurative ears back and digs his heels in, nothing will change his mind until he's good and ready. I knew not to press it.

Richard's words rushed on. "We need to think about Mom. And especially Jenn and the kids." I thought of Stephen's wife, Jennifer, and their two preteen boys — fine boys, lovable boys.

"How are they doing?"

"From what I understand, she and the kids are coping as best they can. They saw it go down." His voice was soft but husky.

"Oh God, they did?"

Something like this could scar children for a lifetime. Hell, I don't think Richard or I will ever get past our father's death, and we were grown up when Dad died.

I looked over to the house and saw movement from one of the drapes in the family room. I was sure Lila was watching us, but our mother is the type of person to give her children a moment to be together, to say things only for one another's ears. "Mom's flying to Phoenix to help out," Richard said, updating me. "You know how Our Lady is. She's been on the phone with the funeral parlor several times already. She's trying to get through this by concentrating on the rest of the family."

"Wait a minute. When did this happen?"

"Jenn called Mom from the hospital around seven thirty last night, when he was officially declared dead."

"You've known all this time, and you're just telling me now?"

"What could you have done, Lee? Besides, Mom insisted. We knew you were tied up on the Video Pops case and wound up being out half the night.

I was going to come over around nine this morning to tell you, but then Vicki saw it in the *Chronicle*, what with Mom's side of the family being prominent and from this area. I called you as soon as..."

His voice tapered off, sounding apologetic, but pressured and defensive. I touched him on the shoulder.

"I understand. Sometimes a family can't share sorrows at the same time. Forget it. Before I go in, how's Mom doing? What should I know?"

"She's taking it hard, Lee. Even Tío broke down last night. He was very fond of Stephen. He'd just finished baking his birthday cake yesterday, ready to send off tomorrow."

"Tío always packs it in dry ice, so the cream cheese frosting stays fresh in shipping," I added, momentarily happy in the memory. A bird in a nearby tree began to chirp. We both looked in its direction.

Richard brushed at his eyes, shifted his position, and began to ramble, as people often do at times like these.

"Stephen was the one who got me into running. Said I needed to get outside more, build up some muscles, get some color. Gurn was going to join us for the Palace to Palace. It's a 12K. I've never done one of those before. We'd been planning it for months, laughed about bulking up on pizza carbs right before. Of course, Stephen was a legitimate runner. He'd been doing these races pretty seriously for a couple of years now, won more than he lost too. He loved it." Richard's voice petered out, and he stopped talking. An oppressive, lingering silence descended.

That's when the first rogue wave of emotion assaulted me, and my throat closed up. I leaned my head into my brother's slim shoulder, refusing to drown but feeling lost in the inevitability.

I heard a window open.

"Are you coming *in*?" Mom called out. "Liana? Richard? Come on into the family room. You've been out there *long* enough."

I started to go into the house, but Richard grabbed my arm. I turned and faced him, seeing he had more to say. I shouted out to our mother, "We'll be right there, Mom."

"Lee, promise me you won't say anything to Mom just yet. Right now, it's only a suspicion but if —" Richard broke off and swiped at a slight five-o'clock shadow. "If what I think is true turns out to be, it's pretty mind boggling."

"Is something *wrong*?" I heard Mom question with growing impatience. "Aren't you coming *in*?"

"Yes, Mom. We'll be right there." But I stood perfectly still, studying my brother's face. He looked directly into my eyes, unwavering.

So there it was. If Richard found Stephen's death to be suspicious, it was suspicious. As DI's director of Information, Technology, and Research, Richard's personal raison d'être is the compilation of data. Sometimes on the surface of it, the facts appear to be disjointed or erroneous, but they never are. Nobody can connect the dots better than my brother.

In his early teens, he'd created several innovative programs propelling DI to the forefront of investigative services. Between us chickens, I'm not sure all aspects of them are legal. Some dip into confidential information gathered by impressive, initialed agencies, such as the IRS and CIA. But Richard maintains, while it may not be strictly within the letter of the law, if you don't use the info for personal gain, it's not unethical. We don't question it. Frankly, my brilliant brother runs his part of DI any way he wants.

Without uttering another word, Richard and I went around to the back of the house and into the deserted, retro '30s kitchen, with its inviting whipped-yellow and white color scheme. I paused, reluctant to leave my favorite room in the house, and looked for our Uncle Mateo, called Tío by almost everyone.

Nearly every hour of the day, ever since he moved in, there's been the delicious aroma of something Mexican cooking. But not today. Not that it mattered. I don't think any of us had an appetite.

"Where's Tío?" I asked.

"He's probably in the basement feeding those two rabbits he's fostering until the SPCA can place them," Richard said, forcing a more normal tone to his voice. "By the way, who's parked at the end of the driveway? Nice looking Land Rover."

"You're not going to believe this one. It's Nick's wife, Kelli. Seems he's missing."

"Hmmmm," my brother said, not nearly as surprised as I thought he'd be. "Nick again."

"What do you mean, 'Nick again'? Until this morning, Nick has been out of my life for some time, even before his marriage to Kelli."

Richard shook his head instead of answering. "You'd better get into the family room before Mom gets upset. Tell her I've got some work to do, something that can't wait. She started that thing with her earrings again last night. You know what it means, Sister mine." Richard gave me a knowing look. I nodded.

Two years before, between the time our father died and his funeral, Mom took on a temporary but annoying habit. She'd either clip on and clip off a pair of pearl earrings Dad had given her for their wedding anniversary, or she would roll them over each other again and again in the palm of her hand. They would make this clicking sound, sort of like the steel balls Humphrey Bogart played with as Captain Queeg in *The Caine Mutiny*. Except, of course, if Bogey had been worrying pearl earrings instead of steel balls, it would have been a completely different movie.

I started for the family room but turned back. "Aren't you coming in, Richard?"

"No. I'll be on the computer in the study, but don't disturb me. I'll get back to you when I know something."

The rubber heels of my running shoes made a squeaking sound on the travertine stone as I entered the silent room. Mom stood in front of the bay window.

Backlit by shards of sunlight breaking through the cloud cover, she turned to face me, her long-sleeve, high-neck black sheath contrasting dramatically with a room of beige, light stone, and golden oak. She'd recently had the wood stripped in this room, lightening it from a dark to light golden oak. It so worked.

Her initial look was one of perfection. Living on the ice princess side of life, the woman who bore me elects to show the world her beautiful and in-control porcelain face despite what underlying cracks may exist beneath.

The neatly coifed, shoulder-length, ash-blonde hair was a little too lacquered. Pale-blue eyes were slightly puffy under artfully applied liner, and pink lipstick almost, but not quite, shielded a mouth pinched from the strain of self-contained grief.

Sure enough, I noticed her playing with the clip-on earrings in her hand. She saw me notice, so with a flourish, Mom put one earring on, covering a slightly swollen right lobe, and then walked over and embraced me.

I held her tight and took in a whiff of Bal A Versailles, her favorite fragrance. "You know, Mom, one of these days you're going to scratch the pearls if you continue to rub them together like that."

"Liana, *darling,*" she said, ignoring my comment, as she is wont to do, "I'm sorry we got you up so early. I know you were working until all hours last night. How are you?" With a jerky movement, she pulled away and scrutinized my face. "You *look* ghastly."

"Thanks, Mom."

"You know what I *mean,* dear. You can't have had more than *four* hours sleep. I knew Richard *shouldn't* have called you just yet. And where is he? I *told* him to wait a few hours. You need your rest. Otherwise, I *know* you would have at *least* put on matching clothes."

She caught me unawares.

I looked down.

Sure enough, a green sweatshirt topped a pair of hot-pink pants from another set, the first two items I grabbed. Knowing the way she feels about my sweats in general even when they match, I had committed a cardinal sin.

She went on. "Maybe a trip to the *day spa*. Leonardo does a *wonderful* mineral wrap." Mom was stressing more than her usual words in a sentence, which normally drives me crazy. However, I would have forgiven her anything right then.

"I'm fine, Mom. I don't need a mineral wrap. Richard is... he... needs to do something. He'll be in directly."

"He's such a loving, giving son."

"I know, Mom."

"We were together *most* of last night. I'm sure he does have other *things* to do." In an uncharacteristic nervous gesture, she struck at a hair lying perfectly in line with the rest of the coif and turned away.

"How are you doing, Mom?" I said, moving on. I decided not to let Mom's preference for Richard get to me. After all, I had been Dad's favorite when he was alive, and Richard was Mom's. That's the way it was. Some things never change.

"Maybe you need to lie *down* soon, Liana, after we... *after* we..." She paused, reached up, and clipped the remaining earring on the other lobe.

"After we what, Mom?"

"I don't know," she mouthed, shook her head, and turned away.

I reached out to her, tried to find words of comfort, anything, when the connecting door to the kitchen swung open. Tío, my father's surviving older brother, entered the room, obviously having returned from the basement.

Tall and refined, Tío is a retired executive chef. You'd think I would have inherited more from his side of the family than just the height but no such luck. In the case of cooking, not only did the fruit fall far from the tree, it catapulted clean out of the orchard.

Despite the hour, he was dressed more formally than usual, dark gray slacks and a cotton Mexican embroidered shirt, white on white. In his own way, Tío exuded as much class as Mom. He carried a carafe of coffee as well as a look of sobriety. When he saw me, his eyes lit up for his only niece.

"*Buenos dias, sobrina mia,*" he said, setting the carafe down next to a tray of mugs, cloth napkins, milk, and sugar on the square golden-oak-and-glass coffee table. I went into his arms for a quick hug. He kissed me on the forehead.

"Such sad news, Liana. *Muy triste.*"

I nodded and changed the subject, feeling too much weight and unhappiness.

"How are the bunnies, Tío?"

He smiled briefly. "*Bien, bien*. Tomorrow they go to a farm in Marin to live a happy life. *Queries* coffee?"

"No, Tío, but thanks. Actually, Tío, I drank some coffee earlier, but it's not sitting well." I rubbed my forehead with a careful hand. He stared at me for a moment. I went on. "Last night I had a little too much alcohol on the job and—"

"Ah! *Entiendo.* The hangover of the head." He turned around and headed for the kitchen. "*Un momento.* I have something the former mayor of San Jose, a good friend of mine, would drink when there was such a need. But this is between ourselves. Shhh!"

He looked over at Mom, who sat down on the sofa. "*¿Mi hermana, mas café?*"

Even though they are related only through Mom's marriage to my father, through the years, Tío has become like the older brother my mother never had. To Tío, Lila is the little sister he always wanted. Their bond became even closer after Dad died. When Tío moved in last year and took over the kitchen and first floor, Mom went to the upstairs rooms. In a fourteen-room house, that's easy to do. They keep to themselves and their own busy lives but usually meet for companionable meals once or twice a week.

Mom looked at Tío with warmth. "Please don't be concerned about me, Mateo. I'm fine."

"You are not fine," Tío chided gently. Mom started to protest. "I will not hear the 'no' from you. You did not eat breakfast. You will at least eat the fruit compote I made. You need the strength."

Tío takes food and the eating of it very seriously. Until he retired, he ran a stylish Mexican restaurant in San Jose called Las Mañanitas. He'd also been a minor celebrity, one of *Gourmet Magazine's* favorite chefs for new and traditional south-of-the-border recipes. Using a little of this and a little of that, Tío can whip up a culinary masterpiece which has dropped better than me to their knees in supplication. He left for the kitchen just as the phone rang.

Mom picked up the small beige phone from the coffee table and spoke in hushed tones to the person on the other end of the line. I lay my head back and closed my eyes. Thoughts of my last phone conversation with Stephen swirled in my mind. I felt my eyes grow hot under closed lids.

"Liana."

I opened my eyes at the sound of my mother's voice. She was no longer speaking on the phone, and I saw her face drained of what little color she'd previously had.

"That was the Maricopa County medical examiner in Phoenix. Jennifer had asked me to deal with the coroner's office for her as well as the funeral parlor. It's all she can do to cope with this tragedy and the boys."

"What did the coroner want?"

"He says he wants more time and is not releasing the body until at least Friday."

"Why?" I asked, on the alert. "Do they suspect foul play?"

"Foul play?" Lila repeated. "He didn't mention foul play. Why on earth should they suspect foul play? Delays in autopsies can be for a hundred different reasons." Her voice had a forced edge as if she didn't want to question the cause of the delay.

"No reason, Mom. Forget it. Too much *CSI*, I suppose."

"You watch too much of that type of television, Liana," she said, standing up in anger. She tossed her ash-blonde hair. "With what spare time you have, you should be watching PBS or educational channels. Like the Discovery Channel."

"Yes, ma'am," I said meekly.

"Not filling your mind with worthless, inaccurate…"

She stopped talking suddenly and shook her head, then rubbed the back of her hand across her forehead, which I couldn't believe. Mom's big into not touching one's face with one's hands.

"I'm sorry. I seem to be more short-tempered than usual. Forgive me." Lila sat down heavily across from me in a large beige leather chair. Feather pillows expelled soft air around her, and the supple leather molded to her body.

"There's nothing to forgive, Mom."

I don't think she heard me. She was reaching out to the single rose in a silver bud vase on the coffee table, the last of summer's offering. We both knew it had come from a bush Stephen planted ten years ago in our garden. Tapered fingers lovingly touched a petal of the fragrant lavender flower and then drew back almost as if the flower grew hot to the touch.

"Richard doesn't think Stephen died of natural causes, does he?" Lila asked, her voice echoing throughout the silent room. My mother didn't look at me but reached up to the earring on her earlobe, thought better of it, and dropped both hands in her lap.

"Mom, we don't know anything yet. It's just Richard being Richard and me with my usual big mouth. Let's not think about anything like that until after we hear from the coroner." I took a deep breath. "What time are you flying to see Jenn and the boys?"

"Maybe I shouldn't go just yet, what with the postponement of the release of the body."

"Why not ask Jenn if she'd like you to come now? Maybe she needs you. Isn't she still on the outs with her mother?"

Mom nodded. "You're right, of course. Thank you, my dear. I'm not thinking as clearly as I ordinarily do. I'll call Jennifer. I'll tell her the funeral will be pushed back several days. I'll keep the coroner's phone call from her, if I can."

She tried to give me a smile, but it was fleeting at best. Straightening her back, my mother took out a small notebook from her nearby handbag.

"But life goes on, doesn't it? I'll take care of as much business as I can from Phoenix and anything I can't do, I'll let you or Richard know. You can deal with it." Her voice sounded more like the usual, in control Lila. "I've got several agents on the Lascom case, as the company is willing to pay for it."

"Remind me again, Mom. Those are the guys trying to find out who pirated their new interactive game?"

"Correct, Liana. It's now being sold under the name of Carter's Speedway in K-Mart, of all places.

"Lascom will have a hard time proving it was stolen. They waited too long to call us. Three months? Jeesh," I said, once again glad to be talking about work. As much as we loved each other, we often felt safer in work mode.

Mom's smile was genuine for the first time. "I agree. But thanks to your efforts, Video Pops is on their way to… where?" She looked at me.

"Bruce, South Dakota."

"And Video Pops has asked the local authorities to detain the young man in question until they arrive. If you hadn't gotten the information from his girlfriend, I don't know if we would have found him," she said, shaking her head. "In any event, the company is in the process of doing damage control."

"Are they pressing charges?"

"No. They don't want the publicity."

"In that case, you don't suppose they'd be willing to send me to the Betty Ford Clinic to dry out, do you?" I asked. "I mean, after last night, it's the least they can do."

"My dear, you do have a tendency to become irreverent at the slightest provocation," she said, the corners of her mouth reaching upward in a smile nonetheless. "The Betty Ford Clinic has provided help for thousands. Any one of us may be in need of their services at some point in our lives."

"And one of us is going to be me, if I have another night like last night."

Mom laughed lightly. "I know you're trying to cheer me up, and I appreciate it, Liana, more than you know."

The swinging door between the dining room and kitchen opened again. Tío entered carrying a tray on which sat a small crystal bowl of mixed fruit. There was also a glass of liquid looking a little like tomato juice but suspiciously oranger in color, if that's a word. He set the tray on the table, handed the bowl and a fork to Mom, who began to pick at the offering. Then he thrust the glass in my hand.

"Drink," he ordered in his heavy Spanish accent.

I took it warily and looked at him. "What's in it?"

"*Mi sobrina*," he said, expelling air in exasperation. "Drink it down and do not ask the questions."

"Is there anything in here besides Tabasco sauce?" I forced a smile to my lips while my heart raced. "I hope; I hope?"

Tío glared at me in such a way I took a big gulp before he could say anything more. A fiery inferno exploded on my tongue, bounced off the roof of my mouth, and then blazed a trail to the top of my skull with a quick stop at my nasal passages and eyes. My head felt like a flaming, overheated barbeque grill. Throw another shrimp on the barbie, mate.

I inhaled a jagged breath and lowered the glass, which retained about half of the liquid. Wordless, Tío pushed my hand and the glass back up to my mouth and held it there. Paralyzed by my own personal firestorms, I gave in and drained the glass dry.

The second swallow did far less damage to my innards than the first, and as the fire died down, the old Liana Margaret Alvarez resurrected herself.

I won't say the lark was on the wing, and all was right with the world, but I felt like I might recover.

"Thanks, Tío. That's miracle stuff that."

"One raw, beaten, pasteurized egg, the juice of alfalfa, spinach, red beets, and horseradish mixed with tomato and chili sauce."

"Too much information, Tío."

"*¿Estás mejor?*" he asked, a challenging look in his eye.

"*Sí,* better," I replied.

"*Bien.*" He nodded and strode toward the kitchen door. "I will make for you my fresh herb omelet to cleanse the body and the mind."

"Can you make two of them?" I said, thinking of Kelli. "And pack one to go. I've got company."

"I thought Gurn was still in Washington, DC," Mom said.

"He is, Mom. My guest of honor is ex-husband Nick's current wife, Kelli." Mom raised both eyebrows, and Tío stopped at the door and wheeled around to face me.

I hadn't realized until I'd spoken, and the words hovered in the air, I'd made a pretty loaded statement about a pretty loaded situation. Sometimes you don't face what's going on until you hear what you've said about it. I hurried to give a brief, capsulated version, hoping the more I talked about it, the more it would soften around the edges. It didn't.

My mother donned her "stone" face, meaning she did not approve, and Tío stared at me in wonderment. I seem to arouse stunned silence from a lot of people a lot of the time. I try to think of it as a gift.

"You left her alone in your apartment while you came here?" Mom finally asked.

I opened my mouth with a defensive retort and thought better of it. Now that I was working on all six cylinders, thanks to Tío's miracle elixir, maybe it wasn't such a good idea after all.

Chapter Three

Coping With It All

The morning fog was lifting as I hurried up the stairs to my apartment. I tried not to focus on the wrought-iron banister with the Mayan character insets that ran along the stairs. Stephen had commissioned the artist, a friend of his from Marin, and gave me the renderings two years ago as a Christmas present.

Seeing it, another rogue wave smashed at me. I staved off hot tears and opened the door, looking around anxiously. Kelli lay balled up on her side on the couch, out like a light. Tugger perched on her hip, and Baba snoozed at her feet. The sound of the door opening had caused two pairs of feline eyes to open and look in my direction, but Kelli didn't stir. I breathed a sigh of relief. Everything looked fine. Mom had spooked me for no reason, once again.

On the coffee table sat a ten-gallon, fish tank with a lacy goldfish swimming around in pristine waters, an elaborate filtering system hard at work, and a heat lamp keeping the water at a perfect temperature. I couldn't imagine why those cats weren't in that bowl, water and all, until I saw a sturdy, wire mesh screen topping it.

I tiptoed into the kitchen followed by Tugger, who started yowling at the top of his lungs for his breakfast. He was trailed by a quieter and more docile Baba.

I shushed him, for all the good it did, put the omelet for the sleeping Kelli in the oven on warm, and picked up My Boy, in the hopes of shutting him up.

It worked. He wrapped his front legs around my neck in an embrace, lowered his eyelids, and began to purr.

That's when I lost it. I buried my face in Tugger's sinewy, warm body and sobbed. I tried to be as quiet as possible for fear of waking Kelli, and stepped out onto my back deck, Baba at my heels. I picked up the little girl in my free arm and sat down in a nearby teak rocking chair.

Under the warm California sun and surrounded by plants and colorful flowers, I rocked the three of us back and forth lost in ragged, gulping tears. It wasn't only the horror and unfairness of my cousin's death, it was the loss of Stephen himself. His absence would make the world a slightly colder place in which to live.

"Okay, guys," I said after about fifteen minutes, wiping my wet eyes and nose with the sleeve of my sweatshirt. "Time for breakfast."

At the word "breakfast," Tugger's ears perked up, and he hopped down from my lap, heading for the kitchen door. Who's the idiot who said cats don't understand words? Tugger knows a good twenty of them at only ten months old, and breakfast, lunch, and dinner head the list.

I opened a can of premium cat food that cost almost as much beluga caviar, mixed two helpings with their dry food, sprinkled dry fish flakes on top — sorry Lady Gaga — and watched both cats tuck in with enthusiasm.

With a glance toward the living room, I noted Kelli still slept, lying on her side, arm stretched out under her head as a pillow, covered with the throw from the back of the couch. I had a moment's guilt at not providing linens and towels before I left but figured Miss Manners would forgive me this one time. The kitchen clock stated 9:45 a.m., and I still hadn't done my ballet barre.

Before heading to the second bedroom, where I keep the office and my dance/exercise studio, I gathered some stuff from the linen closet, including a terry-cloth robe, under the "better late than never" heading, and set the pile down on the coffee table next to the swimming fish. She was cute, this Lady Gaga, although how anyone could tell if it was a she or a he was beyond me.

While changing into a leotard and tights for my barre, I thought about how I would pass the time until I heard from Richard. There was no point in bothering him now. I knew my brother; when he had information, he'd call me. Otherwise, I was persona non grata.

* * * *

The regimen of a barre is one of the greatest exhilarations in the world. Some people climb mountains or jump out of planes. Not me. I dance classical ballet. Through fate's twisted sense of humor, though, no matter how hard I try, I am mediocre at best. I discovered in my early teens, I would have been lucky to wind up in the chorus of a second-rate ballet company. Now in my mid-thirties, I've gotten too old to even consider professional dancing. Lousy and old, there's my legacy. Nonetheless, I can't live without dance in its purest form. And each day, as I do my forty-five-minute barre, I'm another Ánna Pávlova, dancing for the sheer love of it.

By the end of my workout, my body dripped with sweat, but I was clear of mind. I knew what I was going to do until I heard from Richard. I took a shower, flipped on my laptop, and started my first round of roster-checking for airlines, bus lines, rental cars, etc., thanks to a series of databases created by Richard. It's grueling work and requires a lot of concentration, but it goes pretty fast. I was done in less than an hour and picked up the phone.

"This is Flint," said a gravelly male voice on the other end of the line. With those three words, Flint Tall Trees, Las Vegas PI, and longtime family friend, let you know you'd better state your business fast and make it good.

"Lonato," I said, using his Shoshone name and pronouncing it as he'd taught me years ago. "It's Lee from California."

"Papoose!" Flint replied, his tone changing from business steel to fond friend. "Did I ever thank you for the birthday card? Not that I appreciate being reminded of another year gone by. Fifty-seven years old. I'm an old man."

"I think you've got a lot of fire left in your teepee."

Flint let out a hoot of laughter. He and Dad met when they were rookie cops and traded to each other's precincts in a six-month experimental learning program, Flint to Palo Alto and Dad to the Shoshone Reservation in Nevada. The exchange changed both their lives. Dad said the Shoshone taught him to pay attention not only to a man's five senses: sight, sound, smell, touch, and taste, but to the sixth and most important one: intuition. All six held him in good stead as a detective for the rest of his life.

Conversely, when Dad found out Flint had a sickly eight-year-old son on the reservation wasting away for want of medical attention not offered locally, he stepped in. Dad pulled a few strings, found a good Samaritan with a plane, and flew the boy to the Mayo Clinic for treatment, for which he fronted the costs. Through the years, Flint paid back every dime but felt he owed Dad for his son's life.

"I know I'm interrupting your Sunday but—"

"I'm just playing touch football with the grandkids. What is it? You wouldn't call unless it was something important." Flint had a way of getting right to it.

"Flint, I don't want to take you away from your game—"

"As an elder," he interrupted, "it is important for my children's children to learn the eagle can only soar because the wind ripples his feathers. You must recompense the wind."

"Are you saying I'm full of hot air?" I quipped.

He sniggered dutifully and moved on. "What do you need, Papoose?"

"You remember my ex-husband, Nick Papadopoulos?"

"Of course. Lives here with his new wife. Does real estate, but I hear it's on a downswing. Times are tough."

"You already know a lot about him."

"Vegas is a small town."

"Nick's disappeared. About a week ago."

"So?"

"So his wife wants to know what happened to him."

"What does his ex-wife want?"

"I said I'd help her find him."

Flint burst out into a full-blown, hearty laugh. "You are so much like Bobby. Always helping the underdog." He stopped laughing. "Of course, I've got grandkids to play ball with because of your father. Otherwise, I would have lost Knoton that summer."

"Knoton? Oh right, Ken's Shoshone name."

"No more Ken for him. And his two boys are named Hakan and Igasho, in the way of the elders. I am the past; they are the future."

His mood changed again, and he became all business. "I'll look around and see what I can find. Did you check his credit cards to see if he's used them recently?"

"His wife says she got the statement yesterday, and there weren't any charges on it since he's been missing."

"Hmmmm." There was a moment's silence. "Are you sure he's still in Vegas?"

"No, but I've done a quick rundown on airlines, buses, and car rentals. Unless he's traveling under an alias, he's not on any lists. There's money missing from the checking account, and his wife suspects he's still in town, so it's a good place to start."

"Most hotels on the strip don't take cash these days. They all want plastic. But downtown, it's another story. I'll get back to you in a few hours."

"Any help you give me, I'm paying you for, Flint. Let's settle that from the beginning."

"Sorry, Papoose, the debt is full up. This is a man's honor. Besides, I can't play touch football for long. I'm an old man. This is a good excuse to get out of it and save face."

We said goodbye, and I hung up knowing I'd done what I could.

My cell phone rang an instant later. I made a lunge for it and saw it wasn't Richard, but Gurn.

"Gurn, hi!" My heart did a small flutter of happiness, but don't let it get around the neighborhood.

"Lee, I'm calling to see how you are." His voice, low and rich, was filled with concern. He'd heard about Stephen; I was sure of it.

"You know?" was all I could get out.

"Yes, I read about it on an APB bulletin just now when I got out of my meeting. I'm so sorry. How is everybody, the family? How are you, my darling?"

It's funny how the man in your life can reduce you to putty. I thought after my cry on the back deck I was fine, but I found my throat closing up again and those danged hot tears threatening a return. I took a deep breath and put on a brave front.

"We're doing as well as can be expected. Mom's flying to Phoenix to be with Stephen's wife and kids and help out. And Richard..." I broke off here, not quite wanting to say what Richard's suspicions and, ultimately, mine were. "And Richard and I are holding up."

"I wish I was there with you, sweetheart."

"Me too." I swallowed. This man was great. What the hey was he doing with me?

Stop it, Lee, I chided myself. *Remember: think positive. Tell yourself you deserve this guy. Repeat it endlessly until it sinks in.*

"When do you come home?" I asked aloud.

"I'm dealing with some tax issues, so I have a few things to clear up here in DC."

Yeah, right. Ha ha. Gurn is a CPA by listed profession. At least, that's what the Yellow Pages say. He's also a lieutenant commander in the navy reserves and was Richard's commanding officer for the four years my brother was in the reserves. They became friends. But what's never talked about is the man in my life has some sort of hush-hush job for the navy, which requires frequent trips to our nation's capitol.

Try as I may, I couldn't get a toehold on exactly what the job was. I met him when Richard dragged him in on the investigation of stolen artifacts by an international racketeering gang out of Mexico. But that's another story.

"I'll be back," he went on, "in a day or two, unless you need me now. Say the word, Lee, and I'll hop in the plane. I know what Stephen meant to all of you. I only met him once, but he seemed like a good man. We were going to run the Palace to Palace together next week."

"I know." I cleared a parched throat. "You don't have to rush back, but I hope I see you soon. It's already been a week."

He chuckled. "And I'm feeling every minute of it. I'll make it tomorrow night no matter what." He paused, then blurted out, "Lee, I have to say this. I've been thinking about us. A lot. I love you. I miss you. I didn't realize how much until this week."

This was the first time the "L" word was mentioned between us. We'd only been seeing each other for four months, not a longish amount of time, and I was taken aback.

Between some of my quirks and what I did for a living, most guys left skid marks when they dumped me. I didn't reply. I was too busy quelling my beating heart.

"Lee, did you hear me?"

"Yes," I found myself saying, "I love you too."

OMG. I'd said the "L" word back. I gulped and started to hyperventilate. "I've got to go now, Gurn. The cats and I will see you tomorrow night."

"I can't wait. By the way, how's Baba doing?"

"Just great. Tugger's quite smitten with her. They're lifelong pals."

"I knew it. Bye, my love. Until tomorrow."

I hung up and continued to hyperventilate for about two more minutes. Then I faced it. I was in love. I'd said over and over it would never happen to me again. Ha!

I felt giddy, invincible, scared, vulnerable, courageous, stupid, and happy. Like Nellie Forbush, I broke out singing something about being as corny as Kansas in August, only gawd-awful. I hate to admit it, but I can't sing.

It was ten thirty. Kelli was still asleep, I was playing a waiting game with Flint and Richard, and there was nothing else to do. The cats and I took a much-needed nap.

True to his word, Flint called back at around twelve thirty. Cats toppled everywhere as I groped for the phone.

"You sound like I woke you up, but you'll be happy I did."

I rubbed the sleep from my eyes and tried to sound more alert than I was feeling. "What have you got, Flint?"

"I found him."

"You found Nick? Already?"

"Not too hard when you know your man and where to look. You gave me the idea when you said the word 'alias.' He's registered under the name of Richard Alvarez—"

"He's what? Why, that son of a—"

"Now, now," said Flint with a snort. "Remember, Lila raised you to be a lady."

"She missed by a mile."

He gave another hearty laugh while I stewed about Nick using my brother's name. Flint went on. "I knew he was an ex-marine, but Nicky Boy struck me as a man with little to no imagination, so I tried a couple of names he might use instead of his own and got lucky after a few calls."

"You're sure it's him and not someone el—"

"I'm sure," he interrupted. "I've seen him. He's at a sleazebag hotel off of Third Street. One thing, looks like somebody else found him too."

"I saw two goons waiting on a park bench across the street, looking mighty interested in the people coming in and going out. They got very excited when they saw Nick walking back from a nearby 7-Eleven. Even started to cross the street, but they got sidetracked by a group of tourists looking at maps outside the hotel door where Nicky Boy went in."

"These men were waiting for him?"

"Felt like it." Flint's feelings were first rate.

"How long ago was that?"

"Not five minutes. What do you want me to do? I'm around the corner. These guys have been talking on a cell phone ever since they saw him. I think they're asking permission from someone to take him."

"I don't want you to do anything. We don't know yet what he's mixed up in. What's the name of this place?"

"Carter Hotel. Want the phone number? I got it. I also know what room number Nick's in."

"Now you're spoiling me. How'd you do that, Flint?"

"You'd be surprised what a twenty can still buy you."

"If you got the room he's in, those men can get it too."

"That's my thinking."

I wrote down the number and called the place, surprised each room had a phone, if only for incoming calls. After a series of clicks and scrunching sounds, the line rang for a long time in room 218. Just when I thought I should hang up and call it a day, someone picked up, but there was silence on the other end.

"Nick?" I said, taking a chance. "It's Lee, Lee Alvarez. If you can hear me, get out of there now. And use a back door, if there is one."

It sounded like someone dropped the phone, picked it back up, and juggled with it, all the while breathing heavily.

"Nick! Talk to me."

"Lee? Is that you?" Nick's voice sounded strangled, confused, and frantic.

"Yes, Nick, move. There are a couple of men waiting for you across the street. They could be at your door any moment. Get out, but call me when you can at DI"

"Okay," he said. "Okay."

Then the line went dead.

Chapter Four

A Miscalculation of Sorts

When I came out of my office, I heard the shower running. Not only was Kelli up, but she had straightened up the living room. She'd even put Lady Gaga's tank on one of the bookshelves, where the little wet devil fit perfectly. I'd never thought of having a goldfish before, but I mulled over the notion Tugger might like the diversion, especially after I had to give Baba back to Gurn. A fish might be good, if Tugs couldn't get at it. I'd look into it.

The guest bathroom door opened, and Kelli came out singing "The Girl from Ipanema" in a sweet, but untrained soprano voice. She was freshly scrubbed from head to toe and wearing a terry-cloth robe that hits me above the knees but came down to her ankles. The word "petite" takes on new meaning with this girl. Without any makeup, she looked around eleven or twelve years old. Her childlike face lit up when she saw me.

"Hi!" she said, grinning and resuming her little tune until she'd finished the song.

"Very nice," I said. "Fun song."

"I like it. It makes me think of beaches and beautiful places."

She pulled off the towel from her wet, white-blonde hair that quickly clustered into ringlets. Had she been around Hollywood in the '30s, Shirley Temple wouldn't have stood a chance.

"How do you feel?" I asked.

"A lot better, thanks. You look better too."

"Due to a combo of Tío's miracle elixir and a nap. Kelli, there's one of my uncle's omelets in the oven, if you're hungry."

"Great!"

Her enthusiasm was disarming. Kelli followed me into the kitchen, where I wrestled the warm omelet out of the tinfoil and onto a plate. All the while, we both said little. It was as if she was content to just sit in my kitchen and be.

I sat across from her while she started to eat, once again, with the zest of a kid. "Kelli, I have an update on Nick."

She put her fork down. "Do you have any ketchup?"

"Ketchup?" I was thrown for a second. "Yeah, sure. Let me get it."

I went to the fridge and opened the door, wondering if she'd heard me. I handed the bottle off to her and watched her drown Tío's fabulous omelet in red glop.

"So what's the news?" she finally said. "Good or bad?" Kelli licked ketchup off her fingers and looked at me.

"Well, both. I found Nick, even talked to him briefly, and —"

"You did?" she interrupted. "What did he say? Did he say anything about me?"

"There wasn't time for a real conversation, Kelli. He had to leave. I told him to call me when he could." I watched her face as I said this. It was devoid of emotion.

"So he split." She chewed on this development, as well as the omelet. "You're sure you don't know where he went to?"

"No, but at least we know he's alive."

"That's a relief. I sure wish I knew where he was," she said, taking another huge bite.

"Do you know if there are other people who might want to know where he is, too, Kelli?"

She shook her head and crammed the last mouthful of egg mixture in her mouth, chewed it, and looked at me. I looked at her. A moment passed with us looking.

"Would you like some toast?" I asked.

"Love it."

I did the chore of toasting and buttering a slice of bread, all the while thinking about what was going on inside Kelli's confusing little head. I couldn't put my finger on it, but something was off. I mean, *pass the ketchup*?

I set the plate of toast on the table and noticed Kelli was studying me for a change. "What?"

"You're wondering why I'm not more upset, aren't you? I mean about Nick."

"The thought had crossed my mind. Jam? I've got guava and strawberry."

"Oooo, guava. I've never had that before. How exotic." She almost clapped her hands in delight. This whole situation was getting weirder by the minute.

"Coming up." Another fast trip to the fridge. "So what is it, Kelli? What's on your mind?"

"I was thinking while I was taking a shower," she said, spreading guava jam on the toast and speaking in the same breathless voice I've come to have ear strain over. "Maybe you're in cahoots with Nick. Maybe you've known where he is all along. Maybe you two planned this whole thing. Maybe he's taken our money and sold my car to go back to you!"

"That's a lot of maybes." I stood up and folded my arms over my chest. "First of all, Kelli, who uses the word 'cahoots' these days? You've been watching too many westerns."

Her eyes narrowed, pretty smile fading. "I know what it means, in it together."

"To answer your charges, there are no 'cahoots' going on between Nick and me. Now you've forced the issue; I think Nick is just about the biggest jerk I've ever had the misfortune to know in my life. I happen to be very happily involved, nay, in love, with another man. Even if I weren't, I wouldn't take Nick back trussed up and roasted on a spit, thank you very much." I drew myself up to my full five feet eight inches and did my best imitation of my mother at her haughtiest, which is pretty danged haughty.

"I think you should finish your breakfast and leave, Kelli. I've done what you've asked. I've found out Nick is still in Las Vegas. I suggest you get back there. And why he doesn't want you to know where he is, that's your problem."

Whereupon, she burst into tears.

Haughty took a nosedive. "Oh, jeesh, Kelli. Stop that. Really. Stop blubbering. It's already been a long day, and it's only a little past noon. I just can't help you. Not right now. I've got... we've had... there's been a family tragedy. I need to focus on my family. I'm sorry."

"No, I'm sorry." She did the grabbing the hand again as if I were the pope or the godfather. "I didn't mean what I said.

It's just I don't understand it." She looked at me with those china blues, tears streaming down her face.

The world's biggest chump sat down with a sigh.

"Why doesn't he trust *me*?" she asked in her little girl voice. "Why doesn't he think *I'm* the best thing that happened to him; *I'm* the most beautiful woman in the world? Why you and not me?"

"The man's an idiot? Let's go with that. But I can't do anything more for you, Kelli. I know I said you could stay here a couple of days, but I need to concentrate on family matters. You're going to have to leave, okay?" I patted, then loosened the hand clutching my own. "I promise to tell Nick of your concern if and when I hear from him. It's time for you to leave."

"But where will I go?" she wailed. "I don't have enough money for gas to get home."

"I'll give you gas money." I got up, went to the cookie jar, and took out one hundred dollars.

"I don't want your money," she wailed again. "I want your help."

I set the cash on the table, wondering just what part of "no" Kelli didn't get. I kept my cool but leaned in, staring into her baby blues.

"I've done what I can. If the man doesn't want you to know where he is, he doesn't want you to know where he is. *El fin*. It's over. You need to leave."

My phone rang. I looked at the incoming number, and it was Richard. Finally!

"Kelli, this is an important call. I've got to take it, and it could be awhile. Why don't you pack up your things, and we'll say goodbye now?"

I got up from the table, asked Richard to wait a moment, ran to my office, and closed the door. My office/dance studio is soundproofed. When I'm dancing, I like to keep the outside world outside. Then there's also the loud music I sometimes play and any private phone conversations. You never know who might overhear what. After thinking it over, I locked the door for good measure.

"What have you got, Richard?"

"I've been looking into the last six months of stats for competitive footraces across the country. Within that time frame, five racers have died of apparent heart attacks, scattered across the US of A. Stephen makes six. There's another one, a seventh. He collapsed three weeks ago, once again, right before the finish line. He's still in ICU, but it could go either way. Keep in mind these are all healthy and youngish men and women. Like the twenty-nine-year-old woman who died in Louisiana, a young woman with no history of heart problems."

"Meaning?"

"I'll get there. Don't rush me."

"Sorry."

"Then there's Central and South America, where it appears eight more races were tampered with."

"'Tampered with?' What does that mean, 'tampered with'?" My voice was sharper than I'd meant it to be.

"Hey, what's up with you? You sound like you got bit by a bear."

"Sorry, Richard. I'm still reeling from my encounter with Kelli. She should be leaving in a minute, so I'll try to calm down. My apologies. Go on with what you were saying about South America."

"Out of eight races, three of the leading competitors disappeared right before the race."

"Disappeared? Just like that?"

"And it's not so easy to do, even in a Third World country. Going on, and please don't interrupt me again—"

"Now who's sounding like he's been bitten by a bear?"

Richard ignored me with the same facility as my mother does. "Two disappeared, two dropped out, one was shot by person or persons unknown from the grandstand, and three others died, once again, from heart attacks. And in every case, a runner no one thought was going to win, won the race."

"Wow. You're saying these races are being fixed by the most dramatic measures, i.e., murder?"

"That's what I'm saying." He paused and took a deep breath. "There's more, and you're not going to like it."

"What?"

"I was talking to Jenn, and she said the night before Stephen died Nick called their home to speak to him."

"Nick? Called Jenn and Stephen? Why would he call them? He only saw them years ago at family gatherings when we were married."

"He asked specifically for Stephen. Jenn told him Stephen was staying at a hotel in downtown Phoenix to be ready to start the race at five thirty a.m. She gave Nick the number of his cell. That's all she knows."

"Did he call? Did Nick talk to Stephen?"

"Appears not. The police turned over Stephen's personal effects a little while ago. I asked Jenn to check the messages on his cell, and Nick's was one of three in voice mail. One was from the kids, another from a work associate, and the third was from Nick. I don't think Stephen ever heard them. Jenn said he often turned his cell off the night before a race, so he wouldn't be disturbed. It was off when Jenn got it back."

"Do you know what this supposed unheard message said?"

"I asked Jenn to play it for me over the phone, and I wrote it down.

"*Stephen, this is Nick, Lee's ex-husband. Don't run the race tomorrow morning. Your life may depend on it. Don't run the race.* And then he hung up."

"Jeesie peesie, what's going on?" My mind flashed to Nick's wife, sitting in my kitchen. "Is Nick being in Las Vegas somehow tied to Stephen's death in Phoenix? Even with everything you've told me, it's hard to believe."

"I know, but everything points that way, Lee. At least, right now. Where is Nick? Did you find out?"

"Yes, but I was going to leave it alone. Now I'll pursue it. Flint was helping me out initially. I'll give him another call. See if he can follow up."

"Good. I've asked Jenn to Fed-Ex me Stephen's phone. I'll take it apart and see if I can get Nick's location or something."

"Let's talk in about an hour," I said and hung up. I leaned back in my chair. Nick had called Stephen the night before he died to warn him. Did Kelli know anything about this? Before she left, I'd have to grill her.

I put in a fast call to Flint. He didn't pick up, but I left a message, asking that he call me back ASAP.

I went for the door, unlocked it, and tried to push it open. It didn't budge. After about thirty seconds, I gave up. I called my home number from the cell, hoping Kelli would pick up. Maybe she could come and help open the door. I let it ring about twenty times. No answer.

It began to dawn on me that Lila Hamilton-Alvarez may have raised a stupid child after all. I threw my body against the door, nearly broke my shoulder, and it still didn't move.

Frantic, I phoned down to the house. Tío answered on the third ring.

"Tío! Don't ask any questions, drop whatever you're doing, come over to my apartment, and let me out of the studio. I think the door is blocked. I can't get out. *Pronto*, Tío."

With a "*si*," he hung up.

Two minutes later, I leaned my ear against the door and heard shuffling of some kind coming from the other side. This soundproofing worked a little better than I'd counted on. Maybe nobody could hear what was going on in the studio, but by the same token, I couldn't hear what was going on in the outside world either.

Once the door was opened, I burst out and saw Tío holding one of my kitchen chairs, it having obviously been what was jammed against the door. I raced into the living room like a maniac, trailed by Tío, who asked questions I was too busy thinking about to answer.

Everything of Kelli's, including the fish tank, was gone. I tore into the kitchen, where one hundred dollars lay on the floor, mocking me. Back in the living room, I looked out the window to an empty driveway. How long had I been in the office? About twenty-five minutes, including the time after I knew I was trapped. She'd moved quickly. I stopped running as abruptly as I'd started and tried not to panic. The house was very quiet. Too quiet.

"Tugger! Tugger! Come on, boy. Come to mommy." Silence. "Baba! Tugger! Come on, you two. Treat! I've got a treat!" The call of a treat will rouse Tugger from even a deathlike sleep from the top shelf of a closet. It's never failed. I stopped breathing, hoping to hear the patter of little feet coming from somewhere. All I heard was my uncle coming up behind me.

"The cat carrier, it is gone," Tío said, his hand on my shoulder, "as well as the litter pan."

"*Dios mio!* She took the cats. She took the cats!"

Chapter Five

I'm so Duped

I ran to the phone, just as it rang. Looking at the number, I saw it was Richard. I didn't even let him speak.

"Richard, Kelli stole Tugger and Baba. She's kidnapped the cats!"

"Oh crap. I saw her careening down the driveway about ten minutes ago. I wondered where she was going in such a hurry."

"I need to call Frank, have him put out an APB." Frank Thompson, chief of the Palo Alto Police and my godfather.

I heard a beep in my ear, announcing a call waiting. I looked at the name. Kelli! "Richard, she's on the other line. I've got to go."

"I'll call Frank, Lee. She can't be far. He's good at finding people who've had a much bigger head start. And it's pretty hard to miss a red Land Rover." He hung up, and I went into the call with Kelli.

"Where are you?" I didn't add the word "bitch" to the end of the sentence even though I felt like it.

"I'm on my way back to Las Vegas, just like you told me," she said in a voice that carried an edge of assuredness and one-upmanship.

"I don't know what you're playing at, but bring back the cats before I get mad."

She actually laughed her stupid little laugh I once thought so cute. "Here's the deal, Lee. You get me Nick; I give you back the cats."

"Oh, really?" I asked, playing for time. "What do you want Nick for? If he doesn't want to be with you —"

"Just get him," she interrupted with a snarl. "You go to Vegas; you find him, but this time you hang on to him. I'll contact you later."

"You harm one hair on those cats —"

"Lee," she interrupted again, and her little girl voice was back again, a voice I'd come to despise. "Now you've hurt my feelings."

"I'll hurt more than your feelings if anything happens to them. I can promise you that."

"Don't you know I would never do an injury to an animal? But you'll never see either one of these kitties again unless you get me Nick. I can promise *you* that."

And then the bitch hung up.

The phone rang the instant she disconnected. It was Frank.

"Know anything else about this red Land Rover?"

"It's a late model, with Nevada license plates. She just called me. She's holding them ransom, Tugger and little Baba." I fought back a sob. My uncle, nearby, patted my shoulder.

I heard Frank's voice say, "That's Gurn's cat, right?"

"Right."

"Well, I've listed them both as stolen property, very rare breeds, worth several thousand dollars. It's the only way I could put out an APB. We normally don't send out alerts for missing cats. What does she want in exchange?"

"What about an Amber Alert?" I asked looking in my uncle's grave eyes, not paying attention to what Frank had just said.

"Let's not push this, Lee," was Frank's steady reply. "You know it's for missing children." I started to protest. "I know, I know. Tugger's like your son, but on the books, he's still a cat. I repeat, what does she want in exchange?"

"She wants me to find Nick. He's somewhere in Vegas."

"Why does she want him so bad?"

"I'm not sure, but he's been hiding out for a week. Maybe from her." I gave him a capsulated version of the story, knowing with Frank's brain, bare bones are all he needs.

"I've got the All-Points Bulletin out," he said, when all he heard on the line was my heavy breathing. "We should know something soon. She hasn't been gone long, right?"

"Right."

My mother's voice at the front door broke into my thoughts. "Liana, what's going on?" Lila asked, coming inside.

"Call me when you learn anything, Frank."

"Will do." He hung up.

Tío looked at me. "Try not to lose the control, *mi sobrina*. You will get Tugger back. And the little girl too. The woman, she took the litter pan. That means she will take care of their needs."

I crossed the room to my mother, whose questioning eyebrows arched above eyes filled with concern. "Mom, I'm so sorry to be dumping anything more on you than you're already dealing with—"

"Don't be silly, Liana. Richard told me what happened. I'm here to help," she said, taking the phone out of my hand and setting it down on the end table. I stood frozen in place, my mind racing. Mom enveloped me in her arms as only a mother can do. "We'll get the cats back."

"You don't understand, Mom. This is my fault. I never should have let her in the house. Or believed her. She manipulated me, and then she took the cats as hostages until I hand over Nick. Somehow Nick is tied in with Stephen's death. I don't know how, but he is. I've got to find him."

Fifteen minutes went by with me pacing and chewing the inside of my lip. The phone rang. I made a lunge for it on the coffee table. It was Flint.

"Flint! You don't happen to know where Nick went, do you? This time it's vital."

He chuckled as only a man who was on top of things would. "I know right where he is. I'm across the street. That's what I calling to tell you."

I tried to breathe normally and felt my first surge of hope. "You are amazing. Do you know if those other men followed him too?"

"No. They were too busy talking on their phones. What's going on, Papoose? You sound upset." I told him while I checked my watch. Nearly an hour had passed since Kelli took off.

"Well, if this don't beat all," Flint said. "Catnapping. I've never heard of such a thing. Never been a cat man myself, but she must have known she had you by the short and curlies when she took them."

"I practically packed them in the car for her. As long as she's got the cats, she's calling the shots."

"In that case, do you want me to grab him? Give you some leverage? I can do it."

"No, not yet. It's looking like I'll be flying to Vegas later this afternoon. If so, we'll take him together. Meanwhile, keep an eye on him. Something is going down. I don't know what it is yet, but I will. Thanks, Lonato. I owe you a big one." I heard the call waiting beep and saw Richard's name. "Got to go. Don't lose Nick, whatever you do."

"Not to worry." We disconnected, and I went on to Richard's line.

"Richard, I got her mobile phone number." I looked at the received calls on my phone. "It's 555-872-5478. Can you track it?"

"I can try, but I'll have to do it from the office. It's not as easy as it looks in the movies. At best, it could take several hours. I don't carry that kind of equipment with me."

"Then go. But before you do, are you calling with any update?"

"Not a good one. I just talked to Frank, and he said they found the Land Rover abandoned on a side road of the Oregon Expressway about two minutes ago. No sign of her."

"The cats?"

"No sign of them, either."

"What about a fish tank?"

"Come again?"

"A fish tank with a goldfish. Was there one in the car?"

"No."

"So, then, she's got an accomplice. Or this was so well planned she had another car stashed where she dumped the Land Rover. Either way, there's no way she could carry two cats in a carrier plus an awkward fish tank on foot very far."

"She's on the lamb with a fish tank? What kind of a lunatic is this?"

"A lunatic who is seriously good at deception. Richard, Kelli could be anywhere. We don't know what kind of car she's in, who she's with, or where she's going. We might never see Tugger again. And there's little Baba; she's such a sweet little girl." I almost gave in to the overwhelming sense of helplessness at the fate of the cats. Then something rallied inside me.

Don't give up. If you do, you've already lost. And no Alvarez is a loser.

"Okay, I'm hanging up now. I've got to talk to Frank. Then I'll get on the laptop for a list of flights to Vegas."

"I'll do it," offered Mom, heading for the laptop on the coffee table.

I turned to Lila. "Thanks. Mom, are you still going to Phoenix?"

"Yes, the boys are asking for me. And I want to see Jennifer face-to-face. Maybe she knows more about what's happening than she thinks she does. But if you need me to go with you to Las Vegas..." Her voice dropped off.

"I'm okay, Mom. I spun down for a moment, but I'm okay. I'll find out who killed Stephen. And I'll get Tugger and Baba back too. I promise you, Mom, and I promise myself."

"There's the Liana I know and love," she said and blew me a kiss. She went back to her search on the internet.

"Maybe we'll be leaving at the same time. If so, I'll drive you to the airport."

"I'll drive you both," said Tío, entering from the guest bathroom. "And *mira, mi sobrina!* See what I find on the sink." From a fingertip he dangled a large silver ring with a huge red stone.

"Kelli must have taken it off when she took a shower," I said, as he dropped it into my open hand.

"I thought this could not be yours. It has the cheap look."

I appraised it. "Maybe not, Tío. This might be a genuine stone. Mom, would you look at this and tell me what you think?" Lila got up and crossed over to me, handing off a handwritten list of flights to Vegas for the remainder of the day. At a quick glance, there was a flight leaving in two hours. Perfect.

Mom took the ring from my other hand and gave the stone a once-over with a practiced eye. Not only can she shoot the backside off a gnat at fifty paces using any weapon with bullets, she can tell a gem's worth from nearly the same distance. Lila Hamilton-Alvarez has many gifts.

"I don't have my loupe with me, but this looks like a Burmese star ruby. It's in an atrocious design, so one might think it was set in silver or worse, but I can assure you, this is the finest platinum."

"Worth what?"

She let out a slightly annoyed sigh. "Liana, I told you I don't have my loupe with me. I can't be sure."

"Guesstimate, Mom."

"Seven, eight thousand dollars. Maybe more."

I whistled, took the heavy clunker of a ring back, and put it in my pocket. "A possible bargaining chip."

I heard a knock at the door the same time as it opened. Frank walked in, dressed in his uniform, looking crisp, important, and no nonsense. Frank Johnson, a black man who started his life in East Palo Alto, met my dad, a Latino, when they were freshmen at Stanford, both having gotten there on good grades and scholarships.

In those days, Frank liked to say his granny ran a brothel in Harlem, just to see people's reactions. The truth was, his granny's family owned a mom-and-pop grocery store in Jamaica. I've seen pictures of Sidney Poitier in his heyday, and Frank could have passed for one of his brothers.

"That was fast," I said.

"I thought I'd come over in person and see what kind of mess you got yourself into this time." He looked over at Mom and Tío. "I don't know how you put up with her."

He wore a forced grin, and I knew he was trying to lighten the situation. He also played with his hat, rolling it by the band back and forth with his long, expressive fingers. This alone showed me he was more upset by what was going on than he wanted to reveal. Frank Thompson is one tough cookie on the outside but a marshmallow on the inside.

"The taking of the pets seems to be tied into Stephen's death, Frank. I don't know that Liana did anything inappropriate," Mom said before I could open my mouth. She stepped forward, not only in a protective manner but also defiantly. I saw Frank stiffen.

Frank had been Dad's best friend since they met in the late '70s. Actually, more than that, they'd been heart brothers. When Dad married Lila, Frank and she had to contend with one other. Even after Dad's death, as godfather to both Richard and me, Frank will always be family. I love Mom and Frank to pieces, but they just don't "get" one another.

Tío, the family peacemaker, jumped in. "Now, we all know Liana; upon the occasion, she leaps in with the heart before she thinks with the head. But we would not have her any other way, ¿*verdad*? Still, what is done, we cannot undo. We must try to recti-recti—"

"Rectify, Tío," I said. "Rectify the situation, if that's what you're trying to say." He nodded his head to me with a smile.

I saw warmth spread over Frank's face. He opened his arms and stepped forward.

"This has been a helluva day for you already, hasn't it, pumpkin?"

I nodded and stepped into his embrace, and for one shining moment, I was comforted by his very being. For one shining moment, I felt closer to the father I'd lost too soon, too fast.

"Okay," I said, swiping at my hot eyes. "Enough of this feeling sorry for myself. It's getting us nowhere. Let's sit down and talk."

I reached back for Mom, while still holding on to Frank with one arm and embraced her with my other. I felt her relax somewhat. The three of us walked over to the seating area arm in arm, followed by Tío.

"Frank," I said, guiding him to the leather easy chair before sitting down next to Mom on the sofa, "I'm beginning to think Kelli told me a lot of half-truths. If that's the case, unless she rented a car and somehow maneuvered both cars where she wanted them to be for the disappearance, I think she had an accomplice, maybe one who drove her Mercedes here while she had the Land Rover. I'd like you to put out an APB for a late model, yellow Mercedes, probably Nevada license plates. With a little luck, she's in that car."

"Where do you think it's heading?"

"Gut instinct: back to Las Vegas. In her search for Nick Papadopoulos."

Chapter Six

The Trail Leads to Vegas

There is nothing pleasant about flying these days. Forget the friendly skies. Now it's the pissed-off, you're-being-stripped-searched-back-to-last-week's-laundry skies. Bring on the long lines, pulling things out of carry-on, putting things back in carry-on, taking coats, jackets, hats, shoes, and belts off, putting them back on while you and your luggage bump to the end of the conveyor belt, throwing away your bottled water, cold cream, and anything else that's liquid and weighs over four ounces. By the time you get to your gate, you're usually a mere shell of your former self. If you still have everything you came to the airport with, it's a miracle. I personally am still missing a bra. I have yet to figure that one out.

This time, though, worrying about Tugger and Baba's fate made the above travesties excruciating. Frank hadn't any good news yet regarding the yellow Mercedes, and I found myself sending up a few prayers to St. Francis, the patron saint of animals. Anything I could do to help the cats, I was going to do.

Mom had left for Phoenix a few minutes earlier. I was booked on the 5:30 p.m. flight to Vegas. While waiting, I must have paced six years of pile off the terminal carpet. Right before I boarded, the phone rang, and it was Richard, so excited he didn't even let me finish saying hello.

"Lee! Tío just told me Kelli took the cats in the cat carrier. Why didn't you tell me?"

"I don't see—"

"Don't you remember a couple of months ago when I came up with this idea about making those identity chips they insert into an animal's neck where you could not only identify the pet but track their whereabouts?"

"Richard, what are you droning on about? What you so laughingly call a chip was about the size of CD-ROM. You couldn't put that into an animal under the size of a tyrannosaurus rex on steroids. Why are you bothering me with this? You can come up with more idiotic ideas—"

"Will you shut up and let me talk? Besides, the chip is not in the final stages. It's just a rough prototype."

"Get to it, Richard, before I hang up."

"I tinkered with Tugger's carrier."

"What?"

"I put the chip in Tugger's carrier."

"You put a chip in Tugger's carrier?"

"Are you going deaf? Yes, a tracking device. Tugger's carrier. About a month ago. Don't you remember when Tío took Tugger to the vet for his checkup? You were out of town or something. Tío said I could," Richard added defensively before I said anything. "He said you wouldn't mind. I think we both forgot about it. I've got so much going on these days I only remembered when Tío said Kelli took the carrier and litter pan. Anyway, I tracked the carrier to the vets and back."

"Don't tell me it worked."

"Well, it did for an under six-mile radius. I don't know—"

"Does that mean you can find Tugger?" I practically screamed out. Nearby passengers looked up from newspapers, magazines, laptops, or conversations, and stared at me. I shrank down into my chair. "Richard, can you?" I asked, containing the volume of my voice.

"First, I have to transfer information to a tracking system within a program then to a satellite. Then with a certain booster, maybe I can—"

"Never mind the yada yada. Can you do it or not?"

"Always the black and white," my brother said with a sigh. "Lee, I'll know in fifteen minutes. The satellite comes back in range, so I can test the theory."

"Oh, Richard. If you could save Tugger—" I broke off because I heard a noise. "What's that?"

"Vicki is back. She's been doing this mega-sale at the Obsessive Chapeau. Speaking of Vicki, we've got some news…"

Whatever Richard said got lost in the boarding call for the flight to Las Vegas. I interrupted him even though I couldn't hear a word.

"Richard, the flight is boarding in about five minutes. Should I go or not? I don't want to go to Vegas if Tugger and Baba are still in the Bay Area."

"It's not scheduled to be within range for fourteen minutes, thirty-seven seconds. There's nothing I can do before then, Lee."

I chewed this over. "Okay, we're not scheduled to take off for twenty-five minutes. I'll get on, but if you find something here, and I should not be heading for Vegas, I'll get off, if I have to knock down the crew to do it."

I sat on the plane, listening to everyone board and watching the time. Latecomers were still boarding when Richard called back.

"Lee! I've got it! It works. I've got to fine-tune it, so I can get a more detailed scope. I—"

"You've found Tugger? And little Baba?" I broke in, so elated, my voice registered about an octave above a birdcall. "Where are they?"

"I found the carrier," he clarified. "Somewhere between here and Fresno, probably on I-5, heading south. As I said, I've got to fine-tune the system."

"So we know she's heading for Vegas for sure." The steward came on over the loudspeaker telling us to buckle up and turn off all electrical apparatus.

"Seems so. I alerted Frank to look for a yellow Mercedes. If they find it, do you want them to apprehend her?"

I thought about this, weighing my options. "No. Let's not do anything yet. I'll stay on the plane. Richard, can you keep tabs on the carrier all the way to Vegas?" The plane began to taxi on the tarmac.

"I can but try. Gotta go. Vicki needs me. But call back when you land. When is that? About an hour and twenty-five minutes?"

"Yes. Thanks, Richard. Let's hope this is one step closer to finding Tugger."

I turned the phone off and tried to close my eyes during the short flight for what lay ahead of me. I must have dropped off because the next voice I heard was the captain telling us to prepare for landing.

The new night was crystal clear, hovering between twilight and darkness. The descent into Vegas was spectacular. Even in the fading light, I could see the glowing pyramid of the Luxor Hotel, which is so strong astronauts have commented on seeing it from space. The glowing lights of the Eiffel Tower of the Paris Hotel, a detailed, half-size replica, and the rest of the dazzling, colored lights of The Strip became even brighter as daylight began to wane. It had been a couple of years since I'd been to Vegas, and I would have been more impressed if I hadn't been so heartsick over the cats.

Flint was meeting me at the airport. With his help, my plan was to flush out Nick and use him as leverage to get the pets back. The bigger job was to find out what he had to do with the deaths of the runners, but I could concentrate better once I had Tugger and Baba in my care. I'd even staved off my anger and outrage at being bamboozled by Kelli, who took me in like a pro. I needed to think clearly and not let my emotions run away with me.

Flint had an extra gun waiting. I wasn't sure what plane I'd be on, and firearms have to be left in baggage unless you're working for the carrier.

I hate borrowing and I don't like guns—mine or anyone else's—but I had a feeling this could get pretty messy, and I wanted to be prepared. Besides, whatever I had to do to get the cats back, I was going to do.

The plane landed in an hour and fifteen, and the first thing I did was to check my messages. One from Flint said he had one of his best men watching Nick's hotel, while he came to pick me up at the airport. Then I called Richard for an update, but his VM picked up. I didn't panic. It usually means he has his proverbial nose to the grindstone and won't allow himself to be distracted. I left a message, knowing he would call me back as soon as he could. By the time I walked outside to the arrivals pickup area, Flint was already waiting for me in his highly polished, black Jeep Wrangler.

"Nicky Boy's holed up and hasn't moved," Flint said as he pulled out into heavy traffic. We're about ten minutes from the hotel." McCarran International Airport was built in 1948, when Las Vegas was a sandy blip on the radar. The city has grown around the airfield, and it's one of the few in the country only minutes from a downtown area.

"What did you bring me?" I asked.

Vague though the question was, Flint knew what I meant. "A nine-millimeter Glock. It's under the seat."

I reached under, found a paper bag, and pulled it out. While I examined the Glock, larger than the one I'm used to, he went on. "I know you like your snub-nose detective thing because Nick and Nora Charles had one like that. Or was it Dick Tracy?"

"I like the grip of the Colt, but this will do." I checked to see if it was loaded, then twisted and turned the gun in an effort to get used to it. It was bottom heavy. The balance of the snub-nose special is mainly what makes the Colt work for me. It's also easy to conceal, something I often have had to do in the skimpy designer clothing Lila requires her agents to wear on the job. I shoved the Glock into the front zipper of my knapsack for easy access.

"And Tracy used a tommy gun, smarty pants."

"He did? Well, no wonder he got his man."

"And anybody else within a two-block radius," I added.

"Yeah, those things cover a lot of ground."

We both laughed, me more out of nervousness than anything else. Flint glanced over at me from the corner of his eye. "I spoke to Richard. He told me he's tracked the cat carrier to Bakersfield and on to 237. They should be here in a matter of hours. So what's the plan?"

"We pay a visit to Nick, and he tells us what's going on."

"And if he doesn't?"

"He will."

"Or what? You going to shoot him over a couple of cats?" We stopped at a red light on Las Vegas Boulevard, and Flint turned and stared at me. "What's the game plan, Lee?"

"Flint, seven people are dead that we know of. There may be more. I'm thinking Nick knows something about this, or he never would have called Stephen. And would I shoot him if it meant getting Tugger and Baba back? Probably."

"Good 'nuff." The light changed, and Flint depressed the gas pedal. We lunged forward.

"Just wanted to know. From what I can tell, Nick Papadopoulos is the kind of man who gives the rest of us a bad name. If we have to shoot him, there's no real loss there."

"Well, his mother might not agree, so let's try not to do it." I laughed, uncomfortable with all this chitchat about shooting someone, even Nick the Jerk.

Minutes later, we pulled up to a narrow, seedy-looking hotel, wedged between a strip joint and a pawnshop. A peeling white-and-black painted sign hung over the door, announcing the Langford Hotel, which looked like it had seen better days, if only marginally.

Flint flung open his car door and dropped his feet to the ground in one svelte move. His were easy moves for a man so large. Standing six foot four or -five in his cowboy boots, he had an enormous chest, massive arms and legs, and a neck like a tree trunk.

He probably weighed in at two forty if an ounce. Reminiscent of a Kodiak bear I'd once seen from the safety of an Alaskan train, Flint was used to going through life pretty much like one of them, with all living things stepping aside.

Now he was standing up, I noticed the strap of a caramel-colored, buckskin leather pouch thrown over his neck, and crossing his mighty chest from left to right. Pinned to the strap, a glittering piece of metal caught my eye. Familiar, a flood of memories came back to me.

"Flint! You've still got that thing?" I looked at the large, fake US Marshals badge I'd found in a thrift shop when I was nine years old. I'd purchased the badge with my hard-earned allowance for fifteen dollars as a Christmas present for our family friend. Engraved on the thick brass were the words, Nevada District US Marshal. To the nine-year-old mind, it seemed like a perfect gift.

"I'm never without it, Papoose. It's my lucky charm. I wear it all the time when I'm working a case."

"And no one razzes you about it?"

Flint gave me an incredulous look.

"Right," I said. "Lost my mind for a moment."

He reached for his ten-gallon hat on the back seat, plopped it on a head of straight black hair, with silver strands intermittently running throughout. A leather thong deftly wrapped around a short ponytail at the nape of his neck. Flint straightened out his deerskin-fringed jacket with a shake and realigned himself. A rugged, sincere-looking man with coarse features, Flint always wore an easy smile and brandished the scent of an expensive, lemony cologne. A lot of women who were into the Wild West look fell hard for this Native American, and most men considered him a man's man.

Leaning on a nearby parking meter, reading a paper, and chewing on a toothpick, a short, stocky middle-aged man looked up. He received a cursory nod from Flint, returned it, folded his paper, and strolled away.

"The only exit in the back is blocked by about sixteen boxes loaded with DVDs and other stuff. I think the manager has a sideline of selling stolen goods," Flint said as he walked toward the open door of the hotel.

"Where is he?"

"Room 310. He paid in cash, two days in advance."

"More of what a twenty will buy you?" I said, stepping over a cracked and filthy doorsill into an even filthier hallway. The smell of urine and rancid bacon assaulted my nostrils.

"A ten-spot," he responded. "I told you, this place is even seedier than the last."

I looked around at the crumbling, graffiti-covered, dirty walls, once painted a color now unidentifiable and felt a pang of pity for the humanity crossing this threshold. Some places should be razed to the ground, just on general principle.

We passed a counter, also nasty looking and littered with used paper cups, booze bottles, and trash. An emaciated-looking man sat on a stool behind the counter watching a small black-and-white television, topped off with a wire clothes hanger instead of rabbit ears. The man saw us and grinned a cadaverous smile, a few missing teeth completing the picture.

Flint threw another ten-dollar bill on the counter, bothering a nearby cockroach that scuttled away. The manager made a lunge for it, the bill not the roach, and winked at us. He went back to his television show, while we headed for a rickety staircase farther back. I guess he thought Flint and I were planning to use one of the rooms on an hourly basis. As we started up the creaky staircase to the third floor, I turned to Flint.

"Nick must really be scared to be hiding out in a place like this. It could make him dangerous. Let me handle him. Don't say anything. Stay in the background. I want him to consider you the silent but ever-ready plan B."

"We're going to play good cop, bad cop?" Flint asked with a lopsided grin. "I make a great bad cop."

"Okay, but let me lead the way."

At the top of the stairs, a small, twenty-five-watt bulb hung from a frayed electrical wire in the center of the narrow, dark, and oppressive hallway. I felt something small scurry by my foot and was pretty sure it wasn't someone's bichon frise out for an evening stroll. I managed not to scream but stood on tippy-toes the rest of the way down the hall. I remembered a small flashlight I keep on me and pulled it out. For the record, this is a part of an investigation that is sooo not me.

Even with this pinpoint of light, what with the dark and so many door numbers broken or missing, it was hard to make out which room was which. We arrived at what I thought was room 310, and I looked at Flint with a shrug, hoping for some kind of reaffirmation. He shrugged back as un-reaffirmed as me. I decided to go for it and knocked on the door. The knock echoed through the silent and gloomy hallway like someone had hit a cymbal with a baseball bat.

Nothing. I waited a few seconds and then knocked again. More nothing. I put my mouth to the crack, which I was loath to do given what I'd seen loitering in the cracks around here.

"Nick," I whispered hoarsely. "Nick. It's me, Lee. Let me in."

Just then, my phone rang out with the New York Philharmonic's version of Beethoven's Fifth. I really need to rethink that ringtone. While I struggled with my pants pocket to relieve it of the phone before it blasted us with yet another surge of "Bum, bum, bum, bum," I stumbled against the door. Nearby, Flint backed up into the shadows, swallowing laughter. The phone blasted again, and leaning against the door, I looked at the number.

"Richard," I squawked. "I'll call you right back."

While fumbling to close the phone, the door opened, and I fell inside with a yelp. I sat on the floor and looked around. It was a tiny room, only able to hold a single, lumpy bed, a beat-up wooden chair, and a sagging chest of drawers, with no knobs and one missing drawer. A miniscule, chipped sink with a loud water drip hung on a battered wall next to a tiny, doorless room with a toilet, sans lid and seat. Charming.

"Well, if it isn't Liana Alvarez. And where she goes, can the rest of the Alvarez clan be far behind?"

From a shadowy corner, an older, thinner, and stressed-out Nicholas Papadopoulos stepped forward. He still had the same thick, dark, curly hair, but now the hair was flecked at the temples with gray. His face wore a two- or three-day stubble, also slightly flecked with gray, and one of his eyes — those dark velvety-brown eyes I used to find so irresistible — was recovering from a pretty bad bruise. Something looked different with his nose, too, but maybe I wasn't remembering everything right. It had been at least four years since I'd seen him.

Fear dominated his being even though he tried to hide it. His whole demeanor was the same as when he'd relive some of those raids he went on in the Persian Gulf, where he knew he stood less than a fifty-fifty chance of coming back alive.

I opened my mouth to say something and was stopped by Flint, pushing his way into the room, more like a tsunami than a man.

Terror tracked across Nick's face. He backed up the full length of the small room, which was three steps more or less, and banged into the wall, where he froze.

"Jesus Christ!" he said.

"It's all right, Nick. This is Flint. You may remember me mentioning him to you when we were married. He's a friend of mine."

Flint grunted a greeting, something like a Kodiak bear would do right before it eats you, and folded his arms across his enormous chest, the fringes of his deerskin being the only movement in the room.

"W,-what do you want?" Nick stuttered. He looked at me and then at the glaring Flint. I think if he could have climbed up the wall to get away, he would have done it.

"I want to know what's going on, Nick."

"I don't know what you're talking about."

"Why did you call Stephen the night before he died warning him not to run the race? What were you trying to warn him about?"

"How did you find me?" Nick countered. "Go away. Go away."

"Not happening, Nicky Boy," said Flint, his deep voice filling the room.

"Go away and leave me alone, can't you?" Nick visibly shrank next to the wall, looking around for an escape.

"I'm not going anywhere, Nick, until you tell me why you're here," I said. "Why did you disappear on Kelli a week ago?"

"Kelli?" he said, his voice became high pitched, filled with panic. "What do you know about Kelli? How do you know Kelli?"

I'd said the wrong thing, apparently.

Flint moved forward, and Nick slid to the floor, arms flailing to protect himself. My big friend bent over, grabbed Nick by his rumpled polo shirt and hauled him up.

"Let me rough him up a bit, Lee, just a little bit."

Slack jawed, Nick stared at me. I didn't see anything of the former marine in him, which shocked me, but I tried not to show it.

I put a hand on Flint's arm drawing back in preparation for a punch. "No, no. Even though you could say he done me wrong, let's not get rough." I paused dramatically. "Not yet."

Flint let go, and Nick fell onto the unmade, crumpled bed, although how he could do that considering what might be sharing the space with him, I'll never know.

I stared down at Nick, who sat up and cupped his face in his hands, rocking back and forth. I had never seen him this scared, this pitiable. What had happened to the man I'd known and loved?

I crouched down and put my hand on his knee, trying to look into his face. No matter which way I moved my face, he turned away.

This was the time to be gentle, I knew instinctively, even though I wanted to kick him in the groin for somehow being involved in Stephen's death.

"Nick, you need to tell me what's going on, and you need to do it fast. If we found you, whoever you're afraid of will find you too. It's only a matter of time."

He looked at me with tear-filled eyes. "How do I know you're not here to kill me?"

I got angry. "That's not my style, and you know it. Since when did I turn into a thug? But I can't help you if you won't talk to me." He shook his head and lowered it into his hands again, all hunkered down into himself.

"Okay," I said, exhaling and standing up. "Let's go, Flint. If he won't talk to us, he won't talk to us."

"You mean, let those other guys have him?" Flint said with a straight face but a twinkle in his eye. "Sounds only fair. I got better things to do with my time than watch a grown man act like a scaredy-cat." We both turned for the door.

"Wait a minute," Nick said, looking up at us. Then he stood. "You're just going to leave? Leave me like this?"

I gazed at him for a moment. "That's the plan." I turned for the door.

"Okay, okay. I'll tell you. But not here. What if Lou's men come? You can't fight them off. There's too many of them."

"Who's Lou?" Flint and I said in unison.

"We have to get out of here," Nick whined. "I can't stay here. Like you say, if you found me, they can too."

I looked at Flint and nodded. In the car, we'd discussed where we might bring Nick for safety, if it came to it. While my first choice for lodgings in Vegas would have been the Bellagio, this wasn't the time or place. Besides, I'd rather go there one of these days with Gurn.

"I know a safe place," said Flint, "but you'd better not bring any bedbugs or lice with you. I run a clean establishment."

Chapter Seven

I Don't Know Who's the Bigger Idiot

Without much conversation, we jostled Nick out of the room and down the stairs. As a precaution, we used the back exit: Flint flinging boxes of DVDs every which way so fast, the clerk only managed one "Hey" before we were out the door. The exit led to a narrow back alley filled with garbage, trash, and more small scurrying animals that should be calling the SPCA to complain about the conditions under which they're forced to live.

While Flint went to bring the car to the side of the alley, I waited in the shadows next to Nick and pulled out the Glock. The irony of the situation hit me like a double charge on a credit card bill for shoes not only too tight but last year's style.

On the left, a disgusting dumpster, on the right, an even more disgusting ex-husband. And me stuck in the middle as usual—a reluctant PI if ever there was one.

Rather than inhaling the stench of fly-ridden garbage, I'd really rather be sniffing out dastardly doings of computer sabotage or thievery, in particular, long after said dastardly deeds have gone down. It's my idea of a good job, especially when I get to zip off whenever I want and have a great lunch.

The part I like best—besides the food—is sitting at a highly polished, recently vacated mahogany desk in an air-conditioned office, sifting through the rubble of high-tech deceit and betrayal.

I like gathering enough evidence to point a manicured fingernail at the culprit and shout *j'accuse!* Backlit by enough briefs, memos, emails, and other telltale papers, the culprit is mine. That is a real high.

This was a real low. But I had to think about Stephen. My cousin was dead, and Nick knew something about it. Hell, maybe he even had something to do with it. And, of course, there were the cats. If Nick was in any way responsible, I might do him in myself and save whatever goons there may be the trouble.

All these things were flitting through my mind when Nick — the stupid idiot — made a lunge for my gun, muttering he could take better care of himself than I could. Sometimes an ex-marine, like an ex-husband, needs to get over himself.

One of the first lessons you learn as a PI is to not to carry a gun if you're going to let anybody take it away from you. All the years I've been carrying, ten to be exact, people have taken all sorts of things from me — including my virtue — but never my gun.

So when Nick came at me, my knee went up fast, strong, and accurate. Ex dropped to the ground in a fetal position. God only knows what else was lying there with him, but I left him on the dirt, anyway. He was busy moaning while I cocked the Glock and gave a 360-degree spin, prepared to do whatever was necessary to keep the jerk safe. At least for the moment.

Fortunately, no one showed up except a passing rat or two, excluding the one I stood over. After what felt like a lifetime, I saw Flint's headlights, although I'm sure it didn't take him more than three minutes to get there. I helped Nick up. He limped to the car, and Flint, bless him, raised an eyebrow over Nick's condition but didn't say a word. What a guy.

During an uneventful fifteen-minute ride to Flint's apartment, I rang an excited Richard back and learned he had commandeered a piece of software, which overlaid a grid onto his tracking map, enabling him to pinpoint the whereabouts of Tugger's carrier within five hundred yards. According to Richard's calculations, the cats should arrive in Las Vegas in about an hour and a half.

I was mightily impressed, not to mention hopeful, but couldn't respond with much enthusiasm on my end. I didn't want Nick picking up any information, him being a first-class louse. Said louse was quiet once I'd bested him, sitting next to me in the back seat of Flint's Jeep. I watched him lean his head against the window with his eyes closed. I whispered to Richard that Nick was in the car, and after he told me Lila had landed without incident in Phoenix, we ended the conversation.

* * * *

Flint resides in a two-story apartment complex, complete with gardens and pool, in an upscale residential area of Vegas. Sometimes I forget people actually live here. Being a transient visitor, I tend to think of Vegas as a transient place, but there's a large population willing to call this gambler's paradise home. Flint was one.

He'd left the police force and reservation, where he had been until his early thirties, and set up shop in Vegas. He was still committed to his people, donating money, sponsoring kids for college, contributing funds for tuitions, all that good stuff, but he'd moved off the reservation twenty or so years ago and never returned. His son once mentioned a falling out with the elders over the burial of his wife, who committed suicide after being diagnosed with ovarian cancer. As far as I could tell, he'd never returned to the reservation.

We entered a two-bedroom corner apartment on the second floor, with enough sophisticated locks on the front door to make the picking of them pretty undoable, further aided by an alarm system which could wake the dead. The back door had been cemented up years ago, and each window wore interior bars, released from an inside latch. There was only one way in or out, and that's how Flint liked it. When he came home, he once said, he wanted to know it was his castle and not his crypt. It's the downside of doing his type of work, with divorce and bond jumping being a major part, but nobody does it better than Lonato, aka Flint. He makes a very good living.

I gave the living room a quick once-over and saw a room heavily decorated with Native American art, blankets, and crafts. Nick ripped my attention away from the décor, his whole demeanor changing once inside this restful space. He stood taller and wore a smug grin.

"I could sure use a shower," he said, turning to the bigger man.

Before Flint could reply, I gave Nick a shove, throwing him off-balance, and onto a sofa covered with intricately woven and colorful blankets. He fell down, with a surprised look on his face.

"Not until you answer some questions, Nick. Now who's Lou?" I sat on the edge of a sturdy-looking coffee table across from Nick and leaned into his face.

"All right, all right. Don't get your liver in a quiver."

"And you can drop the cocky, smart-assed routine, too, before somebody does something to you I'm not going to regret." Flint played along with me and scowled at Nick in a menacing way. "Now, who's Lou?"

Nick licked his lips and ran a fast hand over his stubble. "Okay. Okay. Lou Spaulding."

He paused and looked down at nervous hands. Out of the corner of my eye, I saw Flint react to the name.

"Who's Lou Spaulding?" I looked from one man to the other.

"Believe me," Nick said, "you don't want to know."

"Yes, I do."

"He's bad news, Lee," answered Nick.

Flint came forward, folding his arms across his chest. "He came to Vegas about three years ago from Chicago and financed the new hotel across from the Encore, the Fantasy Lady. It's for serious gamblers. No families, no penny slot machines, just big players from all over the world. Rumor is, it's part of a syndicate coming out of Dubai, run by some of the world's wealthiest businessmen. They're into heavy betting, and they play for keeps."

"You don't want to mess with them, Lee," said Nick, looking down and picking at a scab on his hand.

"We messed with them when we took you out of that hotel room, Nicky Boy," said Flint.

I glanced at him and then back at Nick. "Right," I said. "So what's Kelli got to do with this Lou Spaulding?"

Fear washed over Nick's face again at the mention of his wife's name. I smacked him on the leg to get his attention again.

"Talk to me," I yelled into his face.

He looked up, and I saw the teenage boy I'd known so many years ago, the one whose father had run off with another woman never to be heard from again. Once again, Nick reeked from betrayal, loneliness, and fear.

"How does she fit in, Nick?" My voice was softer but firm.

"She started fooling around with Lou about two or three months ago. At first, I didn't catch on. She told me she was working at the casino late, visiting with friends, you know, girl stuff."

"I thought she quit working once you got married," I said, the words popping out of my mouth before I thought better of them.

"Where'd you hear that?" Nick asked. "She never stopped working. She didn't want to, and I've always liked a working wife; you know that."

Score another one for the nefarious Kelli. "Never mind. Go on."

"Anyway, the bottom had dropped out of the real estate market by then, and Kelli, well, I think Kelli thought I had more money than I did." He paused, picking at the scab again. The sore started to bleed, and he wiped the blood away with an impatient gesture.

"Maybe I gave her that impression. I was… I was in love with her." He took a ragged breath. "Right before we got married, I'd bought her a new car for her birthday, ninety-five grand, but I couldn't keep up the payments after I closed the office, so the collection agency came to take it away. The next day it was sitting in the parking lot again. I asked her about it, but she said she had some savings and went and paid for it in cash." He shook his head. A look of sadness came over him, almost heartbreaking. Nick blinked his eyes rapidly as if unsavory memories ran amuck before them.

"Right before I met Kelli, I was doing a pretty big deal with Lou on a penthouse condo on The Strip he wanted. I had a year's exclusive on it, one of the last deals I made before the bottom dropped out of the market. Otherwise, a man like Lou Spaulding is out of my league. I knew it; he knew it." Nick shrugged and inhaled another tired breath.

"That's how she… Kelli… met him. We went to a couple of parties he threw. After the deal was done, he stopped answering my calls. Looking back on it that must have been the time she started seeing him. She got the money for the car from Lou. I know it. After a while, she didn't even hide what she was doing. She'd come and go as she pleased, staying out all hours, coming home mussed up, or smelling of another man's aftershave. About two weeks ago, I confronted her, and she said, 'Screw you, Nick. You don't like it? Get out.'" Nick looked at Flint. "You got a drink? I need a drink."

"Finish your story first," I said. "What happened then?"

"I started sleeping on the couch. Last week while she was at the casino, two men showed up at the door.

They shoved their way inside and started knocking me around, demanding I give them back what I took from Lou Spaulding."

"What did you take?" I shot at him, the words flying out of my mouth.

"Nothing. I didn't take anything." He spread his arms out wide as if offering up his life to the truth. "I hadn't seen Spaulding in months. And what the hell would I take? I told them, but they didn't believe me. They ripped the place apart looking for I don't know what. Then they broke my nose and told me nobody messes with Spaulding and his races."

"They used the word 'races'?" I asked.

He nodded. "They said I had twenty-four hours to return it, or I was a dead man." Nick paused and looked at me. "And they weren't kidding. I didn't know what was going on, but I knew Kelli had something to do with it. I sat in the dark waiting for her to come home. When I told her about the visit from Spaulding's men, she looked me up and down and laughed. She just laughed. Here I am with a bloody nose, a black eye; they threatened to kill me, and she's laughing. Then she did a turnaround—she does that a lot. You know, one minute she accuses you of cheating on her, lying to her, or something, and the next minute she's saying she loves you, hugging you, kissing you. Anyway, she tried to hug me, but I'd had enough. I pushed her away, took off my wedding ring, and threw it at her feet. Then I left, with her yelling at me to come back. I hadn't packed; I didn't take any keys, just the clothes on my back. I must have walked for hours trying to figure this out. And I've been in hiding ever since."

"How does Stephen fit into this? What made you call him?"

"Right after Lou's men left, I found a piece of paper with his name on it in the mess in the bedroom those two left."

"You mean Stephen's name?" I asked.

"That's what I said, didn't I?"

His voice was sharp and annoyed.

Flint stepped forward protectively. Nick became docile again. "I think the paper fell out of one of Kelli's drawers when they pulled everything out. I'd never seen it before. At the time, one of the names on the list seemed familiar, so I picked up the note and put it in my pocket. I didn't remember Stephen was your cousin until the night I called his wife, when it came back to me. I'd met him at a New Year's party back when you and I were married.

"Once I realized, well, seeing Stephen's name on anything connected with Lou Spaulding was scary, so I called to warn him. I would have kept calling until I reached him, but my phone ran out of juice, and I didn't have my charger. I didn't have any money to buy one either."

"Tell me about the races," I said.

"What races?" His voice gained an exasperated edge, adding to the fear and impatience. "The first I learned about any of this was the day I found that paper. I don't know what the hell's going on, but I'm scared. Those men find me... I'm dead. I know that much."

"Show me this piece of paper." I put out my hand.

He thought for a moment, reached inside his jeans, and hesitated before turning it over to me.

I unfolded the three-by-five-inch lined sheet, torn from a small notepad. On it were written seven names. The top one was Stephen's. I scanned the rest of the list and found the name Gurn Hanson at the bottom. I fought to keep my cool about the man I loved being on a possible dead-man's list. No small feat for a Latina who wears her emotions on her sleeves. Besides, I had talked to Gurn several hours ago. He was fine.

Ignoring the thudding heart inside my chest, I studied the list. After each name was a date, some past, some future. Then the phrase "take out" and a set of numbers, followed by the letter "K." The date next to Gurn's name was the Sunday coming up, seven days. Whatever was going on, we had to stop it by then.

"Whose handwriting is this?" I asked. "Do you recognize it?" Nick shook his head and looked down.

I passed the note to Flint, who studied it, while I turned back to Nick. "What do the numbers mean? The ones followed by the letter 'K'? Does the 'K' mean the length of a race?"

"I'm telling you, I don't know. I wish I did." His impatience, fear, and frustration rang true. He knew nada.

Flint jumped in, saying, "It could be a race. I've heard high rollers on the top floor of the Fantasy Lady will literally bet on anything, with the minimum bet being a million dollars. Maybe they're into footraces now. They've sure been into soccer for a long time."

I absorbed the info and turned back to Nick. "Why did you tell Kelli about me? Why did she show up at my place early this morning?"

Nick's eyes got huge as he stared at me. I could see the wheels turning inside his head. "I don't know why she'd come to you. I've never said one thing about you to her, ever." He thought. "Wait a minute, once, when we first got together, she asked me about my ex-wife. I told her you and your family ran a detective agency in the Bay Area, a pretty successful one. Other than that, I've never said one word about you to her."

I crossed one leg over the other and considered this. So either Kelli had made up all the malarkey about Nick thinking I was the most beautiful, wonderful, yada yada in the world, or Nick was lying now. I looked at him. He wasn't lying. He was too scared. Besides, he'd just admitted he loved her. So it was Kelli. She knew by making it sound like he still had a thing for me, she'd hit me in my ego. Ex-husband still pines for ex-wife and admits it to younger, newer wife.

I'm such an idiot.

"Spaulding and his men are still after you, Nick," I said, uncrossing my legs and standing. "So they must think you have whatever they say you took from him. Get up and strip."

"What?"

"I said, get up and take off your clothes. You can have a shower while Flint and I go through your things."

"Are you crazy?" He looked at both of us. "I'm not going to stand up and take off my clothes just because you say so."

Flint came closer. "Yes, you are, Nicky Boy, or I'll take them off for you."

Nick studied me for a moment, and I glared back. Then he shrugged and pulled the wrinkled and stained polo shirt over his head. His marine dog tags clinked against themselves, protesting the rough treatment.

"You still wear those things, Nick? After all these years?"

"Never take them off," he said, throwing the shirt to the floor and unzipping the fly of his jeans. I averted my eyes and looked down at the floor. "What's the matter, Lee? You've seen it all before."

"Yeah, but I don't want to see it again." Both Nick and Flint laughed, Flint's laugh hardier than the embarrassed chortle Nick gave out. I kept my eyes down but joined in the laughter after a moment. His movements ceased, and there was silence. "Done?"

"Done," said Flint. "Naked as a jaybird."

"Can I take that shower now?" Nick asked. "I haven't had one in four days."

"And you smell like it, Nicky Boy," offered Flint. "Sure. Second door on the right, towels in the linen closet. Take the blue ones: those are my guest towels."

Wordless, Nick strode to the bathroom, my eyes flitting to his backside. I had to admit, he still looked pretty good, although out of condition.

While we listened to the running shower, Flint and I search through his shirt, jeans, and boxers. Nothing but sixteen dollars and fifty-one cents and a receipt from one of the dives.

"Well, if there's anything here," said Flint, "I can't find it."

"There has to be something." I looked at my watch. An hour had passed. Only thirty minutes more until the scheduled arrival of Kelli's yellow Mercedes and the cats. Nick strode out of the shower, his middle wrapped in a blue towel. The light caught the glint of his dog tags.

"Give me those tags, Nick," I ordered, reaching out my hand.

"You know, you are nuts." Nick came to a stop in the center of the room. "I'm not giving you my dog tags. They always stay on me. Always."

"Are you sure? They've *always* been on you?"

"Sure, I'm su—" Nick stopped talking, and his face reflected an incident. "Except the time a while back when the chain broke, and Kelli offered to fix it for me. She was only gone an hour or so, went to a jewelry store, I think, and she came back with the new chain."

"How'd they break, Nicky Boy? Were you both in the heat of the moment, and Kelli ripped them off your neck?" Flint stepped forward with an extended hand.

Stunned, Nick took the tags off his neck and dropped them into Flint's large hand. Meanwhile, I'd pulled my flashlight from my knapsack and crossed over to a reading lamp on an end table, where the two men joined me. I took the tags and began to examine each one.

"What's on my tags so small I can't see it?"

"We're going to find out." I flipped the tags over and examined the other side of each. "Here's something," I said. "Flint, you got a pair of tweezers?"

"You bet." He crossed to the kitchen and opened a drawer, bringing out a rolled-up black-leather pouch. I knew at a glance they were for the fine art of picking a lock but said nothing. He unrolled it and pulled a small pair of tweezers from one of the pockets. He handed them over.

With care, I pried free and lifted the tiny square metal from the tag. "Now I need a magnifying glass."

"Coming up," said Flint, returning to the leather kit and pilfering through another pouch.

"What's that?" asked Nick, leaning in to see what I had trapped on the end of the tweezers.

Flint handed me the round magnifying glass, and I peered through it.

"It's a plastic-coated, miniaturized data chip. Maybe even one of those new ones weighing next to nothing. If I were to release it right now, it probably would hover in the air for a time."

"Are you kidding?"

"No I'm not. Apple, Sony, Toshiba, all the big companies have been working on a 'lighter than air' concept for some time now. At least, that's what Richard tells me. Not only would your phone and laptop weigh literally next to nothing, these chips can hold enough information to fill a library."

"How would Kelli get something like that, and why would she put it on my dog tags?"

"And an even bigger question," I said, "is what information is on this chip that's important enough to engage in such an elaborate subterfuge?"

Chapter Eight

Caught in the Crosshairs

The phone rang. It was Richard. I answered it by saying, "Got anything?"

"The carrier is in Primm. You've got twenty-five to thirty-five minutes before the car hits Vegas. So you know, I've locked on to your phone. This way I can tell how far apart you are from the carrier."

"Thanks. Did you manage to lock on to Kelli's phone?"

"No signal I can find. She probably destroyed it. She's a pretty smart babe, judging by what's transpired so far."

"True. Along those lines, I've got a microchip, looks plastic coated, about one-sixteenth of an inch, silver in color with brass lines running through it. Found it attached to one of Nick's dog tags. I think Kelli put it there."

Richard let out a low whistle. "Bet it's important."

"I think so, yes."

"Any idea what's on it?"

"No."

"Then we're going to need to scan it. It sounds digital, but I don't know of any company out in your neck of the woods with anything like that, except MAPLAB, IDE."

"What's that when it's at home?"

"MAPLAB is self-explanatory."

"Not to me."

"Never mind, let's move on to the relevant part. The IDE stands for Integrated Development Environment.

An integrated toolset for the development of embedded applications employing microchips and microcontrollers."

"Richard," I said, dragging out his name in annoyance, "you're talking in a foreign language again."

"Lee," he said, imitating my tone, "they deal with microchip compilations for medical timed-release chips, intelligent power supplies, smart bombs, things like that. Exacting and detailed information stored on the virtual head of a pin. Not too many places can."

"This MAPLAB can?"

"Yes, their lab is about fifteen miles outside of Vegas. But it's top secret. I'm not supposed to know it's there—nobody is—so we can't go to them for help. Besides, odds are it's probably where the chip came from in the first place."

"If I get this to you, can you extract the info off it?"

"Sure, I've got a friend at the Linier Center at Stanford. He's a proud papa of every scanner known to man. I'll give him a call. Meanwhile, Tugger's on the move. What are you going to do?"

"First order of business, get the cats back. We'll plant ourselves on the outskirts of town, wait for the Mercedes to come by and follow it. You say you're locked on to my phone signal as well as the cat carrier?"

"You bet."

"Can you correlate the two signals?"

"Duh."

"Right, just checking." I hung up and turned to Flint. "You got any clean clothes for him to wear?" I gestured to Nick. "If not, it's back into the old ones."

"My son left some things that might fit. I'll go get them." Flint headed for a hall closet and began pulling clothes off a hanger.

"Then, gentlemen, we need to move. They're on their way."

* * * *

Flint said it was best to stay on the side of I-215 before the first exit into Las Vegas, called South Point. New buildings dotted here and there fed warm light into an otherwise dark and cold landscape. Cars zoomed by, many going over the allotted seventy miles per hour.

The waiting was excruciating, worse than at the airport. I don't wait well. I tend to go the worst-case scenario as the seconds tick by. I gnawed on nails, which only the day before had been groomed by a woman who devotes her life to the condition of your cuticle. What my hands looked like now would send her to the nearest bar.

Behind the wheel, Flint's eyes were closed, and it looked like he was asleep, but I knew better. In the passenger's seat, Nick fidgeted so much, the car actually rocked back and forth from his movements. I wanted to smack him, but I'd already done that several times before. Don't want to develop bad habits.

My phone rang. In my excitement to answer it, I nearly dropped it. I flipped it open but didn't have a chance to say a word.

"It's there," Richard said. Your two signals are almost one."

Anxious, I looked out the window at the cars whizzing by. "I don't see a yellow—"

"Hey, look," interjected Nick, pointing at a passing late-model station wagon. "That BMW station wagon. It looks like… It is. It's Eddie's car."

"Who's that?" Flint asked.

"Eddie Crackmeir, Kelli's uncle," Nick replied.

"Let's go!" I slapped the back of Flint's car seat. Flint peeled out into the nearest lane and fell two cars behind the wagon.

"Okay, I see everybody's on the move, Lee," said Richard.

"Richard, I know you're doing a lot, but do you think you could check on a Nevada plate?" I read the plate as we followed behind, darting in and out of traffic. "One, seven, four, P for Peter, A for Alpha, G for George."

"Got it. I'll have Andy run it."

"Is he there? It's almost ten p.m." Andy was one of two of Richard's assistants. A real whiz kid, if ever there was one.

"Everybody's here. You think I could do all this by myself? Vicki's even brought us sandwiches. This might be an all-nighter."

"In that case, run a check on an Eddie Crackmeir; don't know how it's spelled. He might be driving the car." I hung up.

"Look at that man! He's passing everybody," Flint said as he watched the wagon weave in and out of traffic. "He has to be going ninety miles an hour."

"Don't lose him, Flint," I said.

"You're paying my speeding ticket, right?" Flint laughed. "Whoa," he said, making a hard right off the I-215.

Nick and I grabbed on to anything we could to stay upright.

"We're going to Tropicana Road. Odds are we're heading to the Fantasy Lady."

"Don't let him see you, Flint. Not yet. Not until we get the cats."

"Cats?" bellowed Nick. "You're doing all this for some stupid cats?"

"Shut up!" Flint and I said in unison.

Both cars stopped at a red light on busy Las Vegas Boulevard, the wagon one car ahead of us. "Duck down, Nick," I said, pushing his head down from behind. "I don't want them to see you." I lowered my head, too, just in case.

We started moving again, but I kept my head down the entire way until I felt us turn left and slow down. "Where are we, Flint?"

"Parking lot of the Fantasy Lady. I'm staying pretty far behind, but I can still see them with the lot lights. They're pulling into a farther away section. There are two people in the car, a man and a blonde woman."

"That's Kelli," was Nick's husky reply.

"They've parked about as far away from the casino as they can get. They're in the shadows, but they're getting out. Now they're in more light. She's little but a looker," Flint remarked.

"Never mind," I said. "Honest to God, you men."

"Where are they going?" asked Nick's muffled voice. I could tell he was still hunched over.

"Heading for the casino."

I sat up and studied the tall hotel/gambling casino standing erect behind the parking lot, while Flint's car crawled in. The façade of the Fantasy Lady wore a brightly lit, fifteen- to twenty-story-tall Art Deco woman, her curvaceous body outlined in shades of pink lights. A slightly darker pink color, representing fabric, was wrapped around her nude body in strategic places. Arms extended over her head, she stretched, fingertips lightly touching a large, blinking red poker chip. A little garish for my tastes, but Vegas has never been known for its subtleties. Kelli and her uncle disappeared inside the casino doors.

"Now's our chance." I opened the car door and got out, running ahead to the five-door BMW station wagon. Flint kept pace, driving his car behind me. In this area of the parking lot, there were only a few light poles scattered here and there. Diffused, stark lighting created eerie, flat shadows without depth, reminding me of pictures I've seen of the moon. In some ways, I would have preferred total darkness. I squinted and studied my surroundings while I jogged to the wagon, which looked like a big, black blob. And try saying that three times fast.

As I neared the vehicle, I heard two different but equally pitiful meows coming from inside. The louder, scared, but belligerent one was Tugger's. The smaller, sad cry came from Baba. My heart did a flip-flop.

In a fury, I tried the doors of the wagon — locked — then I pulled my flashlight from my knapsack, along with the Glock. Seeing the windows had been left open a crack for air, I put my mouth to the back passenger window and yelled inside.

"Tugger, Baba. It's me!" I swung the light into the back of the wagon and saw the cats were loose. Loose and, on the surface of it, okay. Relief swept over me. Hearing me, they both hopped into the back seat following my voice with renewed vigor to their cries.

"Hi, babies! Don't worry. I'm getting you out now."

I heard Nick come up behind me. "Lee? What are you doing?"

"Here," I said, shoving the flashlight in his hand. "Keep the light focused on the lock of this door." I rooted through my knapsack and found the sixteen-piece car unlock set I'd brought with me—ninety-nine fifty on sale.

Flint crept over, scaring me half to death, and whispered in my ear. "I'll watch and make sure no one is coming. I'm right behind their car, and the motor is idling. Let me know if you need any help."

I nodded and felt rather than heard him go away. I chose one of the pieces in the set, maneuvered the slender metal with the curved edge through the crack in the window, and down toward the lock. I was glad I'd paid attention when this exercise was being taught in a class I took on suspect apprehension. I got an "A" by opening a car door in record time and hoped the knack hadn't left me. Within seconds, I heard a click, and the door was unlocked.

I swung it open, leaned down, and Tugger rushed into my arms, caterwauling at the top of his lungs. He groped his way up to my shoulder and neck and clung on for dear life.

Little Baba hesitated for a moment, but when I reached out to her, she leapt up on my other shoulder, meowing piteously. I wrapped my arms around the both of them, half sobbing, half whispering comforting words, and stood up. Glock in one hand, knapsack dangling from the other, and draped in cats, I did a slow pivot and checked out the surroundings. Nada.

Nearer the casino, rows and rows of empty cars sat. The parking lot was deserted except for two tipsy women near the more lit entrance, laughing and calling each other names in pig Latin while trying to open a car door.

"Flint! Where are you?" I whispered hoarsely.

"Over here. The other side of the car. It looks good. Nobody's coming that I can see. Those two gals over there are three sheets to the wind. I don't think they can see the car keys in their hands."

"Good. Nick, open up the back door of the wagon, grab the cat carrier, and anything else in there. I've unlocked the car."

"What? You're kidding." Nick hesitated.

"Nick, just do it, and don't make me shoot you," I growled. "I'm up to here with you and your nonsense."

"Okay, okay." He swung the fifth door open in the back of the wagon and flashed the light inside. "Oh, for Chrissake, that stupid fish is in here."

"Lady Gaga? Put her in the car too."

Nick picked up the small tank and carried it to the waiting car, grousing all the way.

Flint swept in, picked up the carrier and litter pan. "There's water and a food dish in here; you want them? And some fish food. It looks like a pet shop back here."

"Grab it all, and let's get going." The cats wouldn't let go of me, and I wouldn't let go of them, but somehow I reached inside and relocked the driver's side of the car, the one controlling the locking system, so once Flint closed the fifth door, the wagon would relock itself.

Flint threw out the water in the dish but managed everything else, shut the door, and went toward the trunk of his car. I followed slowly, still clutching the clinging but otherwise quiet Tugger and Baba.

I got in the back seat next to Lady Gaga's tank. While juggling the cats, I shoved the Glock back into my knapsack, dropped it to the floor, and tried to control my sniffling. After all, I'm a trained investigator. It wouldn't do to be bawling outright. But I was so relieved and happy the cats were well and safe, I almost didn't care. I struggled to find the phone in my pocket with both arms full, but I wanted to give Richard a fast call. He answered on the first ring.

"I've got them. They're fine. Tugger and Baba are fine. You did a good job, Richard."

Richard let out pent-up air. "I'll let everybody know on this end, including Mom. I've got some news for you about Vicki, but it can wait."

Barely listening, I continued. "Let Tío know right away, too, Richard, we're all fine. He worries so."

"Will do. Still checking on the license plate." He disconnected without saying any more.

Flint got into the car, shut his door, and flipped on the inside, overhead light. Nick was already sitting in the passenger's seat, hunched over and silent. Possibly my threat of shooting him had shocked him. It had shocked me, too, but a girl can only take so much before she gets a little testy.

Flint swung his head around to look at me, wearing a slight smile. I don't know if it was the new neck scarf I sported — the one with four eyes and two tails — or the abundance of cat hair floating about in the air. Cats tend to shed when they get stressed, and the fur was flying. He sobered before he asked, "Where to now, Lee?"

"Back the car up into the shadows, and let's stick around for a while." He turned off the overhead light, put the car in reverse, and backed up several car lengths into complete darkness. We sat in the dark with the motor running, me thinking hard.

After about a minute, I said, "When we get out of here, the first thing I need to do is find me a hotel room for tonight. I'm blown."

"Don't be silly, Papoose. You'll stay in the guest bedroom. You've even got your own private bathroom."

"Are you sure? I mean, I come with a menagerie."

"I'm sure. Now hush."

"I guess I'll take the couch," Nick muttered.

"And lucky I don't lock you in a closet," said Flint.

"Gentlemen, your attention, please." I sat erect and strained my eyes into the gloomy night. Even the cats tensed up. "Someone's coming."

We watched the half-lit figure of a lone man hurry to the BMW, unlock the driver's door, and get inside, not checking the cargo contents. He slammed the door shut, started the car, and drove out so fast you could hear the screech of tires.

"Wow!" I said, "I wonder where he's going in such a hurry?"

"We're about to find out," said Flint, putting his Jeep in drive and heading out.

Several minutes later, the phone rang, and it was Richard. "I've got the owner of that BMW for you. It's Eddie Crackmeir, just like you thought."

"Kelli's uncle, right?"

"Not exactly. Try husband."

I gave a quick glance to the back of Nick's head in the front seat and lowered my voice.

"Say that again."

"Eddie Crackmeir, and that's C-r-a-c-k-m-e-i-r. Her husband. Recorded marriage certificate, Oklahoma, five years ago. Her father had to sign consent. No record of a divorce. In fact, they own a house together in Vegas, and last year they did a joint tax return. They've been married since she was seventeen, and he was twenty-seven. And it gets better."

"I can hardly wait."

"Eddie has worked at MAPLAB for the past two years. He's a technician but a recently demoted one. Seems he made a couple of errors on the screening of micro-components for a smart bomb, which cost the company a bundle in government penalties. They would have fired him if he hadn't been a union man. It's amazing what you can learn from online personnel files when their firewalls aren't adequate. Let that be a lesson to you."

"So a disgruntled employee."

"Seems so."

"That address, is it 1752 Cactus Blossom Lane?" I asked as Flint slowed down, and we watched the BMW pull into the driveway of a modest, single-family house, bright porch light announcing the address.

"Yes."

The car door opened. The short, squat man got out, slammed it shut, and scurried inside the house. Once again, without checking for the cargo contents. Either he had totally forgotten about the cats, or he had something more important on his mind.

"Okay, thanks, Richard. I'll take it from here. And thanks again for bugging Tugger's carrier. We might not have ever found them if it hadn't been for that chip."

"About the chip, Lee." Richard cleared his throat, and I did an inward groan. The clearing of my brother's throat usually meant some sort of lecture was about to ensue. He went on.

"What I was trying to do was find a more economical way of making a smaller, traceable microchip for use in pets. The smaller they are, the more expensive. The chip you found on Nick's dog tags probably runs three to four thousand dollars at a minimum, not including the expense of transferring information, which can be almost as much."

"Hmmm. Does that mean each chip is duly accounted for or numbered? You can't just take one from the factory like a nail and hope nobody will notice?"

"Exactly."

"So there's a sizable monetary investment here, unless they stole it."

"Exactly."

"The plot thickens."

"You still have the microchip, Lee?"

"On me."

"I can check its serial number against MAPLABS records; see what the history is. Try to get it to me first thing in the morning. We need to know what we're dealing with."

"Right," I said, thinking about the list with Gurn's name on it as well. Another thing we needed to deal with ASAP. "First thing in the morning, I'll see what I can do. Meanwhile, thank everyone for a job well done. Now go home and go to sleep." I hung up.

The porch lights to the house went out, but no light inside the house came on. Whatever Eddie was doing inside there, he was doing in total darkness.

Flint had been idling his Jeep across the street for a full five minutes. A nondescript man walking two greyhounds on the other side of the street stopped and stared at us. "Flint, I think we've seen enough. Let's get out of here."

He nodded and pulled out. I leaned back in the seat, covered with cats and cat hair. Tugger started to purr in one ear, and Baba nuzzled the other, when the phone rang again.

Still fisted in my hand, I looked at the number of the incoming call. It was Gurn.

"Hi, sweetheart," I whispered. "We all still love you."

"And who would 'all' be? You, Baba, and Tugger?"

"Yes."

"I can't wait until tomorrow night. I finished my last meeting a few minutes ago. I'm going to catch some zees now. I'll file a flight plan first thing in the morning and be home around nine thirty, ten a.m. West Coast time."

I sat bolt upright. Claws raked at my neck from the sudden movement. I did some of my fastest thinking. Flint must have sensed I needed some privacy because he turned the radio on to a classical station and began to whistle along with "Clair de Lune" to help drown out my conversation.

"Good, good. But listen, how about making a short stop in Vegas and picking us up on the way? That would be Tugger, Baba, and me."

There was a pause on the other end of the line.

"You're in Vegas?"

"Yes," I said, keeping my voice as low as possible.

"You're in Vegas… with the cats?"

"Yes."

"Okay," he said, dragging the word out. "This is doable. I'm not carrying any other passengers or cargo, so I can fuel up there. Dare I ask why you're in Vegas?"

"Let's not go into that yet, but suffice it to say, everybody's fine; we're all well, if not a little tired, and we need to hitch a ride back to Palo Alto tomorrow morning." I turned to Baba clinging to the left side of my neck. With the help of the passing lights of Las Vegas Boulevard, I could see her furry face clearly. Green eyes looked back at me underneath a silky-soft, gray forehead, the rest of her face surrounded by abundant, long and shiny, white fur. She was so cute. I kissed her lightly on her little pink nose, something that if my mother had seen me do, she'd have forced me to use an antibacterial scrub for a month.

"Say hi to your daddy, Baba." And danged if this sweet thing didn't give forth with a charming meow, right on cue. Not to be outdone, Tugger let out one of his, only more along the lines of an air-raid siren with its butt caught in a wringer.

"As you can hear, Gurn, all is well."

"Glad of it."

"I just thought of something. Do you have to do a manifest? Because if you do, put down a three-gallon tank with Lady Gaga in it. But not the singer, a goldfish."

"You have a goldfish named Lady Gaga with you?"

"Yes."

"As well as the cats? I just want to get the lineup right. For the manifest. Anything else?" His voice contained more humor than I thought appropriate, but I let it go. After all, he wasn't mad or upset and that was a bonus.

"I'll have a microchip with me but—"

"A microchip? Man, the things you miss out on when you're in all-day meetings."

"But I don't think you have to write that down. It'll be in my knapsack. And, Gurn darling, you're not running any races in between now and when I see you, are you?"

Another pause. "Gee, I had one scheduled for three o'clock this morning, but it got canceled at the last minute. What are you on, anyway?"

"Nothing." My voice came out a little huffier than I'd planned, but it had been a stressful day. I softened my tone. "I'm not on anything, but please don't run any races before I talk to you."

He laughed and said, "This can be arranged."

"I mean it. No races."

"Not a problem. I'm going straight to bed. I'll see you at North Las Vegas Airport around eight a.m. Do you know where it is?"

"I'll find it."

"Good. I'll call you from somewhere over the Rockies. I'm hoping you will explain all of this in more detail when I see you."

"You got it."

"I love you."

"Backatcha."

* * * *

At Flint's apartment, the three of us struggled inside with our respective loads. Lady Gee — no longer called Lady Gaga because she was now in the witness protection program — was stashed on the desk in the guest bedroom by a reluctant but cooperative Nick. I noticed her water was on the murky side, and she was lethargic. I set the cats down on the double bed, where they huddled in the center, their eyes following my every move. I plugged in Lady Gee's heat lamp and water filter, and she immediately started swimming around again. Flint carried in the litter pan and dishes, set them on the floor of the bathroom, and headed for the door. He opened it and turned back.

"I'm about to order a pizza." He reached into his pocket and pulled out a small, round jar of dry fish food.

"Here," he said, handing it off to me. "You might want to feed this to the fish before you feed the fish to the cats." He winked at me to show he was kidding. "Want anything else?"

"Thanks. Could you order a hamburger for the cats? Just a burger, no bun. Flint, I was wondering if you could hang on to Nick for a while, at least until we find out what's on the chip."

"No problem. He's my new best buddy."

The longtime family friend looked at me with such warmth, compassion, and willingness to do whatever, I felt tears spring to my eyes. I shook my head, looking away for a moment. I turned back with a bright smile and ran fingers through my hair, which hadn't been brushed since early morning. I looked like I got caught in a wind tunnel and felt even worse. Talk about being tired!

He looked down at me. "Lee, the front door is locked from the inside with a combination lock. This way Nicky Boy can't do a disappearing act in the middle of the night. But in an emergency, I want you to have the four numbers in case you need to get out, okay?"

I nodded.

"One, three, six, four. Got it?"

I nodded again.

"And I don't have a landline. The only phone in the apartment is my phone, and it's on me at all times." Flint touched the breast pocket of his jacket.

"I'm glad," I said. "I think it's better if Nick stays incommunicado for a while."

"Trust not the rabbit in the middle of his flight."

The thought of Tío's bunnies came into my mind. Even though Richard promised to call him, I'll bet my uncle was still anxious. I should talk to him in person, relieve his mind.

Flint hesitated in the doorway. "One last thing, Lee, and I only mention this because it may prove useful down the line. One of my nephews works at the Fantasy Lady doing a lounge-lizard act. He sometimes performs in the penthouse. The act's pretty bad, but he owes me a couple of favors, so keep it in mind."

"You're just the gift that keeps on giving, aren't you?" I looked at him in awe. "I mean that. 'Thanks' doesn't even cover it. I couldn't have done any of this without you."

He came back and planted a kiss on my forehead. "Hey, what Bobby Alvarez did for my kid, I try to do for his. I can never pay your dad back, but I can try."

"I think we're even now, Lonato."

"I'll let you know when we are. Keep this door locked," Flint went on. "I'll bring you some food when it arrives. Try to get some rest."

He started to cross back to the door, but my voice stopped him. "In case nobody's ever told you, you're a good man, Lonato Tall Trees, one of the best."

He turned back to me. "There is a Native American saying, Papoose, and one I try to live by: 'When you were born, you cried, and the world rejoiced. Live your life so that when you die, the world cries, and you rejoice.'" He left shutting the door behind him.

I went over, threw the bolt, and leaned against the door. I looked back at the bed and watched the cats separate, gingerly sniff the mattress and its perimeter, come together and touch noses, reassuring one another they were okay. Friendship comes in all forms.

I opened the top on the fish food and sprinkled a few flakes on the water. Lady Gee came running, while I hit the speed dial number for home. Tío answered on the second ring.

"Liana! I recognized the number of your carry phone," he said with pride. "I hoped you will call your uncle."

"Of course I will call my favorite uncle." I tried to keep my voice upbeat and cheerful. "How could I go to bed without saying good night?"

"*Mi sobrina favorita*." He laughed, and I could hear relaxation wash over him. "You are all right, *¿la verdad?*"

"The truth, I am all right."

"And the cats? Richard, he calls earlier to say you have found them."

"The cats are right here, and we're all fine. We're spending the night in Flint's guestroom. We'll be back before noon tomorrow, flying in with Gurn. And it's called a phone, Tío, not that it really matters."

"*Si, si.* I knew it was something like that. Your mother, she flies back tomorrow too."

"She does? Why? I thought she was going to stay in Phoenix for a few days."

"She will tell you tomorrow. You sound *muy cansada, sobrina.*"

There's no fooling Tío. "I am tired, Tío."

"Then go to sleep. *Mañana* comes soon enough. *Te amo.*"

"*Te amo.*"

I threw myself flat on the double bed; arms outstretched, I looked up at the ceiling and tried to free my mind of everything. Cats walked over and around me, stopping periodically to sniff my face, hands, and neck, tickling me with their fur and noses. It was better than a Valium, and I dropped off for a minute or two. Fifteen minutes later, Flint knocked on the door holding a plate with a steaming slice of pizza oozing with mozzarella cheese and a side of hamburger meat in one hand, a cloth napkin, and crystal goblet filled with sparkling deep-red wine in the other. Flint is a wine connoisseur and drinks only the finest.

"Oh, no, I couldn't," I said when I thought about the night before. He looked at me as if I had lost my mind. "Well, maybe just a sip."

A pizza lover from way back, I shut and relocked the door, relishing what I had in store for me. Then I took a swallow of the knock-your-socks-off cab. Ambrosia.

Noting Lady Gee's tank had brightened up considerably, as had her mood, I changed into the large man's T-shirt I often sleep in, fed the cats, and clicked on the remote for the small TV sitting on the dresser across from the bed. After a quick run through the channels, I found the Marx Brother's *Duck Soup* nearing its end.

Ever since I was a kid, I've watched as many black-and-white '30s and '40s movies as I could, much to my mother's alarm.

Having seen *Duck Soup* at least twenty times, I can come into the story at any point. I love it as much today as the first time my father introduced me to one of the best Groucho, Harpo, and Chico films. Cross-legged on the bed, I ate my pizza, laughed at the movie's finale, savored the last dregs of wine, and zonked out around eleven o'clock, with a cat cuddled in each arm. Not bad.

Chapter Nine

Things Are Looking Up… Aren't They?

The next morning, my eyes opened like they were on springs. I checked the watch still wrapped around my wrist. It was precisely 6:30 a.m. I knew precisely where I was, too, which is not so often the case when you're sleeping in a strange bed, and you need to orient yourself. I raised my head, without moving anything else, and glanced down at the warm weight at my feet. Two cats, curled into one, slept peacefully, bodies pressed against me.

I lay there recapping the previous gawd-awful day, not knowing many of the answers but some of them. I tested myself using a pros-and-cons mental ledger, hoping I'd get a decent score.

What I know:

Kelli, my ex-husband's new wife, shows up at my home in Palo Alto yesterday.

Why? She needs to find Nick.

Why me? Probably because he told her my family and I run a detective agency, and we might be more likely to find him when she couldn't.

What did she want him for? Safe to say it revolved around information on the microchip she'd put on his dog tags. Having the chip in my possession, I'll soon know why it's so important.

Why did she take the cats? I'd initially told her I'd look for Nick, which must have been what she was angling for, but threw her out when I found out my cousin, Stephen, had died. Apparently, she had Eddie Crackmeir follow her in his car for any necessary help. Taking the cats, I feel sure this was a fly-by-the-seat-of-your-pants plan.

Wow! This isn't much.

Other side of the ledger — what I don't know:

Putting all the emotions of an ex-wife and current wife aside, I know nada about Kelli other than she is a consummate liar. Like

all liars, she uses the worst of human frailties and weaknesses to her own advantage. Mine, in particular. She's also resourceful and fast thinking. I will not underestimate her again. Even grading on a curve, I'm probably only going to get a C.

Kelli Crackmeir, or whatever her name is, seems to have no shortage of willing men in her life. First, Nick Papadopoulos, a former marine gone to seed. Whatever backbone he'd had seems to have crumbled. Or is that an act solely for my benefit? He and Kelli could be in cahoots, to use her word, and he could be playing all of us. In any event, I know from years ago not to trust him as far as I can throw an overweight bull elephant. My grade is now a lousy D.

Nick says he knows nothing about the races and called Stephen to warn him not to run after he found the list with "take out" written beside my cousin's name. Is that true? Or did he have a case of the last-minute guilts and try to call off what he'd help set in motion? Is Nick innocent of Stephen's death, as he claims, or is he as consummate a liar as his ladylove? He'd lied to me for years about his affairs. Maybe that's why Nick and Kelli were attracted to one another in the first place. Maybe people who lie together lay together. I'm down to a D minus.

Kelli's second man, Lou Spaulding, is an internationally powerful and dangerous man by all accounts. Did Kelli really only marry Nick to get close to Spaulding? Or are Nick and Kelli playing him too? And what info could be on the chip that has Spaulding ready to kill Nick in order to get it back?

Added thought: Why isn't Spaulding going after Kelli with an "i" as well or instead of Nick?

Enter man number three, Eddie Crackmeir, and I'm getting tired of these men, already. What is Eddie's part in all of this? Does it mean anything that he's Kelli's legal husband? Is he in on whatever's going on with Nick and Kelli?

Added thought: Are Kelli and Eddie making fools of Nick and the rest of us?

Face it, Lee, these are only three men I know of in Kelli's life. There could be more. As far as I'm concerned, Cleopatra and Mata Hari were amateurs next to Kelli. I am loath to say it, but I have a deep respect for her capabilities. And of the three men I know about, what did they do for her in the past, and what are they willing to do in the future? I won't underestimate their part in this or trust any of them farther than I can throw an overweight bull... never mind.

What about the names on the list Nick found and I now have in my possession? How many on that list are already dead? Let's not forget Gurn is on that list. Making sure he doesn't wind up dead is something I mean to get an A plus on.

Mentally rerunning my encounter with Kelli Whatshername is like watching one of Boris Karloff's better horror movies. Something dastardly is going on, and you have no idea who's going to get done in, or who's going to be standing at the end. But I promise myself this: I will be standing at the end. And Gurn, my family, and anybody else I care about. It's too late for Stephen, but there is no way I'm going to let anybody else get taken out.

At six forty-five, I got up and went into the bathroom. Before I brushed my teeth, I cleaned out the litter pan and saw the cat's food dish was empty. I hadn't heard the little darlings get up in the night, but apparently they had, ate their dinner, and took care of their business.

I glanced out to the desk and saw that Lady Gee was swimming her little heart out. All was right with her. Should I give her more food? I didn't know. I'd read once that you had to be careful not to overfeed fish. When I got a chance, I would look it up on the internet. Lady Gee was mine now, and I'd try to make sure she had a long and happy life.

That's when it occurred to me I might have gotten more than a D minus on this test. After all, I had the cats, the microchip, an expensive, butt-ugly ruby ring, Nick, and Lady Gee, tank and all.

Momentarily satisfied, I pulled out my black practice leotard, tights, toe shoes, and earbuds connected to an iPod from my knapsack. I had time for forty-five minutes of practice. The few times I wear black is at funerals or when I do my ballet barre. I'm not sure why, maybe it's the solemnity of both occasions, but there you have it. The only addition of color was a short, pale-pink organza tie skirt that wrapped around my waist.

The flimsy fabric is supposed to help the dancer remember that eventually she'll be wearing a costume, 95 percent of the time, a starched tutu. It is important to train yourself to hold your arms out from your body, not to crush the netting. Why this particular dancer — meaning me — wore a flimsy, practice skirt, I don't know. Call it hope. Dancing onstage while wearing a costume could someday happen to me… along with winning the lottery.

I tiptoed out of the room, not stirring cats that were dead to the world, and entered the living room. Last night I hadn't paid much attention to my surroundings, but as I looked around, more refreshed and in the morning's light, I couldn't take my eyes off the walls. Painted a rich, forest green, three of them served as backdrops for various sizes of colorful Native American portraits in oil, acrylic, or pastels. Depictions of warriors: some vigorous and young, filled with the glories of war and old men, memories of long-ago victories and more recent sorrows etched across their features.

I didn't recognize the artist's brushstrokes, and none were signed, but he or she was someone with talent and no small understanding of the plight of the Native American soul. The fourth wall opened into the large kitchen, a long, off-white tile countertop separating it from the living room.

Drawn to one corner of the room, I found a simple hand-chiseled, light wood table held a Frederick Remington cast of a brave, his pony, and a small dog.

It was heartachingly beautiful, each subject exhausted, despairing, and near death. It was the real deal, and I wondered how Flint came to own a museum-quality work such as this. There would be a story, I knew, but it might not be one I should be privy to. I turned away.

Nick was asleep on the sofa, lightly snoring, his left arm over his head and the right holding on to the gray blanket covering him below a naked chest and abdomen, no longer filled with rippling muscles and a well-defined six-pack. Whatever else was going on in Nick's life, he was no longer a slave to his daily workouts. His pants and shirt—correction, Ken's pants and shirt—lay haphazardly on a worn suede overstuffed chair, said chair having seen better days but still exuding its initial expense.

Attaching the iPod to my waist, I walked softly through the room, wondering about the paintings on the wall. Something told me they might be Lonato's work. While I had known him most of my life, it was always as my father's friend. Lonato was a private person, solitary and ruminative. In the past, I often hesitated on asking him the simplest questions, allowing a wall to be built between us, especially when I was a child. No more. After the past twenty-four hours, I saw a man who was giving and generous. I wanted to be more than Bobby's daughter to him. I wanted to be his friend.

I began my barre, freeing my mind of those thoughts and others. For me, this is similar to the reason why many people have a hobby. It's a small allotment of time when you can put everything on a backburner and concentrate on a golf swing, a needlepoint stitch or, in my case, a dance step.

After my stretches and warm-up, I moved on in earnest. On and off for many years, I have been practicing a series of steps, which create one grand movement.

From fifth position, I do a plié, which is French for bend at the knees, then a *relevé*, also French, meaning rise to a toe point on one or two feet. On one point, I raise the nonsupporting leg out to the side, with knee sharply bent so my toe is pointing next to the supporting knee. I say all of this because in the scheme of things, this is about a thousand dollars' worth of ballet lessons right there.

But here comes the hard part. While you're rising up to point, you need to mentally and physically prepare yourself for a series of turns or pirouettes in place, spotting something in the room so you know when you've made one complete revolution. After the turn or turns, the dancer is supposed to relax the body and return to fifth position, exactly from where he or she started. Tack on another fifteen hundred bucks.

Even the most beginner dancers can make one turn in place with a little practice. You need more experience and technique to do two turns, which I've been able to do since junior high. Only the really good can manage three or more turns in place, me not being one of them. One day, if I'm lucky and don't continue to fall on my butt, I might be able to accomplish three turns with a return to place. It is devoutly wished.

Listening to selections of *Swan Lake* on the iPod, I did the preparation, then the turns, and managed to do my usual two and a half revolutions before I lost my balance and came down off toe, not facing the countertop but the sink. Undaunted, I returned to fifth, about to plié again, when I heard Nick's voice, smooth and sultry.

"You always were a beautiful dancer, Lee, but then, you're a beautiful woman."

I hadn't seen him rise from the sofa, I'd been so intent on my barre. I threw a hand towel around my sweaty neck before I faced him.

"That was something you used to say when you wanted to get laid."

"How am I doing?" He flashed a smile and leered at me.

"We're divorced. I don't remember much of our marriage, but I remember that." I returned his stare.

He grinned again. "Maybe I remember enough for the both of us."

I turned away and wiped my forehead roughly with the towel, taking out on my skin what I'd like to take out on my ex. "Nick, don't insult either one of us with this kind of crap, okay?" I faced him again and threw the towel at him. "We've got far more important issues at hand, so don't make me mad. I might forget I'm trying to save your life."

His mood changed abruptly, and he looked down. "Okay. Sorry, Lee." After a pause, he looked back up. "Truly, I'm sorry. I'm not myself lately. I guess having your wife's boyfriend put a contract out on you makes you a little nervous."

I hesitated, and my voice softened. "About that, Nick. The wife part."

"What?"

I moved around to the edge of the counter and stepped back into the living room, heading for the sofa. When I saw it was more or less still his unmade bed, I changed my mind and sat primly on the suede chair. "Maybe we should both sit down."

"Okay," he said, following me, a questioning look on his face. He grabbed his shirt from the back of the chair, pulled it on, sat at the one end of the sofa, and waited.

"Nick, I don't quite know how to put this, so I'll just say it. Eddie Crackmeir isn't Kelli's uncle. He's her husband."

"What?" Nick jumped up and glared at me.

"They were married in Oklahoma five years ago. There's no record of divorce."

"What are you talking about?" Nick began in protest. "She told me he was her uncle. He came over to our condo and introduced himself to me as her uncle." He stopped sputtering and tugged at the neck of his shirt, pulling the collar out. Then he threw himself back down on the sofa, while I went on.

"I understand, but he's not. Richard found a copy of their marriage license online, her father's signature on it because she was underage. Eddie Crackmeir is Kelli's husband." I stopped talking to let the words sink in.

Silence loomed for several seconds. I could see various thoughts and emotions running across Nick's face almost as if he were speaking out loud. He turned to me.

"All this time, she wasn't my wife. I wasn't her husband. She lied to me."

"Yes. I'm sorry."

"You're sorry? You're sorry? Holy shit! I'm married to a fucking bigamist, and the woman's sorry." While he was yelling at me, he pulled at the bottom of the shirt in anger and frustration, one of his old habits resurfacing.

"Hey!" I said, and then I lowered my voice, looking toward Flint's bedroom door. "Stop taking your troubles out on everything and everyone else like you usually do. It's not your shirt; it's on loan, so don't ruin it. And don't take this out on me. You got involved with Kelli, and you married her, Nick, so step up to the plate. Take your strikes like a man. And keep your voice down. We don't want to wake Flint. Although," I said, looking at my watch, "he needs to get up soon if I'm going to make it to the airport by eight."

Just then the front door opened, and Flint walked in carrying a cardboard container with three Styrofoam coffee cups and a bag of donuts on it.

"Morning, all," he said, looking at us. His eyes darted from Nick's face to mine. "I see Nicky Boy just found out little Kelli had not been completely honest about her marital status."

Nick turned to me. "You mean Flint knows too? Am I the last to know about this?"

"Often how it goes, Nicky Boy," answered Flint, unloading the Styrofoam cups from the container. "Look at it this way, son. *The fur of the jackal may be pleasing to touch, but he is still a jackal...* or in this case, she is still a jackal."

Nick stared at him, his face contorted in pain. Despite the fact I was pissed at him, I tried to help out.

"Kelli is good at deceiving people, Nick, something I've experienced firsthand, myself," I said. "You're not alone in being taken in."

"From what I'm learning about the little lady, she's a master of deceit," boomed Flint. "Here's a bonus: since you're not legally her husband, you're not responsible for any bills she may incur or credit cards she may run up."

He threw Nick the bag of donuts. Nick caught it without looking.

"Let's move on to more important business," Flint went on. "Two kinds of donuts, strawberry-or-blueberry jelly filled. Fresh this morning. Help yourself. How do you take your coffee? I brought sugar, artificial sweeteners, and some creamers…" His voice trailed off, and he winked at us.

"God, I'm such an asshole," said Nick, still staring at Flint.

"That's true, son, so pick a donut," said Flint.

I bit back a smile, glad to have the situation diffused, and Nick smiled after a moment, opened the bag, and peered inside.

"Would you look at this?" he said, pulling out a donut. "Real jelly-filled donuts. I haven't had one of these in years." He took a huge bite. Thick, dark blue filling spurted onto his left cheek. "Mmmmm! Yummy," he said, stretching his tongue to clean his cheek of the goo. "I take my coffee black," he said, moving toward the kitchen counter.

From the bedroom, I heard my phone give out with Beethoven's finest. When things slowed down, I'd really have to change it. Before hurrying for the phone, I grabbed a cup of java and a strawberry-jelly donut. I'd have to do push-ups for a week with one of those in my gullet, but some things are worth it.

After shutting the door, I answered the phone and allowed Gurn's voice to wash over me like a warm sun-shower. I assured him the cats and I were still okay, and we arranged to meet at the airport around 8:30 a.m.

Currently airborne in his handy-dandy Citation CJ4, he would do a quick refueling when he picked us up. He'd been kidding about the manifest. Ha ha.

* * * *

Three people, two cats, and one fish tank piled into the Jeep and headed for the airport. On the way, Flint told Nick he would be his guest for the next couple of days. Nick took it like a champ and even offered to do a few household chores. I'm not sure which one of us got through to him — I suspect it was Flint — but he was acting more mature and cooperative.

By the time Gurn landed at the small airport, Flint and I were waiting on the tarmac, me holding the cat carrier, and Flint loaded down with my knapsack, Lady Gee, and all her trappings. Nick decided to wait in the Jeep, probably not wanting to meet Gurn, which was fine with me. Flint and I trusted him to stay put, which was a certain leap of faith, but somewhere along the line, you've got to do that with a person important to an investigation. Besides, if he took off, odds are Spaulding's boys would find him before us. Even Nick knew that.

Gurn taxied to the refueling area, came out and had a few words with the gas jockeys, or whatever they're called, and headed in our direction. Flint and I met him halfway on the runway, and they greeted briefly, the tarmac not being conducive for social chitchat. Flint handed everything off to Gurn and left to get back to his charge in the car.

On the way to his plane, instead of me saying, *Golly gee wimple, I love you and can't wait to jump your bones*, the first words I uttered were, "I sure hope it's a smooth flight home. The animals have been through enough."

"Should be," he said, walking up the stairs of the plane and into the cabin. "The weather looks good from here to home."

With club seating for seven, the interior is sparsely decorated in my mother's favorite color combo, off-white and beige. Yuk. Gurn told me the first time I saw the interior, the plane had been previously owned by a clothing designer. He traveled the globe with his latest line and gave mini-fashion shows to select clients at forty-one thousand feet. Airborne designer wanted a boring but tasteful backdrop for his clothes and got it. As far as Gurn was concerned, the leather seats were comfortable, and the padded interior and rug were pretty much stain resistant. End of story.

We buckled the cat carrier into one of the off-white leather passenger seats. Gurn had a special buckle made for securing a cat carrier to the seat, having traveled many times before with Baba. Lady Gee and the fish tank went on the floor, her air pump and filter plugged into the electrical system. As I'd done five or six times in the past four months, I followed Gurn to the cockpit and buckled up in the copilot's chair.

Less than five minutes later, we were cleared for takeoff and taxied to the runway, where we each went into our usual routine: Gurn flips a bunch of switches while analyzing a bunch of dials. I squeeze my eyes shut and don't open them until the plane has leveled off at four-ten, as he calls it, or forty-one thousand feet.

"It should be an easy flight, so sit back and relax," he said in a voice which makes my knees go weak even when I'm sitting down. After a moment's silence, he said. "So this is the ritual now, is it?"

"What is?"

"The eyes closed until we've leveled off."

"Pretty much," I said with my eyes screwed shut.

"Are you afraid of flying?"

"Don't be silly."

"You are. You're afraid of flying."

"No I'm not. I'm afraid of crashing."

"I don't get it. You fly everywhere. Just yesterday you flew here on a commercial plane."

"A-ha! But I don't have to look out an itty-bitty windshield and know that's all that's between me and the ground. In a bigger plane, I can pretend I'm on a boat, a train, or in my living room."

What followed was the obligatory speech: "Do you know flying is the safest mode of transportation in the world? Why, it's a scientific fact—"

"Yeah, yeah. Yada yada," I interrupted. "I know it all. It doesn't help. It's this windshield. Possibly I'm a little neurotic."

He laughed. "What? You? Never!"

The words were perfect, but the way he said them wasn't.

"I've got an idea," he went on. "Why don't you go back to the cabin, buckle up alongside the cats, and after the plane levels off, you can come back for a visit?"

"Great! Because I really do like looking at those white, fluffy clouds. It's all the stuff below them which makes me nauseated."

I unbuckled and hurried back to the main cabin and sat across from the cats, who were handling this a lot better than me. This time I did relax into the soft comfort of the ergonomic chair.

I thought about Gurn and me using the "L" word. Now that we had, it seemed like we were being a little more honest with each other. I'd been flying in Gurn's jet since I met him. This was the first time he called me on the eyes-closed approach I had to takeoff and landing. Of course, I usually tried to be surreptitious about it, always facing away from him. Maybe I was being more out there too: more trusting. Boy, what love does to a person.

Less than ten minutes later, I heard Gurn's voice on the intercom. "Lee, I've got it on automatic pilot, not that I plan on leaving the cockpit, but I want to give you the bulk of my attention. So come on up and tell me what's been going on from the beginning. Don't leave anything out, just talk. We're not going anywhere for over an hour, anyway."

So up I went, and after numerous kisses by the cockpit door, talk I did, starting from my 8:00 a.m. wake-up call Sunday morning to getting the menagerie and me to the airport Monday morning. I have a photographic memory, when I want one, and gave him verbatim conversations with Kelli, Nick, Flint, hell, even the cats. Wonderful man that he is, he didn't interrupt, didn't ask questions, and didn't offer any comments even though some things went begging for them.

"And that's it. Welcome to my world," I said, letting out a sigh and leaning back in the copilot's seat.

"This Kelli sounds like the ultimate lying machine," commented Gurn. "Not too perfect. Throwing in a few quirks here and there. Sometimes acting a little selfish, a little weird, anything that makes the listener trust what she's saying as real and gospel, no matter how improbable it may seem on the face of it. She has the knack of *not* coming across too good to be true. From transcripts I've read of double agents in the Cold War, it's the same gift they had."

I hadn't thought about it before, but now that I did, I realized it was true. Kelli's whole approach to things came off as scatty but sincere. I turned in my chair to face him. "Does that mean you'll trust me to take care of Baba again?"

He looked over at me in surprise. "After what you went through to get her back? I don't think most people would go through that much to get me back."

"I would."

He reached over and stroked my face with a tender touch. "And that's why I trust you with my life and my cat." I smiled, still wanting to jump his bones. While I wondered if I could be an honorary member of the mile-high club, Gurn released the automatic pilot and took the controls again.

"So once I turn over the microchip to Richard," I said, thinking I had too much caffeine or an overactive libido, "we have to try to figure out what the list means, and why your name is on it. Meanwhile, no more races for you, mister."

Before he could respond, my phone rang. Gurn has the latest of everything known to aviation, and one of them is a cell system allowing phones to work in the plane no matter what the altitude.

"Beethoven's calling," Gurn teased. I looked at the incoming call and saw it was Flint.

"Flint, you're on speakerphone. What's happened?"

"Sorry to disturb your flight, but I've got bad news about Eddie Crackmeir." Flint's voice was loud and clear, sounding like any other normal call and not coming from forty-one-thousand feet below. "Eddie was found this morning in his house, shot in the back of the head, hands tied behind his back."

My stomach lurched more than it did during takeoff.

"Spaulding's men?" I asked. I gave a quick look at Gurn, who was staring straight ahead with grim features.

"Possibly," answered Flint. "There's more. The police found Kelli's Mercedes at McCarran Airport: empty, but traces of blood on the driver's seat."

"*Dios mio!*" Now Gurn and I turned and stared at each other. "Kelli's missing?" I said.

"Apparently, but the cops are looking. Speaking of cops, that's why I'm calling. My bowling buddy from LVPD phoned to say one of the neighbors reported my Jeep being outside of Eddie's house last night around the time he was murdered."

"The dog walker."

"The very one. My license plate happens to be the same numbers as his wife's birthday, so he remembered it and gave it to the police. Buddy said it would be good if I voluntarily came in and told them why I was there. I'm on my way. Am I using client confidentiality? Or am I telling them everything I know? What do you want, Papoose?"

"Flint, tell them everything. DI will deal with the police in Palo Alto. I'll alert Richard and Lila from my end."

"The FBI is going to be in on this," Gurn stated. "It's just a matter of time. This has crossed state lines."

"True," I said, trying to mentally sort things out. "Whatever information is on the chip, they're welcome to, once we make a copy of it. I think we can keep Stephen's death and the footraces out of it for the time being. Although Nick is probably going to have to tell them what he knows. Is he there with you?"

"We're attached at the hip. Want to talk to him?"

"No. Just tell him to be as cooperative as possible; answer all their questions, but not to volunteer anything."

"Got it. Are we supposed to say 'over and out' now?"

I looked at Gurn.

"Roger that," Gurn said with a smile. I was glad to see his sense of humor wasn't gone. Mine was sure flagging.

Chapter Ten

Sharing Information, DI Style

"Before I leave with these affidavits, let's make sure we're all on the same page," said Frank Thompson, chief of the Palo Alto Police Department, when in his official capacity — which was now. He looked around at the rest of us who had been sitting for over an hour in DI's boardroom.

Discretionary Inquiries Inc., lives on the top floor of a Spanish-style, three-story building on one of the loveliest corners of downtown Palo Alto. A designated landmark, the building is constructed of depleted Stanford limestone, its façade ornately carved in relief scenes depicting the settling of California, so detailed they often cause "oohs" and "ahs" from first-time viewers. Late, as usual, I'd rushed through the small courtyard, past the mosaic-tiled, burbling tri-level water fountain under the Tiffany-ceilinged lobby, and up the three floors to the boardroom of DI.

In accordance with Lila Hamilton-Alvarez's directives, the boardroom glowed in timeless, understated elegance. Once the library for executives of a longtime defunct bank, she'd had this dark wood-paneled room recently redecorated in navy and burgundy stripes.

Drapes, cushions, and accessories had not been spared. Copper and brushed glass wall sconces and overhead, indirect lighting gave warmth to an otherwise gloomy, rainy afternoon.

The long, oval, Chippendale mahogany conference table, once enchanting a dining room in the home of a turn-of-the-century San Francisco mansion, now graced us with its presence, including its fourteen matching chairs. All luxuriated on a plush Persian carpet.

Frank looked at home in this setting at the head of the softly burnished conference table. At his left sat Richard. Next to my brother, erect and alert, was surely the world's oldest living attorney, Mr. James Talbot. Mr. Talbot, dressed in his usual charcoal pinstriped suit and flame-red bowtie, arrived moments earlier to protect DI's position with law enforcement. His snow-white hair was well coifed, unlike mine, which was pulled back in a fast, floppy ponytail.

Lila, composed and lovely in a heavy silk dress of a tan and gray swirling pattern, sat at the foot of the table facing Frank. Occasionally raising her head to flash appraising and watchful eyes, she made copious notes of everything said even though we had a video recorder running. Like Mr. Talbot, she'd come straight from the airport, arriving just before Frank started his official questioning.

I had yet to learn why Mom left Phoenix so abruptly and hoped on top of everything else, no harsh words between her and Jenn had been exchanged. Jenn, half Italian and a quarter Irish and French, has a shorter-than-normal fuse. Add Mom, who thinks the world would be a better place if everyone did exactly what she said and when she said it. Pass the powder keg and matches, please. One thing I've discovered, the death of a loved one doesn't always bring out the best in the living.

Gurn flanked Frank on his right. I sat next to Gurn, both of us freshly showered but tired. I wore a burnt-orange pantsuit, accented with a turquoise-and-coral-studded silver jaguar pin. Gurn was in a peach dress shirt and gray slacks, unlike Richard, who has a get-out-of-jail-free card in the clothing department.

Richard, wearing an aged and faded brown *A Chorus Line* T-shirt and ripped jeans on his scrunched-over body, came to attention.

He pulled a pomade-slathered clump of errant fine blond hair off his forehead, pomade doing pretty much nada. Richard pulls on his hair when he's bored, nervous, or antsy: asleep or awake. So basically, it's all the time.

Tío picked up Gurn and me at the airport four hours earlier in the van he uses to transport shelter animals. Richard had also been waiting in his car and dashed off to his friend at the Stanford Linear Accelerator Center or SLAC with the microchip. We'd taken the two cats and Lady Gee back to my apartment, where for three hours we were fed, watered, and fussed over by my mother hen of an uncle who has turned fussing into a fine art. Don't get me wrong. Tío's fussing is more than all right with me; I love it. However, Gurn and I never got any alone time, not that we wanted to do anything you couldn't print on the cover of a *Jughead* comic book, but still.

Having proven his authority over the proceedings, Frank pulled an affidavit from the stack, his eyes resting on Richard.

"Very well. Just to clarify what's been said here, and we all understand one another, let's start with you, Richard."

"As head researcher for Discretionary Inquiries, for about three hours, you were in possession of a missing or stolen microchip given to you this morning by Lee Alvarez. Until hearing about it on the previous evening, you had no knowledge of its existence."

"Right. The ID numbers on the chip match one reported missing by a lab in Las Vegas over a month ago."

"The microchip, which I have in my hand, was examined by you—"

"I had it scanned not examined," Richard interrupted in a pleasant but corrective tone of voice.

"And your findings were?" Frank went on as if Richard had not spoken.

"And my findings were," Richard said after clearing his throat, "the chip contained digital images of what appeared to be the contents of two separate accounting ledgers, plus a list of bank accounts."

"What did you do then?"

"I printed out the pages of information. Gurn Hanson is a CPA, so around eleven thirty this morning, I asked him to look them over to see what they were."

In reality, he barged into my apartment when Gurn and I were eating the delicious grilled skirt steak tacos Tío had set on the table not five minutes before. Not only did Richard insist Gurn leave the table and read the printout then and there, but he sat down and finished Gurn's lunch. Which is a lot of fat nerve in my opinion, but that's an ever-starving techie for you.

"Thereafter," Frank went on, "when you learned what was on the microchip, you turned it and the printed-out pages of material over to the Palo Alto Police Department. Is that correct?"

"Yes, to you about an hour ago."

"Do you have any information regarding Eddie Crackmeir's death or the disappearance of Kelli Papadopoulos?"

"None whatsoever. I never heard of either of them before yesterday."

Frank nodded with approval and turned to Gurn. "Gurn Hanson, you are a certified public accountant in the State of California, correct?"

"I am."

"You examined the pages in question earlier today. What were your findings?"

"It contained images of two accounting ledgers and a directory of numbered bank accounts. The information in the ledgers seems to be deliberately obfuscated, almost in code. However, I could tell the ledgers contain details of the transfer of huge amounts of money from one account to another, going into the hundreds of millions of dollars. I believe it will take several days to understand and verify this information, but the name Lou Spaulding comes up repeatedly within the two books as well as the directory."

"Were there any other names besides the name Lou Spaulding?"

"No."

"What can you tell me about these bank accounts?"

"Not much. But I recognize several numbers that appear to be Swiss bank accounts and one or two in the Cayman Islands. The numbers have a distinctive pattern."

"Do you have any information regarding Eddie Crackmeir's death?"

"None whatsoever."

Okay, so the atmosphere was getting more and more like a rerun of a *Perry Mason* episode during cross-examination. This is what happens when you put Mr. Talbot and Frank in the same room for more than fifteen minutes.

"Everything you've stated is in this affidavit signed by you?" Frank held the affidavit in the air.

"Yes."

Frank turned to me. "Lee Alvarez, yesterday you found this microchip on the dog tags of one Nick Papadopoulos and turned the microchip over to Richard earlier today?"

"Right."

"Is this microchip what precipitated your visit to Las Vegas?"

"No. I flew to Vegas to precipitate the return of two very expensive, rare cats," I said with a straight face. "I discovered the microchip by accident. It's in my affidavit."

Frank gave me a "stop-being-a-smart-ass" look while I grinned at him. Mr. Talbot shifted uncomfortably in his chair and harrumphed before he spoke.

"And as a California licensed investigator representing Discretionary Inquiries," inserted Mr. Talbot, "once she ascertained the import of the information on the microchip, she and the other members of Discretionary Inquiries proceeded to inform the Palo Alto Police Department — you, Chief Thompson.

"Due to the gravity of the situation, with one person dead and another missing, we are confident you will be taking the appropriate steps with this information, and you appreciate the cooperation Discretionary Inquiries is giving to all pertinent authorities in this investigation."

Frank looked at Mr. Talbot and blinked. He'd been out-Perry Masoned by a master.

"Thank you, Mr. Talbot. Your confidence in the law enforcement authorities and DI's cooperation is noted." He turned back to me. "Lee Alvarez, you have no information regarding Eddie Crackmeir or his death?"

"Never met the man," I said.

"Why did you follow him to his home?"

"He was driving the vehicle carrying the stolen cats. I wanted to know where he was going."

"The car was driven by Flint Tall Trees, and you were accompanied by Nick Papadopoulos, correct?" I nodded. "Please answer the question out loud."

"Correct, Chief Thompson. The car contained the three of us, plus two cats and one goldfish."

"None of you made contact at any time with Crackmeir?"

"Nope. Never left the car."

"You didn't see anything suspicious before you left Crackmeir's address?"

"Not a thing. He went inside. One thing though. He never turned on the lights once he went inside. Guess he was saving electricity."

Frank shot me another "don't-be-a-smart-ass" grimace before he turned away. With a hesitant cough, Frank focused on Mom, who gave him an obliging, if not aloof, stare. Frank tried to rise to the occasion but had a harried look in his eyes when he spoke.

"Mrs. Alvarez, as CEO for Discretionary Inquiries, do you have anything further to add?"

"I do not. I am satisfied with everything said."

"In that case," he said with nearly palpable relief, "we want to thank you for the contribution you and your staff have made to this investigation. On behalf of the Las Vegas Police Department, the Palo Alto Police Department, and the Federal Bureau of Investigation, we have no further questions of you or your personnel at this time. However, we are requesting all of the parties remain in Palo Alto until further notice, in case there are any more questions."

He turned off the video recorder and looked around the room. "Okay, so now we've got that crap out of the way, anyone here have anything off the record to say to me? Do it now while you are all still good guys."

We all muttered or murmured in the negative, even Mr. Talbot. Frank looked over at me.

"And you, Miss Smarty Pants, had better stay out of trouble."

"Me? What did I d—"

"Don't play innocent with me, Liana Margaret Alvarez."

"Margaret?" Gurn interjected under his breath.

Not hearing him, Frank went on. "You're in this up to your eyeballs, Lee. Don't pretend you're not."

He turned to Richard. "And she's got you in this one too. I'm sure."

"Not me. I'm just a computer geek."

Frank made a scoffing noise, gathered his materials, and left without looking back.

There was a moment's silence as we all studied the closed door.

"Margaret?" Gurn repeated. I chose to ignore him and turned to Richard.

"So how many copies did you make of the chip?"

"Two. One for the cops and one for us."

"Oh my God," Mr. Talbot pushed his chair back and stood as if he had been bitten on the butt by an alligator. "I cannot hear these things. As your legal counsel and an officer of the court, I can only remind you your duty is to turn all evidence over to the police, copies included."

"Which I did, Mr. Talbot. I am cooperating with the local authorities one hundred percent," Richard said, his face taking on the innocence of a cherub.

"I am glad to hear it." Mr. Talbot turned to Mom. "Lila, I must be going."

My mother rose and extended her hand. "Once again, James, thank you for coming on such short notice."

"My pleasure," the octogenarian said, grasping her hand in both of his. With the formality exchanged between the two of them, you'd never know being her father's law partner and best friend he'd changed many of her diapers when she was born. Lila likes to keep a low profile on that part of her relationship with the old family friend even though you never know when these reminiscences will come out of his mouth.

He turned to me. "Liana, Chief Thompson is right. Try to stay out of trouble. I'm tied up in a custody hearing for the next several days; I won't always be available."

"Why is everybody picking on me? What did I do?"

"What you always do, my dear, put your lovely nose in places it doesn't belong." He smiled, took my hand, kissed it lightly, and looked over at Richard.

"And you, too, Richard. No more bending the law." He nodded briefly to Gurn, who grinned back.

"On that note, I shall bid you *adieu*." He walked out, head held high.

I looked at my kid brother. "Well, of all the nerve."

Both Richard and I giggled like schoolchildren. Gurn suppressed laughter.

"Liana, Richard, stop." Lila rose to her feet, like the queen she is. "This is a very serious matter. You are to do exactly as Mr. Talbot says. We pay him an exorbitant sum of money for his advice, and we should take it. Understood?"

"Yes, ma'am," I said while Richard nodded.

"Tell me again, how many photocopies of the microchip did you make?" asked Lila, looking down at her notes.

"Just the two," Richard answered.

"Run off four sets, one for each of us," she said, gathering up her things and not looking at Richard, Gurn, or me. "Maybe we'll catch something tying in with Stephen's death." She turned to Gurn with one of her breathtaking smiles. "Especially you, Gurn. Maybe with a little more time, you'll be able to find something in those ledgers."

Gurn turned to Lila. "Mrs. Alvarez, you never cease to amaze me."

"I'll take that as a compliment."

I barely heard this exchange as I was too busy thinking. "You know what, Brother mine?"

"What?"

"We need to get inside the Fantasy Lady. Flint mentioned the penthouse floor is where the serious gambling takes place. I would like to get a look at it firsthand. Can you get some information about the layout or what goes on inside the place?"

"I can try." He grunted in thought. "I'll bet I can get the specs on what the architectural firm filed with the county. Maybe even the final blueprints."

"Good. Do it," I said. "I want to see what goes on up there for myself."

Gurn looked at me. "Tell you what, Liana Margaret —" Gurn began.

"Oh, shut up. A man with the first name of Gurn is in no position —"

"Point taken," he interrupted with a laugh. "I'll fly you back to Vegas if you let me in on it. After all, I'm on their takeout list."

I turned to him. "Only if you listen to me and do what I say. I'm the PI here. I know what I'm doing."

Gurn turned to Richard. "She can be difficult sometimes, can't she?"

"And sometimes she's just a pain in the arse," replied Richard.

"Hey, guys, I'm still in the room for crying out loud."

"Children, children," said Mom in her best schoolmarm tone, shushing us into temporary silence. "This is serious business. People are dead, including a family member. Let's ruminate over this for a while and see what we come up with. I know we want to seek justice if someone is involved in the taking of Stephen's life, but we mustn't rush into anything." Lila arranged her notes into a neat pile, placed them inside a black leather briefcase, then stood and crossed to the door.

I got up quickly. "Wait, Mom… ah… Lila." Sometimes I forget in the work setting it's better for us to stay on a first-name basis. I went over to her, took her by the elbow, and steered her into the hallway. Shutting the door behind me, I said in a low tone, "Mom, what happened in Phoenix? Why did you come back so soon? Did you and Jenn get into a tussle?"

Mom clucked her tongue, shaking her head. "Liana, must you use these colorful phrases from old gangster movies? What kind of a word is that for a young lady to say? 'Tussle.' Really. Time and time again I've asked you—"

"Mom!" I interrupted her in exasperation. "Forget the tussle. Substitute any word you want. I've been waiting all day to talk to you. What happened?"

She relented and smiled. "Out of all this sorrow came one good thing. When I called Jennifer's mother—"

"No! You called Fiona?"

"Yes. She got on a plane and—"

"No! She flew to her daughter's side?"

"Yes. After nine long years of not speaking—"

"No! You mean Jenn's mother forgave her about the name?"

Lila's face clouded over. "Liana, please do not interrupt me again. I'm trying to tell you what transpired if you'll only let me."

"Yes, ma'am."

"I've never known you to be a rude person. Please do not start now," Mom said, content she'd done the right thing by Miss Manners.

"No, ma'am. I'm very sorry. Too much caffeine, not enough sleep."

"Apology accepted."

"But Elwood sure isn't a name I'd like to carry around with me for the rest of my life, I can tell you."

"To continue with what I was saying." Mom's voice rose over mine. "Fiona was understandably hurt her only child would not give one of her children a long-standing family name, but she saw spending so many years apart due to this slight was—"

"Was so wrong. Whoops, sorry, interrupted again. Let's blame Starbucks."

"Was best put in the past."

There was a moment's silence. I took a chance.

"You've finished, right? I can talk now, right?"

"For the moment, yes."

"You done good, Mom… ah… did well. You did well," I added, hoping to quell another remonstration on her part.

"Thank you. I would like to believe I was instrumental in helping Jennifer and her mother resolve this long-standing feud."

"Well, take a bow, Lila Hamilton-Alvarez."

I smiled at her, and she graced me with one of her own Madonna-like smiles. Then her gaze locked on mine.

"I know I don't say it often, Liana, but you are a wonderful daughter and I… I… love you very much. I can only hope you and I will never have a misunderstanding of that magnitude."

Actually, I can't remember her ever having said I was wonderful before, forget often. Well, maybe once, but I'd been coshed on the head by a bad guy and was lying in a hospital bed. Madame Blueblood doesn't gush, especially about me, so I was surprised and touched. I felt a warm glow overtake me, like the time I'd sat on one of those new car seats with heated cushions for your backside.

"We won't, Mom. I love you too. And thank you."

I reached for her hand and squeezed it. She squeezed back. Then out of nowhere, I was slammed again by one of those rogue waves coming at me when least expected. I took a deep breath, trying to steady myself.

"Are you all right, my dear? It isn't just the caffeine, is it?" Her voice was probing but kind.

I shook my head. "It's hard to think about Stephen being gone. The fact it looks like it's not from natural causes is almost too much to take in. I've got to keep busy, looking into things, doing something. It makes me feel not quite so… helpless." My fingers struck at a sudden tear sliding down my cheek.

Mom brushed at the tear in a far more gentle way. "I understand, Liana, far more than you could know. You do what you need to do. Only be safe. Promise me that," she added.

Lila turned and with head held high, walked down the hallway and toward her office. I think she pretty much felt the same way I did.

Chapter Eleven

A Game Plan Along the Rambo Line

"Okay, so here's what I've got."

It was the following day, early morning. Richard looked up for a moment from the forty-six-inch computer screen, the likes of which only he and NASA own. This monitor cost more than a new Honda Gold Wing motorcycle, and I should know. I just priced one. On top of that, Richard was using his own pixel-enhancing program, something he created a few years back. Combined, the pixel resonation is in such detail you could see the sideburns on a gnat, should they have them.

Gurn and I stood behind my seated brother in his littered, dark, and cramped office at DI. Richard seemed riveted to the scaled-down specs of the Fantasy Lady's skeletal framework revolving in the lower section of the screen in ever-changing angles. Master plans of her elevators, entrance, and exit doors spun in the top section.

"I've managed to color-code each specific category, so it's easier to see what's what without confusing the eye," Richard said, spinning around and facing us. His own eyes looked tired and red.

"How long have you been up doing this?" I reached out and pushed back an errant strand of hair on his unkempt head.

He grinned half in embarrassment, half in pride.

"Long enough to get this and a few other things done."

He turned back to the screen. "So where was I? Yes. Green for the elevators, blue, the stairwells, and the red is for doorways. I've blacked the rest out."

He isolated a section and pushed a couple of keys. The screen froze, and a green elevator shaft took forefront. The shaft went from the main casino to the penthouse level of the hotel.

"You can see, unlike the rest of the hotel, where there are twenty-six elevators going from the basement to each floor up to the thirty-seventh, there's only one elevator to the penthouse area—floor thirty-eight—nonstop from the main lobby. With the building code being what it is, they had to have four clearly marked stairwells exiting the penthouse to the elevators one floor below. I finally managed to get security specs for the building, a couple of hours ago. That was harder than the county permits and architectural drafts."

"So if you have the security requirements, you know how many guards are stationed at each set of stairs of the penthouse?" asked Gurn.

"Three men on each, if you can believe it, two at the top of the landing and one below. Twelve men in all, all with walkie-talkies."

"What about the lone elevator to the penthouse?" I asked, looking over toward Gurn's serious face. We both saw the turn this caper was taking. "How secure is that?"

"Two men in the penthouse and two men on the main floor. The guys in the penthouse are armed with ARs."

"Assault rifles? Jeesh," I said.

"Wow," commented Gurn. "This is not looking good."

"There's no way we're pushing our way in," I said. "We'll have to use another method."

"Like what?" asked Gurn, turning to face me.

"Need I say I don't like the sound of this?" commented Richard.

I moved away, threw papers and stray bits of computer paraphernalia from one of the chairs, and plopped myself down.

Gurn leaned his backside against Richard's desk and crossed his arms. Both men stared at me.

"I thought this might be a possible scenario," I said, "so I gave Flint a fast call last night. He has a nephew who does a lounge-lizard act with four girls at the Fantasy Lady. One show nightly in the penthouse —"

"You're not thinking of getting into show business, are you? You must be kidding," Gurn interrupted.

"Unfortunately," said Richard, "my sister doesn't kid about things like this. You should know that by now."

I ignored both of them. "This nephew, Johnny Thunder, I think, owes his Uncle Flint a favor, plus he's cash strapped. For a certain price, I can substitute for one of the dancers, who has, all of a sudden, come down with the flu, dollar bills having been flung her way."

"No you're not," said Gurn, pushing away from the desk and standing erect, arms still crossed.

"Yes I am," I said, rising and crossing my arms, matching his stance.

"There is no way I'm letting you go up to that penthouse by yourself."

"Excuse me? There is no way *you're* letting *me*?"

He dropped his arms. "Maybe I should rephrase."

"Maybe you should."

"Children, children, there's no need for this bickering." Lila's voice came out strong and loud. "I'll be there right by her side, Gurn. All will be well."

"By my side? What are you talking about?" I turned on Lila, who entered the room like the grand dame she is, dressed in a Dresden blue suit with navy accessories and her standard pearls.

Lila did her ignoring-me routine. "Richard, did you get the necessary information programmed in?"

"What information?" I asked.

"Oh yeah," Richard said and turned away from me with a guilty look on his face. "Lila had this idea I didn't get a chance to tell you about, Lee."

"What information?" I repeated. "What idea? What's going on, Mom?"

Lila finally turned to me wearing one of her winning smiles. "You remember Alice Farnsworth, don't you, dear?"

"Alice Farnsworth?" A flicker of a memory came to me.

"Such a delightful woman. Your father did her a great service once." The Dresden blue emphasized the color of Mom's eyes, which took center stage and twinkled. Her eyes hadn't twinkled since we learned of Stephen's death. I decided to play along.

"Didn't Dad rescue her son who had been kidnapped and held for ransom? About fifteen years ago," I said.

"One doesn't forget that type of heroism. Your father risked his life to save her little boy. Being a recent widow, Alice became a recluse, buying an island off the coast of France, and having her son tutored privately. She hasn't left the island since then. Now Rupert's grown up and has gone into French politics, but that is another story. The thrust of the tale is—"

"Oh yes, tell us the thrust, Mother," I said, standing in front of her and crossing my arms.

"Now you are doing to me exactly what Gurn did to you." She turned to Gurn. "No offense, dear boy."

"None taken," Gurn replied.

"Basically, I am a grown-up woman, a fully licensed detective, and I will do as I see fit, just as you are going to do as you see fit. We'll both be seeing fit together." She laughed. "A small joke."

"Very small," I murmured. "Now see here, Mom, I'm not sure I like the sound of this," I said, dropping my arms and coming forward. "What are you up to?"

"It should be obvious, dear, especially to one of your intelligence."

"Well, sometimes I'm stupid, so tell me."

"I am going to masquerade as Alice Farnsworth and gain access to the Fantasy Lady's penthouse gambling room.

Alice is a documented billionaire, and as a recluse with no recent photos taken, she is perfect."

"So what Mom had me do last night, Lee," Richard said, "while you and Gurn were off... ah... by yourselves, was to falsify online records making out that Mrs. Farnsworth is a gambling fool. The Principé Casino in Monaco, Monte Carlo, was easy to get into. Alice lost nearly ten million dollars there. The Günter House in Austria, over fifteen."

"Did I?" Lila said, getting into character with a smile. "I thought it was best to keep all the losses in Europe—France and Austria mostly. This way, it's more understandable when no one recognizes me. Richard even altered images in the casinos' surveillance tapes, inserting my picture every now and then. It wouldn't bear detailed scrutiny, but it will suffice for what we require."

"You seem to have thought all this out, Mrs. Alvarez," said Gurn.

"I believe I have, Gurn, and do call me Mrs. Farnsworth." Mom curtsied slightly. Both she and Gurn laughed. I nearly threw up.

I turned to Gurn. "There's no way I'm letting my mother go in there alone."

"Of course not, dear." Mom spoke up before Gurn could say anything. "I won't be alone. I'll have you on the outside, making sure I get out of the interior private casino."

"The private casino where we believe the heavy million-dollar bets are taking place," Richard added.

"See this ring?" Lila offered a hand sparkling with a previously unnoticed large diamond ring. "It's a small microphone and transmitter. Very clever, and it's directly connected to one of Richard's computers."

"It can't be used inside the private casino," Richard added. "After some testing, I found electrical transmissions are blocked going in and out. They're probably using a Faraday cage—"

"Wait a minute," I interrupted. "A Faraday cage. That's like what a microwave oven has to keep the rays inside, right?"

"Right," said Richard and Gurn in unison. Both looked at one another. Gurn gestured for Richard to continue, which he did.

"This is why we need someone on the outside, Lee, at all times. If Lila doesn't come out from the room by a certain time, someone has to go in and get her, like you, Flint, or Gurn. Or call the police. Something like that."

I turned on Richard, leaning down into his face. "You mean you two haven't worked that out?"

"Hey, we didn't get there yet. PS, and by the way, all of this was going on while you were busy elsewhere," Richard said with an emphasis on the word "busy."

What Richard was talking about was when Gurn and I were making like Deborah Kerr and Burt Lancaster in *From Here to Eternity* but in the jacuzzi instead of on the beach. During the previous night, the movie became one of my favorites. Nothing like the personal touch.

"You and Richard work out the details, Liana." Mom looked at her watch. "But keep me posted. I need to get to JFK. Alice has given her staff two weeks off under the premise of flying to the States for a much-needed vacation. At this very moment, Alice's housekeeper — a lovely woman and very trustworthy — is flying to New York disguised as her employer. Alice is hiding out in the gamekeeper's cottage during the interim. The housekeeper will be staying at the Waldorf Astoria as herself for two weeks when I assume Alice's persona later today. Then from New York I need to get to Las Vegas, hopefully by this evening."

"How are you going to do that?" I asked.

"Possibly by commercial airlines, but I thought I'd try to rent a private pilot and jet. It would be more impressive."

"At your service, Mrs. Farnsworth." Gurn stood tall and saluted.

"Gurn, your name is on a hit list probably created by Lou Spaulding," I said. "How can you take Lila anywhere?"

"Once I get to the East Coast, there are several aliases I can use to fly a plane."

"Ah," I mused. "Another perk of being a special kind of CPA?"

"And," Gurn said, ignoring my comment and looking at me, "I know someone who'll rent me one of his Maverick jets under any name I'm using at the moment."

"I'm assuming that, too, is by special arrangement with the board of certified public accountants," I threw in for good measure.

"Liana, there is no need for sarcastic remarks. Let us not question this and merely be grateful for the gentleman's assistance," chastised Mom. She turned to Gurn. "I think you will do admirably. I wouldn't mind having you along for extra protection."

I panicked. "Protection? Hey, this is sounding dangerous, Mom."

"Now, now." Gurn patted me on the shoulder. He took my mother by the arm and headed for the door, saying over his shoulder, "Lila and I are going to be fine. Oh, this means you'll have to make your way back to Vegas today on your own. You might want to give the friendly skies a call," he said with a wink.

"I'll give you some 'friendly skies,'" I muttered, "swinging."

Chapter Twelve

So You Wanna Be in Showbiz?

It was shortly after 5:00 p.m. the same day. I'd finished running through the first two routines, watered-down versions of '50s- and '60s-style dancing with a few step-ball changes and wiggles thrown in. I wiped perspiration from my forehead. Not that it was strenuous or difficult work, but the temperature had hit about ninety-five degrees inside Johnny Thunder's small, windowless rehearsal studio, despite it being November and around seventy degrees in the Nevada desert.

"Okay. So I see you can dance a little, and you're good to look at." The star of the show stared at me appraisingly and then stepped forward and whispered in my ear, "I wasn't sure what I was getting into with Flint, but five grand is five grand. And it's just for tonight, right?"

I tried not to be put out by the "dance a little" crack but nodded in agreement at the time frame. He looked relieved. Johnny stepped back to where he'd been watching me go through my paces.

Dressed in a tight, black jumpsuit, Johnny was a small man with a barrel chest and birdlike legs. Deeply tanned skin, a pockmarked face, and slick, jet-black hair exuded a certain raw, untamable charm. Johnny Thunder, aka Webster Jonathan Tall Trees, probably appealed to a lot of the ladies. The familiarity with which he dealt with the other three dancers led me to believe he'd bedded them all at one time or another.

"Okay, Paisley," he said to me, "let's try the third number."

I tried not to cringe at the name Richard had dreamed up for me. He'd created a driver's license, credit cards, and Social Security card, all in the name of Paisley Putz, no relation to J. J. Putz, the baseball guy. Sometimes Richard's sense of humor gets on my nerves.

"Let's go, girls," Johnny said, turning around and looking at the other dancers in the room. "I'm going to need you on this."

Bobbi, Bambi, and Starlight got up from nearby chairs to line up next to me. In their early twenties, Bobbi and Bambi were mirrors of each other. Taller than me by a good two or three inches, they were thin to the point of emaciation with the exception of huge, fake breasts covered by ripped, midriff-revealing T-shirts. Crew cut, white blonde hair less than an inch all over their heads completed the odd look. With slow deliberation, they sauntered to my left. There they stood as erect as a modern major general, staring vacantly ahead without acknowledging my existence.

Then there was Starlight, the dance captain, who marched to the stage with anger in every step. Starlight LaRue, probably in her mid-forties, had the look of a lady who'd been around the block a number of times, each trip etching itself on her face in ever-deepening lines. Long, dyed red hair, in desperate need of conditioning, hung limply down her back. Two black inner tubes sat on heavy lids, masquerading as false eyelashes. She, too, sported a set of counterfeit jugs, which looked out of place with the rest of her slender, muscular body. I began to wonder if there was a tax cut in Vegas for people with boob jobs.

Sizing the ladies up—and I use the term "ladies" loosely—I wasn't worried about Bobbi or Bambi. Between the two of them, they had little interest in anything other than their apparent cocaine habit and getting through the day. Starlight was another matter.

As dance captain, it had been Starlight's job to teach me the routines. She'd met me two hours earlier armed with the show's music recorded on a boom box and a heavy-duty bad attitude. Along with the routines, I got a crash course in dealing with a snarling dance captain with a chisel-sharp tongue, who could teach an army drill sergeant a thing or two about sadism.

Apparently, she didn't believe for one minute I was filling in for a sick dancer. Hanky-panky with thundering Johnny appeared to be more along the lines of her thought processes. She had a strong sense of ownership for her boss and probably some major history. I would have to watch myself with her.

The one-hour-fifteen-minute review consisted of Johnny belting out loud-and-throbbing '50s and '60s songs while four scantily costumed girls jiggled around in the background, me now being one of them. My part in this cheesy revue was easy to pick up, consisting mostly of dances like the Jerk, Swim, Mashed Potato, and The Twist, while tossing my hair around like an idiot. Two or three numbers actually required knowing your left foot from your right, so I had to pay attention from time to time. Starlight and I stood in a line on either side of the two giant, bleached-blonde Q-tips, we being the two shorter women. We stared at our illustrious leader.

"You sing?" Johnny asked, squinting into my eyes.

"S-sing?" I parroted with a stutter.

"Okay. I'll put it this way. Can you carry a tune?"

"Barely," I said, thinking of all the times Richard and Mom try to drown me out when we go caroling. I'm told I have a three-note range.

"Close enough. Do you know "Yesterday" by the Beatles?" I nodded.

"Good. All you got to do is sing the last word of each line after me and do a little dancing. Watch Starlight. She knows what to do."

Starlight didn't exactly stick her tongue out at me, but I could tell she'd have liked to.

Johnny clicked on the boom box, and the sound of tinny music filled the room along with the pulsing beat of drums.

Johnny spun around and faced a pretend audience. He crooned the beginning lyrics in a not-too-bad voice.

We sang the required backup nasally but in unison, doing two or three steps of some weird dance I was later to learn was called The Monkey. Then we struck a pose. I was only half a beat behind the other women, watching them carefully. But I think I lost consciousness for a moment or two, though, because I suddenly heard him belt out the last two words of the next line, "far away."

"Far away," I caterwauled, giving it everything I had. Then I bounced with the other dancers to the count of four and struck another pose.

I was just getting the hang of it when Johnny stopped singing and turned to me abruptly. "Ah, Paisley, why don't you just mouth the words? Don't sing," he said with an earnest but condescending smile.

Starlight laughed, and even the two Q-tips giggled.

"Sure," I said. *Jeesh, even Johnny Thunder has standards.*

After that horror was over, we ran through several other numbers until we came to the theme from *Peter Gunn*.

"Okay, Paisley," Johnny said, turning to me. "This is where you do your solo with the gun."

"I have a solo with a gun?"

"Oh yeah, I forgot." Starlight walked over to her dancer's bag and took out a small, black wooden pistol stashed inside a holster. The holster was tied to a red lace garter. This had gone from bad to worse, which I didn't even think was possible.

"It's a forty-eight-bar solo, but you got to pull the gun out of the holster on your leg on the last two counts," Starlight said with a nasty edge. "Here you go."

She threw the garter and its companion piece at me. I caught them with one hand and strapped them to my thigh, while she went on,

"We don't care much what you do before you get to the end of the number. Just fill the time, but be sure to pull the gun out on the last seven-eight of the count. We pull ours out at the same time. It's our big finale."

I listened to the horns and drums blaring out the well-known tune once through. The second time Johnny ran the tape, the spot for my solo came up. My heart was in my mouth. Only the day before in Flint's kitchen I'd thought about how wonderful it would be to be dancing onstage in costume. Be careful what you wish for. You may get it.

Johnny and the three dancers moved aside, making room for my ha-ha big number. I commended my soul to God and stepped forward. Then it hit me. Coming into these routines with years of formal ballet training was a bit like using a blowtorch to light a birthday candle. I decided to go for it. I executed an *entrechat, cabriole, assemblé, jeté*, interspersed with a few other easy jumps and leaps. Full of myself, I threw in an *arebesque* — I mean, why not — and ended with several *fouettés en tournant*, a type of turn I do fairly well. My former ballet teacher, Madame Monique, would have been proud.

At the seven-eight count, I grabbed the lightweight toy from its holster, arched my back, and aimed the silly thing to the heavens in what I hoped was a moderately sexy pose. Or maybe I looked like I'd been struck by lightning. I wasn't sure. There was a moment's silence.

"Wow!" Johnny grinned at me with arched eyebrows. Starlight's jaw dropped to the floor. Even the two Q-tips looked impressed. Good dancing, like everything else, is relative. Put me in the middle of a hoedown with fourth graders, and I suspect I would look like another Margot Fonteyn.

"Well, all right," Johnny said with surprise. "Giving the show some class, aren't we? I like it. You see, Star?" Johnny turned to the redhead. "We could use more of that kind of dancing in the show."

"Yeah sure," she answered quietly. "Although I think she could cut it back a little."

"What are you talking about?" Johnny's tone of voice indicated he thought she was crazy. "The girl's a ballerina. I saw that kind of dancing on a PBS special once in The Crackling Nuts or something."

"*The Nutcracker*," Star said through gritted teeth.

"Whatever." He shrugged. "Let's use it."

"I don't mind cutting it back a little," I jumped in with a tremulous smile in Starlight's direction, hoping I could make amends. She glared at me.

"Do exactly what you did there, sweet cakes," Johnny ordered, waving Starlight's comment away. He turned to Bobbi and Bambi. "It wouldn't hurt either of you girls to wake up and do a little bit of that kind of dancing either." He looked back at me, approval written all over his face. "You could learn a lot from her. She's got a lot of class."

The Q-tips stopped looking impressed and glared at me much the same as Starlight had done. Johnny was oblivious. Typical man.

We finished the rehearsal with me feeling like poison oak and being treated pretty much the same way by my fellow dancers. Before I left, Johnny handed me two purple costumes covered in plastic, fresh from the cleaners, a hatbox containing a purple-and-silver Mylar Cleopatra wig, and a pair of beat-up, white go-go boots. Six forty-five, and I was an official Las Vegas dancer.

* * * *

It was now exactly 11:00 p.m., which gave us performers little time to put props and costumes in place once we arrived on the thirty-eighth floor. The penthouse show was scheduled for eleven fifteen. Wearing the first wet and overused costume from the two previous shows in the main lounge, we carried the equally sweat-drenched second costume with us. Yuk.

Johnny pressed the elevator button for the penthouse while I thought about the scenario Lila, Richard, Gurn, and I had come up with. My job, after I had humiliated myself onstage for the third time in one night, was to make sure they came out of the room no later than 1:00 a.m. If not, I was to take appropriate action. This was no time for nerves; just follow the program. It was a matter of timing, remembering what to do, and being in the right place at the right time. I repeated this mantra endlessly.

Lila and Gurn arrived at the hotel around seven, followed discreetly by Flint. They had checked into adjoining suites, she as Alice Farnsworth and Gurn as Rick Maddock, her personal pilot and thinly veiled boy toy. Both had worked their way into the inner sanctum of the private casino around 8:30 p.m. Once inside the metallic cage of the private casino, Lila and Gurn had hopefully been able to break into the electronic, unprotected transmissions, taping them for scrutiny later. I would finish the third set with Johnny and my new best friends by 12:30 a.m. By that time, everything that needed to go down should have gone down, and it would be simply a case of standing by the door and waiting.

I adjusted the purple wig and checked myself out in the elevator mirror, feeling the whoosh in my stomach as we lurched skyward. When the doors opened, two men with AKAs stood on either side, watching us alight.

I looked out into the small but opulent casino room, done in every conceivable shade of off-white, with shimmering touches of soft pink, peach, and magenta. Back, floor, and overhead lighting showcased larger-than-life white ceramic or frosted glass Art Deco statues of slim, long-haired women. Frozen in time, they held vases of cascading water or cavorted with darling, ghostly companions, such as dogs, dolphins, monkeys, and birds, each sculpture surrounded strategically by green gaming tables.

As I stepped off the elevator, the guard closest to me checked the toy gun in my garter and moved up my leg, giving me a screening any airport would be proud of.

I wanted to tell him he could at least buy me dinner first but restrained myself. After, I was free to follow the others to the stage at the end of the room. But I had other plans.

I decided to check out as much of the room as I could and scuttled away. This main casino fed into other smaller rooms, separated by see-through curtains, slats of carved white wood or hidden doors, one of them being the multimillion dollar private casino. Out here in the main casino, well-dressed players, serious in intent, gambled for a minimum bet of a thousand dollars per play. These were the pikers. Behind one of these doors, the minimum was one million dollars per play.

This had to be the quietest casino room I'd ever been in. I looked around at the clientele all intent on playing craps, baccarat, poker, or the roulette wheel in a most dignified manner, like merry old England's Ascot without any horses. Sort of takes the fun out of it, in my opinion. I'd rather be at Circus-Circus with the ding, ding, ding of the nickel slot machines, throwing back a watered down mai tai. But sometimes I've got no class, no matter what Johnny Thunder says.

I finally found what I was looking for on the far side of the room. Discreetly set into an Art Deco wall was a hidden door, with another armed man standing nearby. A man walked up to the guard, showed him a piece of paper, received a nod, and was ushered inside. I tried to amble nearer, just as Johnny bounced over to me. He was covered with enough sweat to have been trapped in a sauna room for two or three hours.

"Paisley! Where did you get to? I was getting nervous about you. You can't take off like that, not up here. Anyway, come with me. We've got to set up."

"Well, what have we here?" We both turned to the sound of the voice, and I recognized Lou Spaulding from Richard's computer images but taller and more colorful in person. He stepped in between Johnny and me and took my hand. "What a lovely addition to your act, Johnny. You must introduce me."

"Oh, s-sure, Mr. Spaulding," Johnny stuttered. "This is the girl filling in for Rita tonight, who's got the flu or something. This is Paisley. Paisley, this is Mr. Spaulding."

"But you must call me Lou," he said, bending over and kissing my hand, a hand I planned on washing as soon as possible.

I forced a smile, which I hoped looked more charming and warm than I was feeling. I gave my hand a little tug. He got the hint and released my paw.

"Nice to meet you, Lou," I trilled, "but I have to go set up for the show."

I countered away from him and crossed in front of Johnny. I kept my smile going until I thought my face would break. I watched Spaulding's leering eyes follow me across the room.

Johnny and I headed to the back of a miniscule stage, maybe able to hold six or seven people, and into one of the two wings, delineated by curtains hung from the ceiling to the floor. Starlight was already setting up. When she saw me, she turned on me with a vicious look on her face.

"Where have you been? Listen, stupid, you can't go wandering around anywhere you want. You stay with the group."

"It's all right, Star. Take it easy," Johnny jumped in before I could say anything. "She didn't mean it. She doesn't know the protocol of this place, right?" He turned and directed the last word to me.

"What protocol, Johnny?" I said, throwing my costume on a nearby folding chair. "I was just looking for the bathroom and got a little lost. What's the big deal?"

"We're only allowed up here because Connie Elsberg likes to hear me sing," Johnny said. "I don't want to say too much, but she and I used to—"

"You don't owe her any explanations about you and Mrs. Elsberg." Star turned to me and snarled. "They're friends, okay? And it's none of your business. Just do the damn show the way you're supposed to."

Connie Elsberg, a sixty-four-year-old widow, owned the lion's share of the Fantasy Lady, having inherited it from her recently demised gangster husband. She now owned a lot of Las Vegas, too, and was supposed to have been quite a vixen in her day. Apparently that day wasn't completely over either. Richard had found an item or two about the widow and Johnny on the net. It explained a lot about this seedy act appearing in such an upscale casino. I suspected Johnny was better at more primal things than singing.

"Okay, okay. Sorry," I said, putting out my hands to deflect her anger. "But where is the bathroom? I really have to go." I knew where the bathrooms were. Richard and I had gone over the locations of all of them. The one I needed was closest to the stage.

"The ones we're supposed to use are behind the backdrop," Starlight said, easing up a little on her attitude. She pointed to a thick, sixteen-foot-high drop curtain behind the stage.

"I'll be back in a minute," I said, pushing the heavy curtain aside and stepping behind it before either one of them could say anything.

A well-lit, off-white wall stood behind with just enough width from the curtain to the wall to create a narrow walkway, allowing people to get from one side of the stage to the other. Two doors, one marked Men and the other Women were cut into the plain stucco wall. I opened the appropriate one and hurried to the third and last stall of the nondescript, basic bathroom. Reaching up behind the toilet tank, I found the small plastic-covered bundle taped to the back, freeing it with a couple of jerks. Clear plastic held a snub-nose detective special. Removed from its wrapping, it felt cool and oddly alive in my hand. Taking out the wooden lookalike from my garter, I threw it in the trashcan and thrust the real gun inside the holster. Aside from the weight, both looked pretty much the same from far away.

It had been another Flint coupe, getting one of the Fantasy Lady's cleaning crew to carry the gun through the metal detector. It cost a lot of money, three thousand to be exact. Whoever did it — and I never got an answer from Flint — took a big chance his or her stainless steel cart would pass through the metal detector, with this weapon hidden between cleaning supplies. So far, this escapade has cost us upward of ten thousand dollars, and we weren't anywhere near done yet. It was for Stephen, I reminded myself. Anything to find Stephen's killer or killers.

I straightened out the purple Ban-Lon go-go dress before I exited the bathroom, all the while hoping it wouldn't come to me having to use this gun. If I did, it meant we were in dipstick trouble. Lost in thought, I opened the door and ran smack into Lou Spaulding, standing right outside. He came toward me. In a natural, reflex action, I stepped back into the bathroom.

Suddenly I felt outraged, embarrassed and more than a little trapped. What the hell? Did he follow me? Even though I could take him on with a few karate moves, did I really want to go that route? No way.

He walked at me wearing a lusty grin, which would have scandalized my mother. I felt my heartbeat quicken but stood still and pulled myself up to my full height. Don't give the impression you're scared, girl. Predators look for just that thing.

I forced a smile. "You know, it's really bad manners to follow a lady into the restroom, especially if you don't know her."

"Well, it's my bathroom. I own this whole place."

Spaulding reached out and took my forearm in a firm grip, pulling me toward him.

No you don't, pal, I thought. *You own 5 percent. The rest is owned by investors like Connie Ellsberg. So stuff that in your turkey baster.*

"You know, Mr. Spaulding…" I began aloud.

"Call me, Lou, baby."

"Lou baby, I have a show to do in about three minutes." I batted voluminous false eyelashes, fanning the surrounding air. "But afterward…" I left the end of the sentence hanging, in a suggestive manner.

"Well, it'll have to do, baby." He caressed the side of my cheek, while I fought the urge to bite off the tip of his finger.

Standing aside but not so much as I could get by him without brushing against him, I fled to the relative safety of three women who hated my guts and a singer with sunflowers seeds for brains.

It was around 12:15 p.m., and Johnny began singing "My Way" in what could only be described as a schmaltzy, melodramatic way. I once heard a recording of Enrico Caruso singing "Vesti La Giubba" from Pagliacci. This type of over-the-top singing can really work, especially if it's a beautiful song sung by someone with an incredible voice. However, I'm here to tell you a so-so song sung by a so-so singer in the same way is just plain painful to listen to. Karaoke singers, be warned.

But his version of this it was, so instead of bouncing around, the dancers were ordered to stand reverently still in darkness at the rear of the stage and watch in rapt attention.

This was my only chance to see if Lila and Gurn were in place and ready. With no light in my eyes, I could see out into the audience, such as it was. A few people sat on stools around a highly polished glass-and-chrome bar, chatting, drinking, and mainly ignoring us. Others were strewn around at nearby tables large enough to hold a couple of drinks and a pseudo candle providing a battery-operated, flickering light. Nobody was paying attention to the singer knocking himself out in what he apparently thought was the performance of a lifetime.

A woman in white stepped into my line of vision. It took a moment for my mind to register who it was. Lila. Wearing a getup the likes of which I've never seen on her before, she stood before me glittering like a crystal chandelier on growth hormones.

Mom is a woman severely into animal rights, yet here she was, dripping in white fox fur, under which was a white suit, molded to the shape of her figure. To make sure you got the message, discreet amounts of fabric were cut out here and there revealing skin beneath. I'd seen a suit like this once on Victoria Principal in a rerun of *Dallas.* It got her into a lot of trouble.

Volumes of curled and upswept hair framed her face as only a do can do when it has been teased and sprayed within an inch of its life. Even in the half-lit barroom atmosphere, I could tell her face was spackled with vast amounts of makeup. When I could rip my eyes from her features, I saw various parts of her sparkling with diamonds — real or otherwise — like a flashy, New Year's Eve float. In fact, she looked like her own personal parade. Kelli would have loved it.

Gurn stepped out from behind Lila wearing aviator style sunglasses and chewing bubble gum. Dressed in white slacks and a silky, half-opened black shirt, gold chains brandished his naked chest. Chewing his cud, he took his sunglasses off and winked at me.

My mouth dropped open, and I gaped. Mom shot me a look that said, "Close your mouth, Liana. It's most unladylike." So I did.

I heard Johnny give out with his big grand finale note, hanging on to it for dear life as long as he could, but ultimately running out of breath. Silence followed and then sparse applause, led by we four women standing behind him. He took a low bow the queen of England would have been proud of. I vaguely thought of how good in bed he had to be for Connie Ellsberg to stick her neck out and bring him up to the thirty-eighth floor. Either that or he had to have a low and dirty secret on her.

Before we went into our next routine, two songs away from my solo dance, Lila and Gurn whispered something to one another. Then they turned and headed between the crowds toward the Art Deco wall, where the mysterious door awaited them.

I didn't get a chance to see if they got in for sure, as I was busy dancing the stroll and other silliness. I had to trust in my cohorts' skills that they knew what they were doing, and all was going according to plan.

I did my big *Peter Gunn* number, only worried for a moment someone would notice I was pulling out a real revolver from my garter instead of the toy. But no one looked at me, including the audience. I probably could have pulled out a food processer for all they cared.

At the designated time, I left the stage with the other girls to change into the second and last costume. After I stashed the revolver in the outside zippered compartment of my dance bag, I pulled on what looked like cut-up pieces of purple-tinted aluminum foil, tactically glued onto a mesh body stocking. I added the purple Mylar-and-feathered boa, plus the headdress weighing in at about twenty pounds, which bobbed precariously on my head. Before I went onstage to finish the act, I tried to adjust what little pieces of foil there were over the more personal parts of my body. I looked at a wall clock. Fifteen minutes from now was the real showtime.

After a grand finale that lay flatter than an overprocessed toupee on a bald man's head, the performance was over. As fast as I could, I changed into my street clothes, threw my costumes to a sulking Starlight, and with sleight of hand, gave Johnny an envelope containing five one-thousand-dollar bills. I was done with showbiz and none too soon.

Once out the stage door, I saw Lusty Lou waiting for me by a nearby Roulette table. He pushed his way through folks dressed in tuxedos, sequins, and sparkling tube tops happily losing their money faster than the speed of light. The number of players had picked up. Twelve thirty at night in a casino is like four o'clock in the afternoon to the rest of the world. I gave a quick glance around to see if Lila and Gurn were nearby, didn't see them, but decided not to panic. I could panic later, if necessary.

"You look great, baby. I like your outfit. Skin tight works for you."

I looked down and remembered I was wearing an emerald-green jumpsuit I'd bought when I was five pounds lighter. After his comment, I vowed to throw it away when I took it off or maybe lose the weight. Naw, throw it out.

Before I could reply, he took my arm in a proprietary way and said, "How about stepping into my office for a nightcap? I've got all the comforts of home there."

Meaning a bed, I'm sure, I thought. I looked down, forced what I hoped was a sexy smile and nodded. He fairly dragged me across the floor to the other side of the casino, jostling players as he moved. He glanced over at me, mistaking my reticence for something else.

"You're the little shy one, aren't you?"

More like nauseated, bub. "Well, after all," I said aloud, "I'm awestruck, being with the legendary Mr. Lou Spaulding."

"So now I'm a legend!"

Not really, Toots, I just made that up. I gave out a hollow laugh and threw my hair around, wondering how Hollywood starlets and ladies of the night deal with such idiots.

Eventually, we made it to the wall on which half-naked pink women forever cavorted amid pale-pink, gold, and lavender Art Deco flowers. A burly, somber man nodded to Spaulding, moved for the half-hidden door and opened it, standing aside. As I suspected and hoped, Spaulding's office was inside this part of the casino seen by only the privileged few. Well, I tried to console myself, this was one way of getting inside. Now if I could just get out with what remained of my virtue intact, dragging Lila and Gurn back with me.

We entered a sparsely furnished circular room, maybe a hundred feet in diameter and two or three stories in height. Overhead a domed ceiling, painted black, faded into the darkened atmosphere. In rows of four, huge flat-screen TVs hung from black walls starting at about ten feet up from the floor, covering the circumference of the room. Over each set of flat screens, liquid crystal displayed banners of information.

Below in designated areas, people lounged on white leather lounge chairs, wearing a headset or small earbud, giving their full attention to the screens before them and the LCDs. Some were being catered to by scantily clad women in pink gossamer costumes serving drinks or croupiers dressed like Gopher on *The Love Boat*, i.e. black slacks, white shirt, black bowtie, and short white jacket trimmed in gold piping. The croupiers carried what resembled an iPad, entering stuff into it after chatting with an individual lounging on a white chair.

I ignored Spaulding's nudges and spun around the quiet, intense room. Given the hour, most of the overhead LCDs announced events from the other side of the world. There was bowling from Hong Kong, a game of bocce ball from the Greek island of Corfu, track-car racing from Bucharest, and the beginnings of a tennis match in Amsterdam, all reverently being scrutinized by the lounging, expensively attired customers.

Other games or contests were going on, but I lost focus trying to find Lila. In this half light, I knew she would be hard to find given we were dealing with white on white, but I needn't have worried.

Just as Spaulding grabbed my arm, Lila's voice trumpeted in pseudo distress above the other sounds of this relatively quiet room. Much of the activity stopped, and people looked in her direction as she faltered, draped around Gurn's mighty chest. One thing about Lila, she knows how to make a dramatic entrance or exit.

"Really, it's nothing, nothing," she warbled to one of the attending croupiers, walking right by Spaulding and me. "I have these sudden attacks of asthma and just need to take my medicine." She sent a fleeting glance in my direction and let out an "Ooooo" sound, almost sliding down Gurn's chest. What an actress!

I loosened Spaulding's grip on me and bolted forward, grabbing her.

"Oh my gosh," I said in my best Pollyanna voice, "Let me help you."

I flung an arm around her waist, and she leaned on me, belting out in fortissimo, "Why, aren't you sweet? What a lovely young lady. Thank you so much, my dear. What a comfort you are."

A small crowd of concerned people gathered around the three of us. Spaulding's henchmen kept watch from a safe distance, nervous glances thrown, now and then, in their boss's direction. Spaulding himself looked like a cat watching a juicy mouse scuttle free to the safety of a nearby mouse hole, me being the mouse.

Gurn piped up, looking at me. "Could you help me take Mrs. Farnsworth to her room?"

"My pleasure," I said.

The three of us moved forward as one, parting the masses like a boat going through water. We passed through the door into the main casino, Spaulding and his men at our heels. The elevator to freedom was within sight, and my heartbeat dropped to a near normal level.

"Lee! Lee Alvarez!" shouted a voice from the throng. Horace Morgan, our local druggist, stepped forward wearing a plaid suit and tie, his mustache twitching in excitement.

"I thought it was you on the stage wearing that purple wig. What are you doing here in Las Vegas? My wife and I are here for our fiftieth wedding anniversary." He noticed Mom and looked at her in confusion. "Mrs. Alvarez! Are you all right? Can I be of assistance?"

He stepped forward only to be pushed aside by three larger members of Spaulding's men, who attached themselves to us like metal to a magnet.

I gaped at Mr. Morgan, who stared at me with an "uh-oh" look on his face. I think it occurred to him as an afterthought what the Alvarez family did for a living. Meanwhile, Lou Spaulding, his face dark with fury, stepped in front of Mr. Morgan and glared at me.

"Why, you bitch," he growled.

Spaulding gestured to two other men, who glommed on to each side of Gurn. Spaulding was taking no chances. I maneuvered the dance bag around so I had access to the gun, my heart pounding again. I saw Gurn draw himself up into combat mode. This navy pilot is a formidable opponent, gold chains and all.

Even Mom, who has been studying karate for only three months, went into a defensive stance. Within a split second, the tension became almost palpable. A small portion of the nearby crowd, including our druggist, began to disperse in an uneasy way as if not wanting to become involved in something taking an unpleasant route.

Spaulding noticed the crowd's reaction and put on a phony smile, saying in a loud voice, "Surely, Mrs. Farnsworth, you don't want to travel the distance to your suite feeling as poorly as you do. Boys, help the lady and her two friends back inside and into my office, will you? She can rest there."

"Mr. Spaulding," said a commanding bass baritone voice interrupting the proceedings. "A moment of your time." We all froze at the emanating authority of the voice, even Spaulding. In unison, we turned to the newcomer, a tall but bland-looking man, with dishwater-blond hair and pale-blue eyes, a man somehow not easy to disobey.

The speaker pulled out a wallet from an inside pocket of his plain black suit and dropped it open, flashing identification. He lowered his voice but still spoke with crystal clarity. "Agent Ed Reinhardt, FBI. I'd like you to come with me, sir."

Suddenly Spaulding was surrounded by five lookalike men, even down to the suits, who stood two or three feet away but watched him in an intimidating manner. His men had surrounded us, and the FBI men, in turn, surrounded them. There was a lot of surrounding going on.

"W-what for?" Spaulding stuttered. His men, thrown by the sudden lack of power from their leader, shuffled their feet and became ill at ease.

"It's regarding two accounting ledgers in your name."

Spaulding at first was puzzled but seemed relieved. "See my lawyers. That's what I pay them for."

Reinhardt shook his head.

"No, sir. There's also a matter of a recent execution-style killing. My superiors would like to see you now, sir."

He reached over and placed one hand on Spaulding's shoulder. Spaulding pulled away and grew taller and larger as if by sheer will. Both sets of secondary men tensed even more. With a sharp breath, I reached inside the dance bag and felt the cold steel of my detective special. If a shootout was imminent, I wanted to be ready.

Reinhardt removed his hand and grinned, diffusing the situation. He looked around at customers in the casino having a good time. "I'm sure your business partners wouldn't like a scene, Mr. Spaulding. We all have to answer to somebody, don't we? Let's do this the easy way, sir."

Spaulding looked at his own men. Shaking his head subtly, he dismissed his underlings, who melted into the crowd. The five FBI agents clustered around Spaulding and ushered him toward the elevator.

Reinhardt stayed behind for a moment and turned to me with a nod. "Thanks, Lee."

"Anytime, Ed," I answered with a dry throat.

Reinhardt followed his men and Spaulding, disappearing within the crowd.

"You know this guy?" Gurn asked me.

I nodded, too relieved to speak. This had been a close one.

"I think I need a glass of wine," Lila said in a whisper-soft breath, which caught in her throat. "Right now."

"I could use something stiffer," said Gurn. "What happened just now? I was sure it was going to get ugly."

"I called Ed this morning," I said. "I told him what was going down, and he should consider showing up for it. Fortunately, he did. I take it you got the info Richard needed?"

Mom patted her small clutch bag.

"I started transmitting to Richard the moment we were free of the metallic cage. It should almost be done by now."

I looked around for the discreetly labeled set of stairs.

"Let's take a walk down to the thirty-seventh floor, then one of the elevators to the street level. While I don't think we're in immediate danger, it might be wise to leave here sooner rather than later. If all went as planned, Flint took the things from your rooms and is waiting for us outside in his car. I'll check." I looked at my text messages. "Voila! All is well. Let's go."

No one said anything going down in the elevator. I glanced up once in a while at the surveillance camera. I'm sure Gurn and Lila did too. Once outside the revolving doors, we visibly relaxed and began a two-block walk to Flint's car parked on a side road.

"What's that?" Lila said to nobody in particular and pressed at her ear. She turned to me.

"Liana, Richard says we've got more than enough to tie Spaulding in with the rigged footraces and wants to know if Ed Reinhardt was the friend of yours from the Mercer Savings sting of a few years ago."

"The very one, Mom. The FBI has been working on cracking those ledgers, and Ed said they made a breakthrough around five o'clock this afternoon. With all the evidence they have, he knew if he could take a bigwig like Lou Spaulding into custody before his lawyers went into their dog-and-pony show, it would mean a promotion for him."

We finally hoofed it to Flint's Jeep and piled in. "Where's Nick?" I asked, looking at the lone occupant, Flint.

"Believe it or not, Nicky Boy is at my gym working out. He started going the day you headed back to California, and he's there four, five hours a day. Going to get those six-packs back." He turned around to the back seat. "Your bags are in the trunk. I don't think I missed anything. Did you get what you wanted in there, Lila?"

"More than we expected, Flint. At least it's what Richard is indicating from the data I transmitted a short while ago."

"Once you're inside the inner casino, the system has no protection whatsoever," added Gurn. "We were able to tap into minute-to-minute information their mainframe was relaying to the croupiers. Ties the Fantasy Lady and Spaulding into illegal betting on a lot of things, especially competitive footraces."

"You didn't make any bets, did you, Lila? Lose any money on a tennis match in Outer Mongolia or something? If so, we'll need to let accounting know," I teased.

"I'll have you know I won fifteen hundred dollars at baccarat. Otherwise, I made no bets."

Flint turned back to me sitting in the passenger's seat. "Where to now, Lee?"

"The airport. We got what we came for and then some."

"What?" said Flint in mock surprise. "You're not sticking around for tomorrow's show? Johnny said you were a good dancer and could come back anytime."

"He just wants another five thousand bucks," I said. Everyone laughed, including me.

I sobered, thinking out loud. "You think Spaulding will do anything to Johnny? He looked very angry, seething, in fact."

The atmosphere of the car became serious, each one of us thinking our own dark thoughts.

Finally, Flint spoke. "I would say, Papoose, if Spaulding has a vendetta toward anyone, it's going to be with you. He took a shine to you, and he's not a man who likes being duped by a woman. Watch yourself."

Chapter Thirteen

And Yet Another Meeting

"Fer cryin' out loud, Richard," I said, stepping out on my deck and into the bright sunlight. "Not another meeting. I've done nothing but go to nonstop meetings for the past two days, ever since we got back from Vegas. Everybody wants to debrief. First Frank, then the FBI, the state's attorney's office, the gaming board of Nevada, and the—"

My brother interrupted me. "This meeting is just the three of us, you, Gurn, and me."

I let out a martyred sigh. Carrying the phone back into the kitchen, I sat down in the kitchen chair facing a wall, not wanting to be distracted by the gorgeous morning. Feeling lost for the moment, I fussed with the hand-loomed and colorful Mexican tablecloth, smoothing out slight wrinkles and looking for residual crumbs of my morning's lone breakfast.

It had only been a couple of days of sharing my apartment with Gurn, but it's surprising how fast you get used to doing something when it feels right. We both knew he couldn't stay indefinitely. After all, he had his own place, and I had mine. However, I didn't realize how empty my apartment would feel after last night's farewell kiss and departure.

"And it's important," Richard added, bringing me back.

"Important? How?"

"The results of Stephen's autopsy came back this morning."

There was a moment's silence, and I felt my body tense.

"What did it say? And skip to the chase."

"Stephen's heart received a jolt of electricity strong enough to cause it to stop beating."

I nearly dropped the phone. "Electricity! You mean a voltage of electricity killed Stephen? But how —" I broke off, unable to finish the sentence.

"Exactly," he said, expelling air. "Nobody knows how it could have happened, not a clue."

"The prosecution isn't going to have much of a case if they can't prove how everybody got done in, Richard."

"I guess the good news is Spaulding and his men don't know we're looking into these races or that we're going after them for premeditated murder. They think everything revolves around money laundering and falsifying their tax returns. In a sense, they've been lulled into a false sense of security."

"What about Eddie Crackmeir? Any more on him?"

"No. I spoke with Frank last night, and he says no one saw anyone near Crackmeir's house that night except for Flint's car. No other fingerprints in the house but the decedent's and Kelli's."

"Speaking of Kelli, have they found out anything more on what might have happened to her? If she's been…"

I couldn't finish the sentence. Yes, I was livid at her for lying to me, taking advantage of me, and stealing the cats. Every time I thought about it, I wanted to wring her neck. But I didn't want her dead, and it had been five days since her car was found at the airport with fresh blood on the driver's seat. Usually, if the police don't come up with something within the first thirty-six hours, there isn't much hope.

"Nothing," Richard said. "She seems to have vanished into thin air. Or she's at the bottom of Hoover Dam. Spaulding's men probably gave her the same treatment as Eddie Crackmeir, only they took her somewhere else to do it."

"*Dios mio*, it's all so gruesome. Sometimes I wonder why we're in this business, Richard, I really do."

"Hey, we do software piracy ninety-eight percent of the time. This is because of Stephen."

"Of course," I said, trying to get back with the program.

"So to recap," Richard said, "all we know is who, what, and why, right?"

"Right. Who—Spaulding and Company. What—fixing races. Why—huge buckos. What's missing is the how, Brother mine, the how."

"There might be something in the recordings I've got. That's the reason I'm calling. I need another pair of eyes to look over the footage."

"You mean you have recordings from each of the races? How did you get those?"

"It wasn't easy, and I've been working on it whenever I could for the past two days. But I need you to look at them, too, in case I'm missing something. I have to warn you though. One of them is of Stephen."

I chewed on my lower lip, a bad habit I had yet to break, but it's one of many and at the bottom of my list. "What are you looking for?"

"I don't know what I'm looking for. That's the problem."

"You need to take a break. You've been at this ever since Stephen died. Gurn and I went to a dinner and concert last night. It was great."

"What did you see?"

"Rachmaninoff."

"Vicki's been after me to take her to it."

"You should go."

"Speaking of Vicki, I don't know if you heard me the other day but—"

"Richard," I interjected, hearing a beep from call waiting. A glance at caller ID showed me it was Frank's private number at the precinct. "It's Frank. Do you want to hold?"

"No, I'll see you in about an hour." We hung up, and I went to the other call.

"Hi, Frank. What's up? Richard was just updating me —"

"Lee, Spaulding made bail," he interrupted. His voice sounded low and grave. "Two million bucks bail, and he had it fifteen minutes after his arraignment."

I kept quiet and waited for him to go on.

"Late last night. I only got the information a few minutes ago. Spaulding packs a lot of power in Vegas, for certain."

"I guess I shouldn't be surprised."

"You talk to Flint lately?"

"Not since the day before yesterday. Why?"

"I tried to reach him right before I called you. He didn't pick up his cell, that's all. I left a message." He paused for a moment. "You know, his face was on the hotel room surveillance tapes. Flint is not an easy man to overlook."

My heart lurched. "Meaning what? You think he might be in danger?"

"I don't mean anything, Liana." His answer was sharp and quick. "I left a message only a few minutes ago. I'll keep trying. Take care of yourself, Lee. Watch your back."

Without saying goodbye, Frank hung up, proving to me he was more upset than he was letting on.

This was the second person to tell me to watch out, within the past few days. The first one had been Flint. I felt uneasy, filled with unexplained trepidations, but I had little time to think about it. I needed to get dressed and over to the office for my meeting with Richard.

I took a fast shower and had just finished throwing on a hot, new lavender-and-pink pantsuit found at my favorite outlet store — label removed, but you can't fool me — when I heard the doorbell. I raced to the door, but Tugger beat me, showing up out of nowhere. Last seen, he'd been sunning himself in the middle of the kitchen floor, where the cupola allows the sun to stream in.

I might have known by his reaction to the doorbell it was Tío. If I were the jealous type, I would think my cat loved my uncle more than me. For sure, he obeys him more than me, but nobody listens to me, human or otherwise, so I can't take offence.

"Good morning, Tío," I said, swinging the door open wide and offering an even wider smile. "How are you? I haven't seen you in a while."

"*Sobrina,*" he said, taking me into a bear hug. "You have been so busy with all the meetings and your *novio,* you have hardly been here. It has been the cats and me."

"Thank you for taking care of them while we were busy, Tío. Both Gurn and I appreciated knowing they were well taken care of."

"*De nada.*" He broke free from my embrace and looked down at Tugger. "There is the good boy, the Rum Tum Tugger." He extended his forearms and gestured for the cat to jump up. "We have something to show you, Liana. Tugger! Come."

I've seen this little trick before, but I am never unmoved by it. My four-footed roommate, the same cat I can't get to do squat, made a lithe jump and perfect landing into the tall man's arms as if he did it every day. Which he almost does. It is a rare day Tugger and Tío don't practice one trick or another.

Tío says Tugger is one of the most intelligent cats he's ever met and needs to keep his mind sharpened daily by doing little tricks and puzzles. I once said I would do the *New York Times* crossword puzzle with Tugger but was met by a blank stare from my uncle. When it comes to animals, Tío has no sense of humor.

"*Sobrina,* Tugger and I have been working on this for the past two days."

With a certain amount of pomp and circumstance, Tío carried Tugger to the center of my living room and struck a pose, reminiscent of Siegfried and Roy in their Las Vegas days.

This looked like it was going to be a long, drawn-out affair.

"Tío, I hate to say this, but I'm in a hurry to get to the office. Whatever you want to show me, can it wait until later today or tomorrow? Richard needs to have a meeting with me."

"So many meetings, Liana! Oh, of course. Little Tugger and I can wait. It is not so important."

But he looked so crushed and dejected, I immediately jumped in with, "What am I saying, Tío? Will it take more than fifteen minutes? I've got fifteen minutes." I looked at him and smiled. He returned my smile ten-fold.

"*Bien, bien.* It will take no more." His long-fingered, elegant hand took Tugger around the midriff and placed him on the floor.

"Tugger, sit," Tío said. Amazingly, the cat sat down on his haunches and stared up at the man intently. That stare always impresses me, especially as I can never get My Son the Cat, to do much of anything, other than eat.

Tío turned back to me. "*Sobrina,* when Tugger and the little one were taken the other day—"

"*Dios mío,*" I interrupted, instantly reliving it, "what a horrible day. I'm so glad it turned out all right. It could have so easily gone the other way."

"*Exactamente!*" Tío said, holding a finger up for emphasis. "It could have so easily gone the way of great unhappiness." He cleared his throat, and I sat down in the nearby red leather chair, giving my uncle my full attention. "This is why I think to teach our Tugger to defend himself and you, of course."

"Beg pardon?"

"All Tugger knows is goodness and kindness. But sometimes to protect oneself and those we love, is something it needs to be taught. It is not always instilled in one so innocent."

"After seeing what Tugger has done to some of my shoes, I wouldn't label him as innocent." Tugger took his eyes off the man, looked over at me and blinked, an upward turn to the corners of his mouth. Did he know what I was saying?

"This is not the time for the jokes, *sobrina.*"

"Sorry."

We both paused and studied the slender, golden-eyed, white-and-orange cat sitting perfectly still. Tugger glanced first at Tío then at me, all the while in a waiting mode. Small flickerings of skin beneath fur belied the outward look of ease and tranquility. The cat was ready for something, but what?

I looked over toward my uncle. "What is the latest trick you've taught him?"

"I will show you, but I want you to first not be afraid. You can see I am wearing the long sleeves of the sweater and underneath I have the long-sleeve shirt. But even that is not enough."

Tío reached behind my sofa and pulled out a padded material with Velcro on one side. "I left this here yesterday when Tugger and I practiced. I think we are ready to show you now what he can do."

Having said that, Tío wrapped the self-adhering pad around his forearm and secured it in place. He snapped his fingers twice over Tugger's head, and the cat's body became rigid in rapt concentration. But once again, for what?

"Tugger! Tugger! Attack! Attack! Now!"

Tío's commanding voice was shrill and tense, unlike anything I'd heard come out of him before. The cat also made a sound I'd never heard—a low, guttural growl. Then he came to a standing position and sprang, his exposed claws and teeth sinking into the padding on Tío's forearm. Tío moved about and tried to dislodge the biting, spitting, and clawing animal, while I sat frozen in horror. My sweet, docile, toy-loving feline was a homicidal maniac trying to chew my uncle's arm off!

This scene probably only lasted for a few seconds, but it seemed like an eternity to me. Tío yelled out over the hissing, growling, and ripping sounds Tugger was making, "Tugger, down. Tugger, enough. Down."

I leapt up and ran over to my uncle, who now cuddled a more relaxed Tugger in the other arm.

"Tío, are you all right?" Anxious, I took his wrapped arm in my hands and looked at it. The fabric was shredded in places, but I didn't see any blood.

"Do not worry, *mi sobrina.*" He took a moment, placing Tugger, who now seemed calm and serene, on his shoulder, and stroking his svelte body. "The padding protects me." He stopped talking and shrugged.

I knew my uncle was all right; I moved on to my pet and snatched Tugger off Tío's shoulder. Except for rapid breathing due to the exertion, the cat seemed physically unharmed by the experience. But his mind, his personality! How had that been affected?

"I don't understand why you would teach him to do such a thing." I said, tears springing to my eyes. I looked at Tío. Here was the gentlest man I'd ever met. Why was he trying to turn my cat into a monster?

I wrapped Tugger in my arms, hugging him, crooning over him. His eyes half closed, but other than that, he remained alert.

"Liana," I heard my uncle say, "Sit down and listen to me." He took me by the shoulders and guided me back to the red leather chair. With my cat in my lap, Tío sat across from me on the matching sofa.

"*Mi sobrina dulce, necessitas* to pay attention to what I tell you now."

I stopped stroking Tugger and looked up into my uncle's warm, loving brown eyes.

He went on. "What you do, what our family does for the living, is not always good. When I say not good, I mean things can happen because of it, bad things."

"You mean like Tugger and Baba being catnapped." I saw where he was going with this.

"*Si.* Among the other things." He moved around on the sofa, settling into the soft, supple leather while marshalling his thoughts.

"You were fortunate Ricardo had put the tracking instrument onto Tugger's carrier and forgot about it being there. Otherwise…" He stopped speaking and looked at me, staring directly into my eyes.

"Otherwise, I might not have ever gotten the cats back." I glanced down at the cat purring in my lap and stroked his forehead, watching his ears flick at my touch. "I know, Tío, I know. I got lucky."

"Sometimes *es necesario* to be prepared, not to count on the luck."

I nodded and Tío went on. "I have taught Tugger how to protect himself, guided by his own instincts or the command of someone he trusts. It was not difficult to teach him these things. He is *muy inteligente*, our Tugger."

"He is smart, Tío," I agreed, a sense of pride replacing the horror of a moment before.

"And he has the *corazón* of a lion. You remember the time the burglar broke in here? Tugger's instinct was to protect you, but he did not know how. Now he knows."

I nodded, keeping my head down, afraid to speak lest my voice betray my deep emotions.

"Do not feel the guilt I see upon your face. He is not suffering or made to be bad. He is wiser now, as all living things must be to survive."

Tío looked around him and smiled. "Even in this world of ease called Palo Alto, even in a home of love, we learn it is not enough to nurture but also to protect. And do not try to deny, *sobrina,* there exists in this house a gun that you know how to use, if called upon. Have you become a less loving human being because you have learned how to protect yourself and *la familia*?"

Tío began to pull the protection from his arm. I sat still and listened to the harsh, ripping sound of the fabric, not unlike what was going on inside my mind. I shook my head, looked up, and smiled at my wise and wonderful uncle.

"Of course not, Tío. And thank you for helping me see that."

Tugger got up from my lap and hopped to the floor. There he stretched, yawned, and went about his business. Seconds later, I heard crunching sounds coming from his cereal bowl in the kitchen.

"Well, I'm glad to see this hasn't interfered with his appetite."

"He has the healthy one, our Tugger. It is true."

I rose from the chair and plopped myself down on the sofa next to Tío, who put an arm around me. He kissed me lightly on the forehead.

"Sorry I got so emotional earlier, Tío."

"No *problemo*," he answered with a wink.

"So I could put up a sign on the front door, Beware of Attack Cat, and not be kidding, right?"

"This is only when *necesario, mi sobrina,* only then. We still have more to do, but he is a good student. He must learn to do it when you make the command, also, not just me."

"I see. You tell me when we need to practice, Tío, and I'll be there." I looked at the uncle who was more like a grandfather to me and had recently become the patient patriarch of the Alvarez family. "*Gracias, Tío. Muchas gracias, por todo. Te amo.*"

Chapter Fourteen

It's All in the Planning

I was late. Richard had already left two "where are you" messages on my phone. They'd gone into voice mail because I, in turn, had been leaving messages for Flint, asking that he call me right away. I tried to tell myself Flint was probably working on a case with his phone turned off, as we often have to do. But it didn't make the knot in my stomach go away or keep me from the shallow breathing, which became slightly labored as I rushed up the staircase to the third floor.

I pulled open the double doors of DI, gave a quick smile and wave to Stanley, our office receptionist/manager, and scurried down the hallway to the back offices housing information technology. Andy buzzed me in instantly. He'd probably been waiting for me under orders from Richard.

When I threw open Richard's office door, it banged noisily against the wall, but neither Richard nor Gurn reacted. Their eyes were glued to the forty-six-inch monitor before them. I scurried into the room mumbling, "Sorry, sorry, sorry" under my breath, finally getting their attention. Richard acknowledged me with a curt wave over his shoulder, and Gurn gave me a quick smile.

Without saying a word, Gurn stood from his chair and gestured for me to sit down. I did, and he leaned in over my shoulder, his focus never leaving the screen.

In silence, I, too, studied the views they were caught up in, eight different rectangular pictures of people frozen in running positions. Filling the screen, each section was of varying digital quality. Some were crystal clear, and others downright fuzzy, but most in between, the enlarging of them causing the pixels to become obvious and almost intrusive. Richard forwarded the sections in unison, frame by frame, allowing us to study each movement of the runners in stop motion.

"Let's put it back to the beginning, Richard," Gurn suggested, "so Lee can see them all." He turned to me, a warm grin on his face. "I can't find anything, but maybe you'll have more luck, sweetheart."

With our noses practically touching, I felt his warm breath on my face. Gawd, he's so yummy! *Down, girl.* I forced my attention back to the screen.

"Okay," said Richard. "Back we go."

With a few keystrokes, the screen went black. Richard pivoted in his chair to face us.

"Eyewitness accounts say the fallen runners dropped within yards of the finish line. What I've done, Lee, is take the last minute of these eight races, synchronizing the foot patterns of the runners and their proximity to the finish line as much as possible —"

"Good going, Richard," I interjected. "That's using the ol' noodle."

"Don't mention noodles or any other food. I've been at this since eight o'clock last night, and I'm starving."

"You bring this off, Brother mine, and I'll get you the largest pepperoni pizza you've ever had." The screen came alive again with the same cast of characters, but the finish line was no longer in sight.

"You'll have to give half the pizza to Gurn," said Richard. "It was his idea. He's been here since about ten thirty last night."

I turned to Gurn, who winked at me. "Is that where you went? I thought you went home."

"Only long enough to drop off Baba and head here. I knew Richard could use someone to bounce things off, and this scenario reeks of something I encountered in Ethiopia three years ago. I still don't know how they did it. Maybe this could give me a clue."

"Wow. So maybe this has been going on for a lot longer than we thought." I screwed up my face in puzzlement. Gurn reached out and rubbed the area above my nose with a gentle fingertip.

"Don't scrunch up your forehead, darling," he whispered.

"It's a bad habit she's got," offered Richard. "Among others."

"Gentlemen," I said tartly, removing Gurn's finger from my forehead. "Let's try to keep this meeting professional, shall we?"

"*Si, mi capitán*," said Richard, turning back to the screen.

"Aye, aye, Captain." Gurn gave me a sharp salute.

"You two are in such trouble," I growled. Both men laughed, then sobered.

Richard rubbed his eyes. "I'm so tired, I'm punchy. Okay. So here's the lineup. At the extreme left-hand corner, Buenos Aires, Argentina; next is Boston, Massachusetts; next is Frankfort, Germany; then Lima, Peru. The second row —"

"Sounds like the United Nations of footraces," I interrupted.

"No kidding." Gurn's voice made us turn in his direction. "They come from across the globe. From what info Richard and I have gathered, the only races affected are the ones attracting top runners, top dollar being offered to the winners."

"But we never heard about any top runners dropping dead —"

Richard interrupted me with excitement. "That's been the beauty of it, Lee. It's never the win, place, or show guys."

"Or gals," Gurn added.

"Exactly," Richard agreed. "The ones who were dropped were people coming in fourth or fifth, the ones showing well but of little concern to the media."

"Or the world at large," I said slowly but thinking furiously. "So illegal bets have been placed, probably at the Fantasy Lady among other places, not on win, place, or show but on the runners coming in fourth, fifth, or sixth."

"That's what we think, yes," said Gurn.

"So Spaulding and his men have been taking in bets, then fixing the races — and in the worst way possible — by killing off the competition."

"Yeah, but how?" both men said in unison.

"Yup, we're back to that one," I muttered.

"So let's get at it." Richard cleared off the remnants of a cannibalized computer from a nearby chair and pulled it over. Gurn plopped himself down, and the three of us stared at the large computer screen.

For fifteen minutes, we said nothing but watched the tedious progression of the last minute of each race frame by frame. My eyes burned in concentration as the runner moved, leg up, leg down, foot touching the ground, foot in the air. Nothing looked unusual.

"Wait a minute," I said, jumping up and touching the screen in the upper right-hand corner. "Who's that?"

"Don't touch the screen with your fingertips," Richard said automatically. Both men got up and leaned forward glaring at the spot I indicated. The grainy image of a man in the background crowd was the focus of our attention. And I didn't remove my finger, no matter what Richard had said.

"Can you keep him on the screen? Then go back to near the beginning with the other races. Somewhere in the lower right side. I think I saw him there too."

"Sure, just a minute." Richard sat down again and pushed a few keys on the keyboard. The grainy man remained, but the other seven pictures returned to the beginning.

"Gentlemen, never mind the runners. Pay attention to the faces in the crowd. In particular, look for this guy." I tapped the screen again on his face.

"Stop doing that," Richard growled.

"Okay, okay. I'll buy you a bottle of glass cleaner."

"I don't use — never mind," he interrupted himself.

Tense and alert, we scrutinized the low resolution and sometimes out-of-focus images of the crowds on either side of the paths or roads for another half an hour, trying not to overlook anyone.

"Stop," Gurn nearly shouted. "Right there!" He pointed to a similar image of a dark-haired, tall, thin man, standing three rows behind a cheering crowd. "That might be the same guy, has the same physical description, height, and demeanor. It looks like him to me."

I peered at the image, and a face half obliterated by a woman waving a multicolored banner directly in front. "Sure does. Although... Richard, where did these two races take place?"

"The one on the top is Lima, Peru. The one at the bottom is Tegucigalpa, Honduras."

"What are the dates? How far apart?"

He pulled a sheet of paper over from the side of his desk and scanned it. "Let's see. Tegus was April fourteenth, and Lima was July fifth."

"He almost could have walked from one place to the other," remarked Gurn.

"Gentlemen, please note. This man is not cheering, waving, moving, or anything. Just standing stock still and watching. Like this guy up here." I tapped the upper right screen again.

"Like he's waiting for something to happen," Richard murmured but saying nothing about my fingernail banging on his screen.

"Exactly. Keep going, Richard. Let's see what this man does at the end of these two races."

"Should I only forward those two and forget the other six?"

"For the moment, yes."

Richard enlarged the Lima and Tegucigalpa frames, each filling half the screen, and eliminated the rest. The remaining two videos, now larger, became even more difficult to interpret. We pushed our chairs back slightly and tried to link the pixilated imagery together in our minds. Unfortunately both videos were apparently shot by amateurs. Right after the victims fell, both videos cut out abruptly, one coming to a jumbled somersault of an ending, as if the shock of the man falling to the ground before the photographer's eyes caused him to lose grip of the camera. The other shooter came in for a close-up of the victim's distorted face, going in and out of focus before going to black.

"That's disappointing," Gurn said. "I thought we were onto something."

"Maybe we are," I answered. "Richard, can you send all eight of those videos to my laptop and phone? I'd like to look at them again."

My phone rang. It was Lila.

"Mom, where are you?"

"Phoenix. With Jennifer."

"How are she and the kids doing? Can you talk?"

"No. We're here in Jennifer's living room coming to some decisions. But in answer to your question, everyone is doing as well as can be expected. Liana, as Stephen had made no provisions for his funeral—"

"Understandable. He was only forty-three."

"Jennifer has decided," Mom went on as if I hadn't said anything. "Since she is moving back to the Bay Area to be near her mother and the rest of the family, to bury him in the Hamilton family crypt in Pala Alto."

"Wow. That's heavy news, Mom, but welcomed. I'm glad Jenn and the kids will be closer to us."

"So the funeral will take place day after tomorrow at Morrison's Mortuary." Her voice lowered. "I would like this situation to be cleared up by then. What is the progress?"

Lila, who is known for making unrealistic demands, still caught me unawares. I was silent for a moment, my mind trying to take in what would have to happen to make her dreams come true, so to speak.

"Don't get your hopes up, Mom. This may go deeper than we first thought. We're still trying to sort out what exactly is going on. We haven't even gotten to the solving part of it yet. One thing you may not know; Lou Spaulding made bail late last night. The charge of murder has not entered into the picture, merely income tax evasion."

There was silence on the other end of the line. If I knew Lila's razor-sharp mind, she was sorting out all the ramifications of our involvement in the Fantasy Lady sting like a first-rate computer.

"I understood it was a possibility. However, we must persevere."

"Yes, ma'am."

"Keep me posted."

"Always."

She hung up. I turned back to my brother and my boyfriend. "Gentlemen, we're being asked to move this along as quickly as possible."

"I didn't know this Spaulding guy was loose," said Richard. "I don't think I like this."

Gurn stood to face me. "There's one way to push this forward." I looked at him with a million questions written on my face. "The Palace to Palace 12K race is tomorrow. I'm going to run it."

"No!" I practically screamed, then lowered my voice. "Gurn, you can't. You can't."

"Yes I can, and will."

"But you're on the list. You might be —"

He grabbed my shoulders with both hands. "Richard checked the other names on the list. There were only two others who hadn't run before Nick found the list. One was a woman who stopped running a couple of weeks ago because she was having problems with her pregnancy."

"And the other?" I asked because he stopped talking, and both men looked at one another."

"Danny Masamitsu ran last week, Lee, and had a heart attack just as he was about to come in fourth. He didn't make it." Gurn's voice was soft and tender, but the words radiated through me like an earthquake of magnitude 7.1. "That's eight people we know of. I'm the only one left on the list. Honey, this is the only way to stop this."

"Don't do it, man." Richard's surprised face showed Gurn hadn't confided in him. My brother came over and stood next to us. "I thought when I showed you what happened to the others on the list, it would slow you down, Gurn. We can't protect you if we don't know what's going on… how they're killing these people."

"But one thing we know is, they are, Rich. And they don't know we know," Gurn argued. "It gives us an advantage. And don't forget, I'm a military man. I've done in a lot of bad guys. Still do."

"A fine time for you to admit it," I said.

"Lee, I'm the ideal sacrificial lamb. I can take care of myself, and I'm a good runner. Three years ago, before I busted my knee, I placed fourth or fifth in a lot of races, some of them pretty big. Then I had to bow out, but the recent surgery was a success. It's all on record. With a little luck, and if I push myself, I can come in fourth or fifth on this. I know it, and if Spaulding and his men have done their homework, they know it."

"That's probably why he was on the list, Lee," added Richard.

"I know, I know," I said. "But I still don't—"

"This could force their hand." I could tell Gurn felt he was winning us over, and he pushed even harder. "Worst-case scenario, I'll drop out fifty yards from the finish line."

"Worst-case scenario, they'll drop you fifty yards from the finish line." I glared at the man I loved, unconvinced.

Gurn looked back at me, one of his radiant smiles breaking out on his face. "Liana Margaret Alvarez, you're one of the most intuitive PIs I've ever met. You'll make sure they don't."

Chapter Fifteen

Repercussions Are No Fun

I drove home from the meeting and its ensuing revelations, with sweating palms, an acid stomach, and a tic in my right eye. Between not being able to talk Gurn out of competing in the race the next day, and not being able to get in touch with Flint, I'm surprised that's all I had.

Gurn left the meeting and drove straight home, with the idea of working out, having an early dinner loaded with carbs, and getting a good night's sleep before the race. How like a man. I probably wouldn't close my eyes the entire night. The next day, there would be dark bags, adding to the rambunctious tic. A charming combo, but I knew how it would be.

After stowing the car in the garage, I ran up the stairs two at a time and found a scrawled note from Tío taped to my front door.

Mi sobrina, I go to the shelter. Three dogs are having the babies, and I go to help. I have left a burrito in the oven for your dinner and fed Tugger. Rest, mija. Tío.

The landline began to ring from inside. Flint! For whatever reason, he was calling my home phone and not my cell. In my excitement, I tore the note off the door, jiggled the key in the lock, threw open the door, tried to push it closed with my hip, and raced to catch the phone before it went into voice mail.

"Hello, hello?" I was breathless, more from anticipation and tension than exertion.

"Lee, it's Knoton-ah-Ken."

"What's wrong?" I blurted out, less from the sound of his tight and tired voice and more from the feeling in my gut.

"It's Dad." His voice cracked. "He's been shot."

"*Dios mio.*" I let out a soft wail and gripped the phone with both hands as if it might fall from my shaking hands. "When? How... how bad?"

"They just finished operating on him. He lost a lot of blood, Lee, a lot of blood. But he's going to be all right. He's going to be all right," he repeated.

Knoton stopped talking and began to sob.

I joined him. Everything I feared had been realized. I didn't even have to ask what happened. I knew: Spaulding and his men.

"I'll be there as soon as I can, Knoton. What hospital are you at?" I don't think he heard me because he started talking again in between sobs.

"They found him in back of the dumpster behind his apartment. Somebody had dragged him there after they shot him last night next to his car. They left him to die. The trash men heard him moaning this morning and called 9-1-1. They left him to die," he said again.

He burst into tears.

So did I. Words poured out of me before I could stop them.

"This is all my fault, Knoton," I found myself saying. "I pulled him into this Spaulding mess and..."

"Your fault?" Flint's son sounded so surprised, he stopped crying. "Are you kidding? You saved his life. I called to thank you. If he hadn't been wearing his badge—"

"Badge?" I interrupted. "You mean the US Marshal badge?"

"The doctors said it was right over his heart, where the bullet struck. It pushed the badge into his chest, caused a massive bruise and a lot of internal bleeding, but the bullet didn't pierce the metal."

I heard him swallow hard.

"If it hadn't been there, the bullet would have gone straight through his heart. He would have died instantly. Instantly, Lee. Your badge saved him."

I was about to say something when I heard the creaking sound of the front door being pushed open. I wheeled around to face Lou Spaulding holding a semiautomatic at the end of his extended right arm. It was a big gun, dull gray, and heavy looking. Even the hole in middle of its long barrel looked large.

Spaulding kicked the door closed behind him with one leg, never moving his eyes or his gun from me. I stood immobile, my mind shocked but accepting. Wordless, I hung up the phone and dropped both arms to my side.

Spaulding was standing not ten feet away. There was no way he could miss. Sometimes, when you see death up close and personal, you are exceedingly calm.

"Mr. Spaulding. Fancy seeing you here." I was astonished by the easy conversational tone of my voice, my flip attitude. Spaulding's reaction was much the same. I thought I had a nervous tic; his right eye looked like it was sending out messages in Morse code.

"Surprised to see me, huh, bitch? I've been waiting for you. I wanted the satisfaction of taking care of you, myself, seeing the look in your eyes when I put a bullet in your brain. And don't think anyone can save you. I read the note on the door. It's just you and me, baby, just you and me."

He looked and acted weird as if he was on speed, but at the same time, burned out. Sweat poured off his forehead and face. His body twitched from head to toe, breaths coming shallow and rapid. Not exactly the sort of person you want on the working end of a gun.

The phone began to ring again, but I didn't answer it. I decided to go with this easy, breezy, film-noir sort of detective, if for no other reason than its effect on Spaulding.

"Won't you come in and sit down?" I said in my best Miss Manners voice.

He let out a raucous laugh, pulled at the soft collar of his dark gray T-shirt with his free hand, and stretched it to wipe the sweat from the sides of his face. All the while, his eyes never left mine. Nor mine his. I knew exactly how a snake charmer felt facing off a particularly mean-spirited cobra. And I didn't even have a flute.

"You're sure you won't sit down, take a load off?"

"I won't be here long," he said and laughed again, high pitched and raw. "Just long enough to take care of you."

I didn't respond this time. My mind raced to see how I could get out of the inevitable fate awaiting me. It didn't look good. Nobody in Vegas would have taken this bet.

"I already took care of your friend," he cawed. "The big Indian. Now it's your turn."

Some sort of expression must have crossed my face when he mentioned what he did to Flint because a grin grew on on his face.

"That's right. I killed him last night. Coming into my hotel and causing all kinds of trouble with my investors and partners. You shaking your ass in front of me and all the while... Next is that blonde bitch mother of yours. I know where she is. I know all about you and your family."

The phone stopped ringing.

Out of the corner of my eye, I saw Tugger fly into the room and halt abruptly. Maybe the ringing phone had brought him in, I don't know. At first, his ears twitched, moving forward like searching antenna. Then they lay flat against his head. Hunkered down, Tugger advanced nearer and nearer the stranger holding the gun, eyes riveted on the arm extended toward me menacingly.

Spaulding didn't see him. His focus was solely on me.

"Do you? What do you know? Tell me," I said.

"Keep me talking, huh? Think that's going to save you? I didn't think it would be quite this easy to off you, little lady." Spaulding laughed, cocked the gun, and aimed for right between my eyes.

In another moment I knew I would be dead 'cause I don't got no stinkin' badges.

I took a deep breath, maybe my last, and screamed, "Tugger! Tugger! Attack! Attack!"

In that split second, Spaulding seemed to hesitate, either from confusion or surprise.

Tugger pounced onto the man's extended arm, growling, biting and clawing at it furiously. Spaulding let out a cry of half anger, half pain, and instinctively pulled his forearm up and away. The gun went off, sending a spray of bullets into the ceiling with an earsplitting boom. Plaster rained down as Spaulding writhed from the slashing and tearing at his flesh by the small but frenzied animal.

Simultaneously, I seized the top end of the tall brass lamp sitting on the end table, ripping off its shade. Holding it in both hands like a baseball bat, I swung the heavy base into Spaulding's face with all my might. I heard a cracking sound, like the breaking of a bone, maybe his jaw. Pivoting from the impact, he fell to the floor, unconscious.

I dropped the lamp with a thud, ran over, picked up the gun, and knelt down for my pet. Tugger was standing beside the man's limp body, half growling, half meowing, bloody jaws working feverishly. Fortunately, Spaulding was facedown on my hardwood floor. I didn't have to see the damage done by a lamp I can barely lift when there's no adrenaline pumping.

"Tugger, Tugger, come here, baby. Come here." I picked him up and cradled him in my arms, where I felt him begin to relax. I half fell into a chair with the little guy in my lap, grabbed the phone with a trembling hand, and punched in 9-1-1.

Keeping an eye on the motionless man at my feet, I set the gun on the floor next to me, put the call on speakerphone, and waited for the police to answer. After giving my name, address, and a brief description to the police, I concentrated on my four-footed hero, cooing to him, calming both of us down with words of love.

Facial tissue from a nearby dispenser—Mom thinks tissues should be close at hand and everywhere—allowed me to wipe the blood from Tugger's mouth, feet, and legs with shaky, but gentle strokes. Then I searched his little body to make sure the cleaned up blood had belonged solely to the scumbag at my feet. It did. Tugger leaned against me and began to purr, the sweetest sound I'd heard in a while.

I don't remember hanging up on 9-1-1, if I even did, or exactly what answers I gave to the dispatch officer. The police and ambulance arrived at the same time, Frank no more than ten minutes later. Spaulding was still unconscious, having made not one bit of noise. He might have been dead for all I knew.

* * * *

"You sure you're okay, Lee?"

My father's lifelong friend and my godfather stood over me, both hands on his hips. I looked up into Frank's concerned face and nodded. I wore a pasted-on, reassuring smile and went back to stroking a sleeping Tugger in my lap. Personally, I wasn't feeling very reassured. Far from it.

I looked over to the wet spot on the hardwood floor, now clean but darker than the surrounding wood. A thought flashed through my mind. Would it dry to the same color as the rest of the stain, or would I have to get someone in to sand and restain it? Then I mentally slapped myself across the face. Sometimes I get my priorities all skewed. Fortunately, Frank didn't seem to suspect I was having a Martha Stewart moment.

"You didn't have to clean up the blood from the floor, Frank. I would have done it."

"Don't be silly, Lee. It went one-two-three. I don't want you looking at it. I threw the towels away. I'll get you some more."

"Now, you don't be silly. My cup runneth over in the towel department. Mom's been giving me a new set of towels every year for Easter since I can remember."

Frank sat down on the large, plushy leather ottoman at my feet and leaned in with a grin. "Most kids get marshmallow peeps. But that's your mother."

"You're sure she's all right, Frank? You made sure?" I couldn't lighten up no matter how hard Frank tried to make me.

"Your mother's fine." He reached over and lightly stroked Tugger's lustrous fur behind the ear. "More worried about you. I had a devil of a time getting her to stay put even for tonight."

"It's just he said…" I stopped talking, trying not to panic. "How do we know he hasn't got one of his men—"

"He acted alone," Frank interrupted. "My sources tell me there's no indication anyone else was involved in these attacks on you and Flint. In fact, the rest of his henchmen and most of his investors have scurried into holes like the rats they are. Too much publicity."

Nearly an hour had gone by. The ambulance had wheeled out the unconscious man, with the paramedics shaking their heads. Between three policemen, they'd taken my statement, wrapped up the bloody lamp, relieved me of Spaulding's gun, commandeered mine, even though it clearly had not been fired, and searched the place for any further weapons. I keep my jewels and another revolver, my Lady Blue special, in a safe under the floorboards near the dining room table. But I never said a word about it. A girl doesn't like to be left completely nude.

Frank—bless him—didn't say anything, either, though he knew very well about the safe and what was stashed in it. He merely hovered around me making sure things went as smoothly as possible. But as the minutes ticked by, I could tell something was on his mind, something he was bursting to say. I searched his face. He was nearly exploding with it, whatever it was.

"Frank, out with it."

"Here's what I can't let go of, Lee. After everyone warned you to be careful, what with Spaulding on the loose, how could you leave the front door open like that?" His voice raised in intensity and volume with each word. By the end of the sentence, he sounded like he was using a megaphone.

"Promise me you won't lose it when I tell you." I ran my hand through my unkempt hair, catching some tangles, and accidentally yanking them hard enough to hurt. "Ouch. Time for a haircut. Too many split ends."

"Never mind your hair." His voice had gone into the lower register, a place where it goes when he's upset.

"I hadn't heard from Flint, and the phone was ringing when I was outside the door. I thought it was him. I meant to close the door all the way, thought I had, but..." I broke off and shrugged. "I know the rules, Frank. I made a mistake."

"A mistake that almost cost you your life. Liana, if I weren't so tired, I'd haul you over my knee for a good spanking."

"Frank, if I weren't so wiped, I'd let you. Tugger saved me," I whispered. "My little guy saved me."

As if on cue, Tugger opened his eyes, stood, stretched, and hopped off my lap with a chirping sound. We watched him saunter over to his favorite scratching post, the one with the furry mouse on top, and bat at the toy in an amiable, friendly way.

"He doesn't look any worse for wear," said Frank, observing the cat. "The wounds he inflicted on Spaulding's arm were mostly superficial, but I'm sure they hurt like hell. What did him in was the slam to his face from the lamp. His jaw will have to be wired together. Some news is good."

"He was going to kill me, Frank."

"I know."

"He acted so weird. Like he'd shot up with something before he walked in."

I shook my head, baffled. I was suddenly exhausted.

"Why would he take such a chance? Why would he come after Flint and then me, himself? He's got a dozen men on his payroll for his dirty work. It doesn't make sense."

"I understand he'd been taken down, replaced by his second-in-command. Like a certain someone, he'd made some big mistakes lately. His started with the blonde bimbo, what's her name. She got close enough to him to take off with some pretty incriminating evidence worth a lot of dough, now in the hands of the FBI."

"Kelli," I offered.

"Kelli, she's the one. Although she couldn't have been much of a bimbo to pull off what she did."

"Nick's wife. Well, not his wife. Although he thought she was his wife. And now she's gone. Nobody even talks about her anymore and—"

"Liana, you're starting to ramble, and you look beat." He glanced at his watch. "I know it's only six thirty, but why don't you get some sleep? I'll talk to you in the morning."

Frank leaned over and kissed me on the forehead before saying, "Walk me to the door, set the alarm, and go to bed. And double bolt it behind me, you hear?" He turned to leave.

"I hear." I rose, weary and used up, and followed him to the door.

He opened it and turned back to me. "And don't be too hard on yourself for leaving the door ajar. It could happen to anyone." His tone was so gentle and forgiving, I was taken aback. Not the usual Frank I've come to know and love.

"But don't do it again," he growled, and I laughed. He laughed, too, and gave me a quick hug. He looked at me with hesitation.

"One more thing, and I'm not sure I should be telling you this tonight…"

"Oh, go ahead. I can take it." I studied his face covered with determination and guilt. Leaning against the doorframe, I felt curiosity coursing through me, but mainly like I'd been run over by a Mack truck.

"I'm going to do the 12K tomorrow, along with Gurn. Not that I can keep up with him, but it'll put me right on the spot, you know?"

Hearing about the Palace to Palace 12K woke me up faster than a double espresso with an extra shot of caffeine. I stopped leaning and came to attention.

"Frank, I don't like this. There's a lot we haven't figured out yet. How are they murdering all these runners? And even if Spaulding is no longer the head honcho, it might mean it's going to be business as usual for them. It's not over. You *and* Gurn!"

"It gets better. So is Richard."

"Richard! All three of you are running the race? This is just great!" I threw up my arms in exasperation. "Why not Tío too? Take all the men in my life and put them in the stupid race. I'm taking this personally, Frank. I don't need the pressure."

I moved away from the door and began to pace the room in agitation. Tugger stopped playing with the mouse atop his scratching post, sat down on his haunches, and watched me. Apparently, I had become more interesting than his toy.

"Relax, Lee."

"Relax? How can you say to relax?"

"Because Richard and I are likely to come in at around two thousand and fifty, right behind a little old lady with a walker." He turned and went back to the sofa, leaned over, and straightened picture frames on the coffee table, picking and choosing his words with care.

"Gurn, he's a different matter. He's a good runner. I've talked to him, and he's running, no matter what we say. I looked up his record before his knee surgery, and he had some pretty impressive wins in small-time races. Charlie Wright—he's the new sergeant come up from Milpitas—is going to be running the race too. He's not as good as Gurn, but he'll stay close by. We'll keep him covered, Lee."

I shook my head.

"Frank, it comes back to, how are they doing it? How are they striking people down without leaving a mark on them and in front of hundreds of people? I know it's there on the videos. It has to be. But I can't see it." I kicked the ottoman in frustration and felt the reward of a sharp pain in my big toe.

"You will, Lee." He put both hands on my shoulders. "Get some sleep. Tackle it first thing in the morning. The part of the race we need to focus on is the end. Maybe you'll see something by then."

"And maybe not. Then there's Flint. I've never felt so useless, so helpless."

"I know the feeling."

"I should be in Vegas right now, with him. He took a bullet because of me—"

I threw myself in my favorite leather chair. Tugger leapt into my lap, turned around three times, and settled down. "If it wasn't for me…" I broke off, hanging my head.

"Now stop it," Frank said, clicking his tongue. He knelt beside me. "I spoke with the hospital not twenty minutes ago, and Flint's going to be all right. He's alert and talking."

"Is he? *Gracias, El Señor.*" I felt as if the cushions in the wingback chair were wrapping me in an endless embrace, I was so relieved. I shook my head, not able to say anything more, and ran limp fingers across damp eyes, still keeping my head down.

Frank went on. "The doctors say initially it looked worse than it was. Regardless, Flint knew the risk when he went in. We all do. Every day you get up, you know the risk.

It's the business we're in. That's why I never wanted you in it in the first place. But you are and at least…" He paused, and I looked up. He winked at me, throwing out one of his dazzling smiles. "At least, you have an attack cat to help you out now and then."

I smiled back, then let out a faint chuckle. "He's better than a German shepherd and doesn't eat as much."

"That's my girl." Frank tousled my already unkempt hair with a careless hand and got up. "I'll see you tomorrow."

Then my father's heart brother walked out and shut the door behind him, shouting, "And come lock this door! I want to hear them chains going on before I leave this porch."

Chapter Sixteen

A Matter of the Upsets

Somewhere I heard a ringing sound, faint at first but becoming louder. I tried to move, but it was like I was under water, motion was slow and laborious. And there was the weight on my back, which moved and sprung off me with my exertions. Tugger.

I'd flung myself diagonally across the bed hours before and went into one of those heavy, deep sleeps. The ones from which you awaken feeling sluggish and overmedicated even if you didn't take anything at all, not even an aspirin.

My bedside clock said eight forty-five as I reached for the ringing phone, but was it a.m. or p.m.? I groggily looked out the window. Dark — 8:45 p.m. — good. I'm glad we settled that. What a detective.

I wiped the drool from my face. "Hello?"

"*Mi sobrina! ¿Estás bien o no?*" Tío continued to rattle off more words in Spanish — too numerous to mention — a sure indication he was upset.

"I was sleeping, but I'm fine, Tío," I said, interrupting his diatribe. Still in a fog, I asked, "Where are you?"

"Where am I? I am in *la cocina*. I now come back from the clinic to a message from your mama. She tells me to make sure you are all right. You were attacked?"

"Wow, Tío. You finally learned how to use the answering machine. I'm proud of you."

He let out an exasperated and noisy breath of air. "I do not like the flip at these times. *Basta.*"

"*Basta*, Tío. I'm sorry if I was being flippant."

"Do not make the apology. *¿Que pasó? Dime.*"

And so I told him what happened. All in all, Tío took it well. He listened. His only comment at the end was the same as Frank's—how could I leave the door open, given what was going on? Boy, make one little mistake, and people sure beat it into the ground.

"Let's move on, Tío. I've learned my lesson. No more hip action at the door."

"The burrito, you eat it? I left also the flan. I make it with the orange flavor, mandarin. They are good this time of year."

"Not yet, but I'm starving. I'll heat it up right now." I stood and walked toward the kitchen, the cordless receiver plastered against my ear, followed closely by Tugger.

"How did it go with delivering the puppies?"

"Two, they were the normal births. One, a Great Dane, gives birth in the breech. We lose one of the babies."

I stopped in my tracks, tears springing to my eyes. For whatever reason, this news made me feel surrounded by mayhem, tragedy, and death. Even a newborn puppy was not exempt.

"Oh, Tío. I am so sorry." My voice quivered, but I couldn't help it.

"We save the other five. It was not easy, but the mother and pups, they are well and resting."

"You sound tired, Tío."

"*Si.* But I have a good tired. You do not sound like a good tired."

"No. Gurn, Richard, and Frank are all running in the Palace to Palace tomorrow." I brought him up to date, adding, "I'm scared for them, Tío. I'm afraid something is going to happen to one of them." Again, it was hard to keep my voice from quivering. My uncle managed to bring whatever I was feeling right out of me. A super confessional, that man.

Tío was silent for a moment. I almost called his name out when he finally said, "Do not let fear take from you the common sense. Like Tugger, you have the *corazón* of a lion. Now you need to make the brain to match."

"It's a tall order, Tío."

"*Si,*" he agreed, "but you are a tall girl. You see? I, too, can make the flip."

He laughed, and I tried to laugh, sounding more like a bat having a sneezing fit than anything else, but regardless, laughter it was. We hung up, me certainly lighter of spirit.

I heated and ate the delicious beef burrito dripping with cheese, wondering about this thing called common sense. It didn't seem to me there was anything common about it. Tugger continued to hover nearby, either to be near me, or the beef I was dropping to the floor. I suspected a little of both.

Afterward, I gave a quick call to Las Vegas General for an update on Flint. He'd been taken off the critical list and downgraded to stable. I almost did cartwheels. The nurse asked if I'd like to speak to him, always a good sign. Even though he was awake, I said no but asked for her to tell him love from Papoose and hung up. I ordered flowers sent to his room, a dozen calla lilies, a flower of which he is quite fond. Then for Tugger's amusement—or maybe mine—I tried to do an impersonation of Katharine Hepburn from the 1937 *Stage Door*, done by a lot of stand-up comics. Only better.

"'The calla lilies are in bloom again, really they are, really.' Hmmm. Not quite right. Higher and a little more nasal, I think."

I looked at Tugger for approval. He left the room after my third attempt. It was like he was almost saying, "Don't quit your daytime job, honey. I've got a catnip habit to support."

* * * *

Six hours later, I nearly threw my laptop across the room in frustration. I got up and banged around my office a little, straightening this and that in a gruffer-than-usual way. I had watched all eight videos hour after hour, again and again, until I thought my eyeballs would fall out of my head. First, I'd concentrated on the runners, then the crowd. I even scanned nearby trees and bushes to see if anyone or anything lurked in them. Nada.

I sat back down and studied the screen again for all the good it did me. However the cartel was killing off these runners, I hadn't a clue.

Tugger, always drawn to the happening place, hopped onto the desk and walked across the keyboard, demanding some attention. His feet hit a series of keys, causing one of the images to freeze and enlarge. The pristine white bib of a fallen runner, with number seventy-one emblazoned in red upon it, filled the screen. It meant nothing to me.

My pet's earnest, golden eyes and sharp meow took my focus away. Bleary eyed anyway, I was glad to oblige. I stood, stretched, and picked him up, rubbing my face against his satiny, sweet-smelling fur.

With a practiced hand, I slung him onto one shoulder, him facing behind me. He settled in, purring. Tugger's the sort of guy that often likes to see where he's been rather than where he's going, another cat lesson in life. We left the office and headed back to the bedroom.

It was 2:30 a.m. I needed to get some sleep if I was going to be any good in the morning. Although what I was going to be good for was questionable.

Still wearing Tugger like a stole, I set the alarm for five thirty. I tried not to fret or think about Gurn, Richard, or Frank. Plenty of time for fretting in the morning. I lay down and was out like a light.

Five thirty a.m. came in what felt like ten seconds. I awoke, I won't say refreshed, but feeling a lot better than my two short naps should have allowed.

After coffee and the remnants of Tío's burrito, I took a quick shower, dressed in jeans and a T-shirt, and threw on an embroidered jean jacket I picked up at a thrift store. I live for consignment shops and thrift stores.

Tugger lay sleeping at the foot of the bed. When I roused him to say goodbye at 6:00 a.m., his half-lidded eyes gave me a cross-eyed, what-the-hey look. Then he crashed again.

Grabbing my new leather handbag-satchel—two-weeks salary but so worth it—phone, traveling coffee mug, and keys, I opened the door and stepped outside, remembering my laptop only when I'd locked the door behind me. Whatever information was eluding me could still be on the bloody computer.

The day was not starting out well, I thought, as I raced back inside to the office. The laptop's screen still held the frozen, close-up image of the bib. I unplugged it, banged the lid down, and crammed it into my bag. The whole operation took less than fifteen seconds, but how could I forget something so crucial?

As I pressed the accelerator of the car to the floor, the angst and fear surged back. I would be in San Francisco and at the starting line of the 12K Palace to Palace in less than an hour. Three men I loved were depending on me to keep them alive before, after, and during the race. I needed to be focused and sharp. No more thoughtless or stupid oversights, like forgetting an important piece of equipment.

Chapter Seventeen

It's All in the Timing

I arrived at the Palace of Fine Arts slightly before 7:00 a.m., already crowded with people on foot and cars searching for a place to park. Frank had put a promised VIP sticker on my windshield sometime during the night. This opened streets for me otherwise closed to ordinary vehicles. Elegant homes, some unassuming, some screaming their wealth, were jammed into this small, upscale section of San Francisco near the waterfront. In this residential neighborhood, parking was difficult under normal circumstances, but now it was ridiculous.

Hidden by trees and buildings, I knew the Golden Gate Bridge loomed nearby like an orange-red skeleton of a gargantuan, mythical beast. After fifteen minutes of crawling from Lyon Street to Crook Street, I pulled into the VIP temporary parking lot set up on the side of the road. A parking attendant pointed me into a cramped space between two bushes barely wide enough to open the car door.

Once out on the street, I joined hundreds of people making their way to register for the race and pick up their bib. When last checked, the entries had numbered over three thousand. Comfortably cramming so many runners into this small neighborhood was next to impossible and didn't include spectators and "bandits," or interlopers, the ones who ran along at the last minute, sans bib and entrance fee. There would probably be several hundred of them.

The sun was breaking through silvery clouds and loosening the cold's grip on the night. All in all, it promised to be a perfect day for running, the temperature languishing somewhere in the upper fifties, low sixties.

I love this part of San Francisco. Old world and slightly hidden away, it's only a short walk to the Bay and a marina, housing boats from the St. Francis and Golden Gate Yacht Clubs. There's also Crissy Field, a fabulous open park, with drop-dead views of the San Francisco Bay. Families are out here all the time, kids flying colorful kites in the breezes off the water. Turn left, and it's no more than a three-minute drive on Highway 101 to the Golden Gate Bridge, which takes you to Sausalito and beyond. Turn right, a short drive on Marina Boulevard takes you along the Embarcadero, passing the Ferry Building, Pier 39, and a myriad of other buildings, all fronting the Bay. In fact, it was in one of these warehouses where I found the body of Portor Wyler, one cold and wintry day, but it's another story, and one that still gives me the shivers.

From that part of the Embarcadero, you can see the Bay Bridge straddling the Bay, linking San Francisco with Oakland and beyond.

Along with the throng, I scurried to Lundeen Street and toward the cement-covered lawn in front of the curved Exploratorium Science Museum, where registration was taking place. This amazing, hands-on museum was founded in 1969, by a really neat physicist named Dr. Frank Oppenheimer. Built in a semicircle around one side of the rotund Palace of Fine Arts, I can remember coming up here as a small child and seeing what made lightning. In fact, I got to make some. Once I even got to pet a live starfish. You can't make up those kinds of memories.

I glanced beyond the museum at the pinkish Palace of Fine Arts in a small garden alongside a man-made lake, complete with gliding swans. The palace's salmon-colored, domed roof was warm and golden, reflecting the new day's sun and looking almost alive.

I guess if I could live anywhere in San Francisco, right here would be the place, maybe on one of the park benches. Of course, the nights would be chilly, and I would probably be arrested for loitering, but what an incredible living diorama.

Turning my attention back to the upcoming race, I saw last-minute registration and sign-ins were well underway. A light autumn wind ruffled a huge, off-white tent, temporarily set up to house supplies and personnel. Directly in front of the tent, long tables sat side by side. Wearing white skirts of large letters of the alphabet drawn on flimsy, eleven by fourteen cardboard, they boogied in the constant wind. I stepped aside, not joining the registrants as they fell into the fifteen or so lines, according to the beginning letter of their last name.

I studied the busy and upbeat crowd, some in groups, some loners, chatting, pinning on their bibs, or doing light stretches for the big event starting in about twenty minutes. I couldn't see any of my men and was about to press the speed dial for Gurn's number, when I heard his voice.

"Hi, sweetheart! I thought I'd find you here!" Gurn had come up from behind. He wheeled me around and planted a big kiss on my mouth. He broke free and went on, "I figured you'd be here eventually, so I've been hanging around waiting for you." His eyes searched my face with concern. "You look tired. Anything happen? Or did worrying about me keep you up half the night?" Before I could answer, he continued in a rush, defending his position.

"Honey, I'll be fine. Really, I've been in worse messes, and I'm surrounded by Frank's men." He stopped pushing his point of view and looked at me, large question marks zapping at me from his eyes.

That's when it hit me; Gurn didn't know about the previous night's horror. Apparently, neither Richard nor Frank had told him yet. Jeesh, usually those two are the biggest gossips since *Entertainment Tonight*. I thought for sure one of them would have unloaded on him by now.

Driving all the way up, I'd been rehearsing what I'd say to counteract Gurn's reaction. If he didn't hit the roof, he'd probably throw a blanket over my head, toss me across one shoulder, and carry me home with him.

Of course, the last part sounded pretty good, so I was tempted to spill about Flint being shot, Spaulding nearly killing me, and Tugger saving my life. But I hesitated, looking up into his gorgeous green-gray eyes, and a face wearing a million-dollar smile. Gawd, I loved this man.

Even though I wanted to share everything with him, this wasn't the time. If he was going to run this race, he needed a clear mind. But it didn't stop me from making one more feeble attempt to dissuade him from doing so. Every serious relationship needs a certain amount of nagging.

"Gurn, I really wish you wouldn't—" He stopped my words with another kiss.

"Lee, we've been all over this," he said after lowering his voice and looking around. He pulled me over to a roped-off magnolia tree, still holding on to large, creamy-colored flowers despite the onset of fall.

"This is the best way to flush them out."

"I know, but—"

"I'm being careful. I've got Frank, this new guy, Charlie, and even Richard's keeping an eye on me. Although I don't know where he is right now."

"I know, but—"

"No buts, Lee." He looked at me with challenge in his eyes. "You've got a better plan?"

"It's just that—"

"This is the only way, Lee."

"If you interrupt me one more time," I threatened, pointing a finger in his face for emphasis, "I'm going to have to smack you."

Gurn burst out laughing and drew me to him in an embrace. I lost my intent and relaxed into his arms.

"Just promise me you'll be careful," I murmured into his neck.

"Of course I will, darling. I promise," he murmured back. He broke from our embrace and looked into my eyes. "I've got a long, full life planned with you. I'm not going to do anything to shorten it."

I tried to smile reassuringly, thinking about how I'd come close to shortening our life together myself. Sometimes life comes at you like a freight train or a bargain-basement three-hour sale. Bottom line: you'd better be ready.

I felt his warm breath on my cheek and asked, "What corral are you in?"

In this particular race, the runners are organized into corrals. Corrals are designated starting areas for participants with similar, estimated finishing times, set up along certain streets. Each race has its own rules, and in this one, placement within a corral is determined by your running average. You could only be in the first ten corrals if you have impressive finishing times in previous races. For people with no average at all, like Frank and Richard, they were probably somewhere in the back forty.

"I'm in number one. That's right over there." He pointed to the corners of nearby Baker and Bay. "Charlie's in number three, so he'll be close by."

"Wow. You're right in there with the big boys."

"And girls. There are twenty of us, fifteen men and five women."

"Any of them from other countries?"

"You bet. Most of them are from Ethiopia or Kenya. I ran with one man from Eritrea three years ago. He came in first, and I came in fifth. I think it's the run that did in my knee."

He let out a laugh, warm and sweet, and I stored its memory for a later time. Gawd, I loved this man. Wait a minute. I said that.

"I need to stretch out a little and get over to my corral." He looked at his watch. "Yup. Nearly time. We start in fifteen minutes. Want to help pin my bib to my shirt?"

He stripped off his windbreaker to reveal a yellow tank top, somewhat covering his rippling and well-defined muscles. The warm color of the shirt emphasized the green of his eyes and matched his cheery disposition. Gurn ripped open a small plastic bag given to each specific runner, containing his numbered bib and four steel safety pins. He dumped the pins into my upturned palm, pressed his bib to his chest, and stood erect.

"Try to pin it on straight, Lee." He smiled down at me, and I knew he was looking for a truce, for me to cooperate and help make this work. "I don't want to look like a slob."

"As if," I said, grinning back at him. A truce it was.

With care, I fiddled with the bib on his shirt and began to pin it in place. I got a little sloppy with the last pin, and stuck him with the sharp point.

"Ow! Careful, sweetie. If I wasn't awake before, I am now."

"Sorry. I didn't realize these bibs were so thick. It's hard to get the pin through. By the way, have you seen Richard or Frank?" I was still wondering why neither my brother nor godfather had spilled the beans about the night before.

"No, Richard called earlier, but we didn't have a clear connection. He's back somewhere."

The runners were lined up along the length of Baker Street, block by block. Front-runners were placed at the beginning on Bay Street. At the start gun, all runners would take off at the same time but from their different intersections.

As usual, the race would circle the palace on Palace Drive, head west on Lundeen Street and continue through Crissy Field — just to further torture everybody — and then along Mason Street to the end of Marine Drive. The run heads for the underbelly of the Golden Gate Bridge but makes a U-turn at Fort Point. A few hundred yards of retracing their steps, and then there's the climb up and through Sea Cliff onto the breathtaking Lands End Trail, with views to die for. This group will take no time for sightseeing, however, only occasionally making a pit stop for water.

Those still with us will hang a left at El Camino de Mar, where they start an even more arduous climb up to the palace of the Legion of Honor, ending up on Thirty-Fourth Avenue and in the circular parking lot in front of this noble-looking museum.

In between both palaces are hills, bumpy pavement, dirt, wide paths, narrow lanes, rocks, and grass, and a lot of heavy panting. It isn't so much the distance — just a little over seven miles — but the terrain. At least 90 percent of the run is uneven, uphill, and difficult. Some people drop out midway and head over to Greens, a great vegetarian restaurant in Ft. Mason, for a well-deserved breakfast. That would be my route.

Before all these people started running for whatever reasons possess people to do so, I would have driven overland to wait at the finish line. The problem seemed to be at the finish line, and I wanted to be there well ahead of time.

"Okay, sweetie, I gotta go," Gurn said, blowing me a quick kiss.

"Wait!"

He dutifully turned around and waited for what I had to say, running in place.

"Don't forget to look for me at the end of the race. I might need to tell you something. You never know. Keep a lookout for me," I shouted.

He gave me the okay sign with thumb and forefinger formed in a small circle, spun around, and ran to his corral.

Three short blasts from speakers, scattered on posts and on trees, gave the warning the race was scheduled to start in fifteen minutes. Last-minute entrants frantically tried to find the locations of their corrals. The easygoing atmosphere vanished and was replaced by a rushed excitement and tension. Before I left for the car, I whipped out my phone to call Richard.

He answered on the first ring. I had a much better connection than Gurn said he'd had.

"Hey, Lee. Got my Bluetooth in and been waiting for your call. And by the way, Mom told me what happened. You're sure you're okay?"

"Couldn't be better," I lied.

"I'm still trying to take it in. Tugger earned his keep last night. Where are you?"

"I'm near the check-in at the palace. And thanks for not saying anything to Gurn. I appreciate it. Where are you?"

"Standing around with the other losers at Baker and Francisco. And I was going to tell him, but I thought it would be better coming from you. You're going to shut the front door from now on when you get home, right?"

Nagging tendencies seem to be a family trait. "You bet."

"I called about Flint this morning," Richard went on, "and he's doing much better. DI sent him a huge bouquet of flowers. Vicki took care of it. Speaking of Vicki—"

Another blast of the horn drowned out his last words. People started moving fast, and loud chatter broke out among the throng.

"Richard, I can't hear you. Let's talk later," I interrupted. "But first, do you see anything questionable or suspicious?"

"Sis, it's more of a party atmosphere around here than a race. No beer except root, but we've got a couple of people dressed up as horses, saddles and all, and some guy running around as Daisy Mae. I don't know where that one came from."

"Where's Frank?"

"I don't know. I haven't seen him for about an hour."

"You looking for me?" Frank's bass-baritone voice seemed to come out of nowhere. I whirled around, nearly dropping the phone.

Frank sauntered over, dressed in a light gray tank top, dark gray running shorts, and white running shoes, mocha skin aglow from moderate exercise. His bib number read 542. Funny, he still looked like a cop even in a running outfit.

"Richard, I've got to go, but stay close to your phone." I hung up and turned to Frank. "Where did you come from?"

"Been checking things out, Lee. Saw you with Gurn a few minutes ago but wanted to give you some time together."

"Thanks for not telling him about last night."

"Figured it should come from you. But you'd better do it soon." He winked at me after he gave me a fake scowl.

I nodded, grateful everybody thought I was grown up enough to know when and where to tell someone something. "Did you find anything?"

He shook his head. "I don't think it's on this end, Lee."

"Neither do I." I threw my phone into my bag. "The race is going to start in about ten minutes. I'd better head over to the finish line and see what I can see."

"I'll go with you," he said, falling into step with me toward the car less than a block away.

"Aren't you running the race?"

"Me? Not on your life. Just get me to the other end by wheels, please."

"Which reminds me, don't they electronically monitor the runners at checkpoints? You know, to make sure they do the entire race on foot? I think you're disqualified if your foot doesn't fall on certain pads along the way."

"Well, if they don't, they damned well should," Frank said with not a small amount of indignation. "People are going to try to cheat on something like this, especially for twenty-five thousand dollars. I thought you knew I'd never planned on running the race. When we get to the Golden Gate, I'll jump out and scout around. Nobody'll be suspicious of me dressed like this."

"Don't kid yourself, Frank. You manage to make it look like a cop's uniform."

"Yeah?" He looked down in surprise. "Well, don't you worry about me. You just put your thinking cap on, and come up with how these SOBs are doing it."

My mouth formed a grim line as I heard the ten-minute warning blast go off. I opened the car doors with the beeper.

"I guess I'll keep looking at the videos and hope I find something." I slid into the driver's seat of my '57 Chevy. "Good luck squeezing in."

Frank opened the passenger's door and grimaced. "Oh, mama, I need to lose weight."

"If I can't find anything, our job is to tackle Gurn to the ground before he gets anywhere near the finish line. Agreed?"

He got in, nodding gruffly. "Agreed."

I pulled out into the street and followed the streets the run would take, heading toward the Golden Gate Bridge. "How much time do we have? How long before the first runners get to the end, do you think?"

"Less than an hour. It's not a long race, but it's grueling. Glad I'm not doing it. These guys are going to need some TLC after this."

"As long as nobody needs a gurney," I muttered.

Chapter Eighteen

Can't You Pick Another Route?

Five minutes later, I sat with the motor idling while Frank showed his ID to a foul-tempered, thin, dark-skinned man at the latest checkpoint, a man who would have rather been anywhere else but where he was. We had decided to drive as much of the race as we possibly could, just to check things out. I looked out the windshield straight ahead while Frank's voice droned on in laconic tones, courteous but saying only what was necessary.

No more than a quarter mile ahead, the end of San Francisco's land mass sat, sloping into a small, tawny-colored dune next to the sea. Speckled with gray-green weeds, the dune had been created by centuries of wind and rested under the base of this side of the Golden Gate Bridge. Lucky dune, it had a multimillion-dollar view of the sparkling Bay waters, Sausalito, and the Marin Headlands.

This stint of the run was a narrow slope bringing the runners to a flat patch of land, covered overhead by the GG Bridge. If you were directly in the sun or sheltered from the blustery weather, the day had warmed somewhat. Otherwise, the bone-piercing wind off the Bay stressed not only the soon-to-come winter, but also the not-so-user-friendly San Francisco Bay.

"Okay, let's get going," Frank said, his business over. He impatiently tapped the dashboard in front of him as a signal for me to put the pedal to the metal.

I pulled on ahead, going no more than eight miles an hour, heading to the spot where Jimmy Stewart jumped into the water and rescued a suicidal Kim Novak in Hitchcock's *Vertigo*. Knowing what I know about the San Francisco Bay, it made me wonder how on earth anybody—even stunt doubles—could throw themselves into freezing, tumultuous waters like that. Just thinking about it, brrrr!

The car crawled alone this quarter-mile portion of the road, turning back onto itself once we got to the end, the building at Fort Point. Ahead, I saw one of the computerized foot registers each runner would have to be sure to hit if they didn't want to be disqualified.

Avoiding personnel, police, and officials, who were darting all over the place on this narrow portion of the run, I noted the twenty-foot-wide pavement separated by the Bay on one side and a sloping cliff on the other. This was a very vulnerable section of the run, although the security was first rate, with surveillance cameras stationed on platforms every few feet or so. Before I made a U-ee and drove back, I stopped the car and looked across the mouth of the Golden Gate spanned by the world-famous bridge only since the late '30s. Before, people got from one side to the other perilously via ferry or other watercraft. Strong currents and the standard sixty-mile-an-hour winds labeled this bridge "the bridge that couldn't be built." Yeah right. It sat peaceful and imposing, this huge edifice, the deep-orange color contrasting vividly with the robin's-egg blue of the sky and the aquamarine, white-capped waters beneath.

"Beautiful, isn't it?" commented Frank. "But we'd better get going. This looks pretty secure here. The circular parking lot out in front of the Legion of Honor worries me. There could be crowd-control problems there."

We turned around, headed away from the marina area, and passed through Sea Cliff, a residential area of swells where a doghouse costs millions of dollars. Up we went through Lands End Trail, turning onto El Camino del Mar.

As we neared the finish line, dozens of people carrying lawn chairs, blankets, water bottles, many with small children, trudged up each side of the winding, tree-covered street.

They'd stop now and then to enjoy the intermittent but spectacular views of the Golden Gate and the surrounding Headlands. The spectators moved haphazardly as large crowds often do, spilling out into the street, laughing, chatting, even singing. Their goal was not so much to be near the ribboned finish line but close enough to see the passing action.

I turned into the parking lot of the palace of the Legion of Honor, teeming with police and race officials, preparing for the onslaught of runners in about thirty minutes time.

"Park behind the news van over on the right," Frank ordered. "I'll get out and look around. Some of Hank Fenner's men are here undercover. He's in charge."

He turned around and faced me, his mocha-colored bare arm holding on to the handgrip over the door. I inched through the crowd, barely going five miles an hour. I gripped the wheel tighter, just out of sheer nerves.

"You remember Hank Fenner?" Frank went on. "Transferred to SFPD about twenty years ago. Runs the homicide division. Bobby and I went to the academy with him."

"I do, Frank. He's the one who interrogated me several months back when I found Portor Wyler's body."

"Oh yeah. That's right."

"He was pretty nice to me," I admitted. I didn't add I'd been short tempered and curt, but he'd let it all wash over him.

"He should be. Fenner idolized your father. Said he learned a lot from him. We all did." Frank's voice took on the gruff edge it did when he was caught up in an emotion he was trying to push away. He flung open the car door and sprang out, then leaned back inside.

"You coming?"

"No. I want to keep looking at these videos. I've got a nagging feeling I'm overlooking something in them. Let's keep in touch by phone."

He nodded and slammed the car door shut. I reached behind me and grabbed my bag off the back seat.

When I opened the lid of the laptop I realized, although I'd unplugged it when I'd left home, I had neglected to turn it off. The frozen close-up image of the fallen Peruvian's bib still covered the screen.

Annoyed at myself for needlessly wasting battery power, I checked what was left. Another four and a half hours remained. Okay. It was okay. Way before, this whole mess should be over. One way or another.

I clicked on the videos feeling determined, but with a heaviness of spirit. I'd start the whole process of scrutinizing them again, because that's what a good PI does, but I didn't hold much hope. Whatever secret or clue was there kept eluding me no matter how many times I tried to snag it.

Sitting on the dashboard were the remnants of cold coffee from earlier, but I thought better of chugging it down. I'd had no breakfast, and now that it was down to the wire, literally, my stomach was churning up bile better than a milkmaid churning butter.

I reached under the seat for one of the ubiquitous chocolate candy bars I stow there, stale though it might be. Some day I'm going to get ants in the car from all the food I store under the driver's seat, but it sure comes in handy when I'm in a situation like this.

Munching away, I watched frame by grueling frame, lost in my concentration. So much so, I hadn't noticed the lot was quickly filling up with hundreds of people packing themselves five and six deep on the sidelines of the final span. Someone actually jumped onto the trunk of my car, rocking me out of my absorption in the laptop's offerings.

"Hey," I yelled out the window. "What are you doing? Get off my car!"

A teenage boy, possibly sixteen or seventeen, turned and gave me a startled look.

"Sorry," he stuttered, with an apologetic smile. "I just wanted to see when they hit the ribbon. You can't see anything from the ground." He hopped down with no more conversation and disappeared into the hoard.

I looked over to where the finish line was or should have been. I've been to less-crowded rock concerts. A glance at my watch showed it to be 8:30 a.m. The first of the runners were due in ten minutes, more or less. I'd been watching these stupid videos for over twenty-five minutes with nothing to show for it.

I turned back to the laptop, this time to shut it off properly. I'd given up. There wasn't any way I could figure out how the syndicate was killing off these people. But I wasn't going to lose Gurn to them. I'd stop him from nearing the finish line if I had to shoot him to do it. Wait a minute. Not the best of plans.

In my frustration, I banged on a couple of keys. The frozen image of the white bib Tugger had somehow triggered the computer to save came back on screen, stark white against the black dirt of the ground.

My forefinger raised in the air, poised to shut down the program when I saw what had been taunting me the entire time. The bib. Clean and stark white. A stark-white bib, ostensibly coming from a man's sweaty shirt at the end of a long run in a tropical clime. Moreover, what was it doing off on the side of the path? It should have still been pinned to his shirt.

Shaky fingers tapped the frames of the video to the last moments of the Peruvian runner's life. And then I saw it. One moment a bib, sweaty, soiled, and wrinkled was pinned to the pale-green T-shirt of his crumpled body, and the next moment a pristine white bib was laying on the side of the path. Ignoring the images of people hovering over the body, I closed in on what hadn't been obscured by well-meaning bystanders.

Before a do-gooder stepped in the way and knelt down, I had a blurred vision of short, stubby fingers reaching out and tearing the dirty bib from the shirt. I clicked forward trying to keep the image of the shirt in frame all the time then froze it. I enlarged the image, enhancing and filling in missing pixels for a clearer picture. Sure enough, I saw small tears in the fabric of the shirt where the bib had been. Then I backed the frames up, widening my scope. Little by little, I searched for the person attached to those stubby fingers. No luck. I fast-forwarded to the last of the video, back to the pristine white bib lying on the side of the path.

It was the bib! Every official runner in every country had to wear one. And each bib was attached to a sweaty shirt with metal safety pins, a perfect conductor of electricity. But until I knew how the shock was triggered, Gurn was in mortal danger.

With shaky fingers, I punched Gurn's phone number, but it went directly to his voice mail. Crap! Just like Stephen, he'd turned it off before the race. What's with these runners, anyway?

I called Frank, who answered on the first ring. I could tell the first set of runners was coming into the homestretch. Several hundred yards back, yells and screams were going up from the crowds. The whoops almost drowned out Frank's voice.

"Frank, you've got to stop Gurn. Do you know where he is?"

"No," Frank shouted into his cell. "But Charley was trying to keep him in sight. I think Gurn broke free from his group about five minutes ago in a burst of speed. Time to find him and tackle him to the ground?"

"Yes, stop him at any cost. It's in the bib."

"The what? I can't hear you."

"The bib. The bib!"

Frank didn't answer me. It sounded like some sort of tussle on his end of the line, and then the phone went dead.

I leapt out of the car and began to run toward Thirty-Fourth Avenue, while punching the speed dial for Richard. "Richard, I need your help." I said, when I heard him huffing and puffing on the other end of the line. "Stop running, fer cryin' out loud, and listen to me."

"I did stop the minute I saw your number. I'm off to the side. I can't help it if I'm still breathing hard. Holy cow, this is tough. What's up? And speak up. I can hardly hear you."

"Richard, it's in the bib. I think some kind of electrical mechanism, wires or something, put inside the bib and then activated toward the end of the run. Is that possible?"

"Sure it is," he said, gulping in air. "All you need is a remote to set it off."

I looked down at the keys and car opener still in my hand. "Like the ones you use to unlock the doors or trunk of a car?"

"Yeah, as long as you're close enough. Jesus Christ, is that how they're doing it? Someone close by is probably triggering a small battery. When it melts —"

"Never mind the physics lesson. Just get here as fast as you can even if you have to take a cab."

I hung up and redialed Frank while running against the crowds, like an upstream salmon. No answer. I panicked. There were hundreds of people now, all pushing and shoving to get to the front of the two lines on either side of the running path. A burley man steamrollered into me, almost knocking me to the ground, but kept going without a backward glance. So much for chivalry. I should have punched his lights out when I had the chance. So much for being a lady.

My phone rang, and I looked at the incoming number, hoping it was either Gurn or Frank. It was a number I didn't recognize. I answered, anyway.

"Lee! It's Frank. Can you hear me?"

"Barely." I put a finger in my free ear to block out some of the sounds of the crowd. "Where are you?" I looked around the mass of people bumping into each other and me, hoping he was nearby.

"My phone got knocked out of my hand by a group of kids, who tromped all over it. I don't even know where it is. I'm calling you from one of my men's. What have you got?"

"Where are the runners now? Can you see Gurn? We've got to stop him."

"No, but the first group is less than a quarter of a mile away. If he's with them, he should be here in about five minutes. Hey! Look out, lady, and watch your kid too," I heard him snarl at someone. "It's chaos here, Lee, utter chaos. Fenner's got two men looking for Gurn right now, but unless we billy club somebody, we're not going to get them to move aside.

"Where are you?" I wailed in frustration. I turned, and for one split second there was a space in the crowd. I saw Frank's back not twenty feet away. "I see you, Frank. Turn around!"

The crowd closed in again, and he was gone. I pushed my way toward the spot where he'd been. I never saw him but felt him grab me and spin me around.

"Okay, let's go." He held my wrist tight, and together we fought the onslaught of the revelers and spectators. "What's this about a bib?" he shouted back at me.

"It's in the bib, Frank. I noticed Gurn's was extra thick. Probably from the wiring. I think the electrical charge is triggered by someone using a remote control near the finish line."

We stopped in front of two uniformed policemen, the taller one holding a megaphone. Frank shouted something into the ear of the shorter man, who nodded, turned, and fought to get closer to the front of the runners' path. I noticed both men had a walkie-talkie, and they handed a third squawking one to Frank. He listened for a moment before turning to me.

"Lee, I think we've finally got this organized. I've told the cop closest to the front runners to pull Gurn out of the group." His walkie-talkie squawked again. He put it to his ear, and a look of surprise and concern crossed his face.

"What? What is it?" I shouted.

He dropped the walkie-talkie down to his side, looked at me, and bellowed. "Gurn got by him. The cop said he couldn't keep up with Gurn. He's radioed for the next man to take over, but Gurn's so close now, that person might have to be me."

Adrenalin pumping, I fought my way through to the front of the line, despite protestations and occasional shoves in return. Once there, I saw three lean men heading toward us and to the finish line. Two men had copper-colored skin, while the third man was almost blue-black in color and smaller. Their sweaty, sinewy bodies gleamed from the sun's glare, defined muscles moving in perfect harmony to propel them forward. Even as stressed as I was, it was one of the most beautiful sights I'd ever seen. All three were nearly side by side and passed me in a flash.

Maybe ten yards behind came Gurn, also poetry in motion. His face aglow, I could tell in an instant the endorphins had kicked in, and he was in another world, the runner's world.

I tried to spurt out onto the path, followed by Frank. A surprised staffer whose job it was to keep the path free of spectators, caught sight of us, signaling others. A heavyset man wearing an official's blue windbreaker, deliberately tripped Frank. Frank stumbled, not quite falling. I reached back to steady him, but a strong arm grabbed me. I struggled, screaming Gurn's name out repeatedly, screams lost in the hubbub, blasts of horns, and cheering.

Gurn, unaware, passed us in a burst of speed. He was running alone, the rest of the pack far, far behind. Gurn was only yards away from coming in the deadly fourth-place winner. Twisting and turning, I broke free from the staffer's grasp but had lost precious time. I ran out into the center of the path, yards behind Gurn. There was no way I could catch up with him. Frank pushed the heavyset man away and joined me. Together we ran forward, yelling at the tops of our lungs.

"Gurn, Gurn! Your shirt! Take off your shirt! Gurn!"

With the last frantic scream of his name, our voices were in unison. The sound rose above the urging yells of the crowd.

Gurn slowed down and looked around but continued moving. He was within feet of the finish line. He could have loped over, coming in fourth. Everyone could see it. Nobody, including Gurn, understood why he'd stopped. The crowd cheered him on, their spirit instinctively propelling him forward.

I screamed his name again. I could tell he'd heard me but couldn't find me. Confused, he still moved forward. Finally, he pivoted around and saw us coming up behind him. The finish line was only inches away. Now he was backing up, still on his collision course with death.

Frank, in a moment of inspiration, slowed down, tore at his own shirt, drawing it up and over his head. He pointed to Gurn's yellow one. By this time I'd almost reached Gurn's side and saw he comprehended.

Gurn grabbed the garment, pulling it over his head in a fluid, often done movement. With his right hand holding the shirt, his arm stretched up into the air, the yellow fabric nearly free of his grasp. Almost in slow motion, I saw a flicker of something residual touch the tip of his middle finger. His face registered shock. He was thrown to the ground almost as if he had been tackled by an unseen opponent. The shirt lay beside his motionless body, now drawn up in a fetal position.

"*Dios mio. Dios mio,*" I cried out, hurling myself at his side. Frank was on top of us and rolled Gurn over on his back near the sideline. Frank searched for a pulse. I felt the breeze of a woman runner passing me, the muted sounds of her running shoes pounding the dirt. Several of the people close to us stopped cheering and looked down at the small scene unfolding before them.

I pushed Frank out of the way, grabbed Gurn by the shoulders, and pulled him onto my lap, fighting back sobs. Gurn's eyelids fluttered, then opened. A grin spread across his face.

"Now this is the way to finish a race, in a gorgeous woman's arms."

I felt a freeing sound of laughter leave my body. I hugged him so tightly he almost couldn't breathe, but I wouldn't let go. Finally, I looked down at his wonderful, still alive face.

"Gurn! You scared me to death. I thought you were —" I broke off speaking. Out of the corner of my eye, I saw nimble fingers stretching out from within the crowd, reaching for the yellow shirt.

I threw myself at the hand, grabbing the unknown assailant's forearm, and locked myself around it. Gurn let out a yelp. In the shuffle, his head hit the hard, packed-down dirt.

What followed was just like the nursery rhyme "The House That Jack Built." I was attached to the arm that was attached to the hand that was attached to the shirt that lay on the ground that Gurn wore. Using the arm, I pulled myself off the ground, then gave it a fast yank. A smallish, nondescript man fell forward to his knees but quickly rose again. He struggled, but it was useless. I was major mad, and I wasn't letting go for anything.

I heard Frank shout out a curse word and lunged forward to assist. Meanwhile, Gurn had rolled over on his stomach, got up, and came to help, wobbly though he might have felt.

In a spurt of anger, and to end any more struggling on the man's part, I kicked him in the gonads as hard as I could. It was a totally un-PC moment, but the crowd went wild. They didn't know what was going on, but they sensed this guy was the villain. With a cry of pain, said villain doubled up and fell to the ground. I felt the whoosh of several more runners at my back, one clipping me on my shoulder.

Assisted by my two shirtless guys, I dragged the man by the scruff of his neck outside the running line. The crowd cleared a space for us, paying rapt attention to everything we did. We had become much more entertaining than the race itself. I saw news cameras pointed at us out of the corner of my eye. I knew we would be on the six o'clock news.

Oh, goody, I thought. *Mom will just love that. Another lecture coming up about my unladylike behavior.*

Chapter Nineteen

To Recapitulate

"So tell me again how it was done. I don't quite get it." Flint leaned back against the myriad of pillows in his hospital bed. He reached up and straightened one behind his head, the bandages on his chest peeking out from underneath an incongruous, paleblue hospital gown dotted with small flowers. An IV was dripping into his left arm, but otherwise, his face was robust and his manner alert.

Nonetheless, I was apprehensive and not just a little guilty. We had already done fifteen minutes on Spaulding's break-in and attempt to kill me.

"I don't want to tire you out." I looked over toward Knoton, seeking his take on whether or not I was sapping too much of Flint's energy. Honestly, though, you'd never have guessed he'd been at death's door three days before.

"You must be joking," the slighter version of Flint said. Then Knoton laughed. "Right now you're entertaining him and keeping him from driving us all nuts."

Flint joined in the laughter. "I think I'm what they call a bad patient."

"He's already threatened to get up and walk out twice," Knoton said. "And the first time was when he was wheeled back from the operating room."

He took his father's right hand, squeezing it hard. "You're one tough man, Dad. A Shoshone brave if ever there was one."

There was no small amount of pride in Knoton's voice, or on his face, as he looked at his father. "But I don't like this getting-shot business."

"I'm not so thrilled with it myself, Son, but it's a hazard of the game." Flint smiled at his son and turned back to me.

"But go on with your story, Lee. How did you figure out how they killed all those runners?"

"Well, I have to thank Tugger for pointing me in the right direction."

"Ah, the cat that saved your life strikes again." Flint looked at his son. "And I thought cats weren't good for much except catching mice."

"The boys think our Fluffy is one in a million, Dad, and she's never even seen a mouse," Knoton said with pride. He looked at his father. "My sons just love our tabby cat. You should get one, Dad. You need the company."

Flint rolled his eyes. "If I ever get a pet, it'll be a Pinto pony. But go on, Lee. How did you do it?"

"It was pretty straight forward once I discovered they did it with the bibs. The syndicate had to be sure to recover the rigged bibs after each race during the commotion. Then they'd toss the original one on the ground nearby. This way no one would find the wiring hidden inside. Spaulding and the co-owners of the Fantasy Lady are being indicted as we speak."

"So it was right in front of everybody the entire time." Flint shook his head in disbelief.

"Let me get this straight," said Knoton. "They ran wiring inside the bib, attached to a small, high-voltage battery triggered by... what? Remote control?"

I pulled out my car opener attached to my keys. "Right. A garage door opener or an auto fob like this." I waved my keychain around. "There is actually a small radio transmitter inside this. Who knew?"

"Well, I did, for one," said Flint. "The world's first remote controls were radio-frequency devices directing German naval vessels to crash into Allied boats during WWI."

I raised eyebrows. "That's pretty nasty."

"War is pretty nasty," said Flint, shrugging.

I went on. "And every runner has to wear a bib with his or her number on it, pinned in place on a T-shirt. And every runner sweats."

"So it revolved around the electricity, pins, and sweat," observed Knoton.

"Yes," I said." I read on two different autopsy reports, there were small burn marks on a couple of people, but nobody thought it was connected to their deaths."

"How did they get a specific bib on a specific runner?" asked Knoton. "They'd have to get that right or what's the point?"

"It was highly organized," I said. "Down to paid-off staff members who'd register the runners, package the bibs and pins, and substitute the lethal bib for the real one when instructed to do so. The syndicate would take bets on sure fourth- and fifth-place runners and then alert their lackeys to fix the race, for which they were paid handsomely."

"I'm taking it, someone on the lower rung sang," said Flint.

"Like the third act of *Aida*," I replied.

"You two sound like an old gangster movie," observed Knoton.

"Thanks. We try." I winked at Flint and he winked back. "The songbird in question was the man I caught with the remote control in his pocket, trying to take back Gurn's bib."

"I understand you kneed him right in the groin," Flint said with a smile on his face. "At least, that's what the newspapers say. Nick had a good laugh about it, I can tell you. I'm thinking you might have done that to him, once upon a time."

"Old habits die hard," I joked. "Where is Nick, anyway?" I looked around the small hospital room as if he might pop up from behind the privacy screen.

"Probably at my office fielding calls or at the gym working out. He's still trying to get back in shape. He's turned out to be a not-so-bad guy, our Nicky Boy.

I'm going to need some assistance until I get back on my feet, and he's offered to help out," said Flint. His eyes searched mine before he said, "It going to be okay with you if he turns out to be a PI, like the rest of us?"

"Just don't let him date any daughters of your clients. He's not always so good with women."

"I'll remember that." Flint hooted with laughter, took a deep breath, and grimaced. "Man, my chest hurts when I breathe or laugh." He looked at me with mock sternness. "So don't make me laugh."

"Wouldn't dream of it."

As if on cue, Nick strolled in, carrying a large brown bag. He looked more like the old Nick I remembered. He had a good five pounds of weight back on him and was buffed up but not overly so. He sported a new haircut, and his clothes were fresh-looking and ironed. My ex seemed surprised and pleased to see me. I almost didn't mind seeing him. What a difference having another and better life makes.

"Lee! I hoped you'd still be here."

He set the brown bag on the moveable tray table at the foot of the bed and opened it. The mouthwatering smells of Chinese food filled the room.

"Have some moo goo gai pan," he said. "There's plenty."

"Ah," said Flint, propping himself up in bed. "Lunch has arrived."

"Are you supposed to have this stuff?" I was concerned and looked over at Knoton.

Knoton stood up and walked down to the edge of the bed while Nick pulled out cartons of food.

"The doctors said it was all right now and then, Lee," said Flint's son, opening one of the white boxes and taking out a set of chopsticks.

"Nothing wrong with my digestive system," Flint said, reaching out for the carton with greedy hands. "I'm here for another week. All I got to look forward to are these meals. Tomorrow is pizza."

"In that case, I'm going to leave you to today's lunch." I gathered up my things and went to the head of the bed. "I'll see you in a few days, Flint, after I get back from a trip." I gave him a quick kiss on the cheek.

"Can't wait to see you again, Papoose," came Flint's garbled reply, shoving rice into his mouth with plastic chopsticks. "Just bring me some eggrolls, will you? They got better ones in San Francisco."

"Don't eat with your mouth full, Dad," Knoten chastised his father.

"Sez you," Flint replied but closed his mouth.

I laughed and headed for the door. Nick followed close behind.

"I'll walk you out, Lee."

I turned and looked at him. Something had to be on his mind. The Nick I knew never extended himself for anyone, in particular me. But those were days of old, I reminded myself. No use holding a grudge about what once was.

We walked down the corridor toward the elevator, the smells and sounds of the hospital rampant and everywhere. The walls had been painted the same pale blue color as Flint's hospital gown. Somebody on the board obviously liked the color, or they got a good deal on paint and supplies.

"Let's go into this room here." Nick pointed to a small waiting room filled with chairs and a sofa for patients' friends and family. The large pane of glass inset into the wall revealed the emptiness of the room, a place which promised to be quieter than the noisy, busy corridor.

I walked in and turned back to Nick, curious. "What is it? I've got a plane to catch."

He looked ill at ease, licking his lips a few times, glancing everywhere but at my face.

"Lee, I wanted to apologize... for... apologize for everything."

"That's a little broad. Everything, what?"

He came closer and looked directly into my eyes. I felt and smelled his breath on my face. The scent of your first love is something you never quite forget.

"I did a lot of bad things to you. Those other women, they never meant anything to me."

"Nick, this is old news. It's history. What's done is do —"

"No, I need to say this, Lee. More for me than for you. Okay?"

He looked like he was asking my permission to speak, so I nodded in assent, not saying anything more.

"I had a lot of problems when we first met. My father had just left Mom and me, the stint in the marines was over, and it sounds stupid to say this now, but I was feeling worthless. I..." He stopped speaking, his mouth opening and closing in quick movements as if the words came forward to his lips but rushed back inside again.

"You," I prompted.

"I thought being with other women would make me feel like more of a man. When you fell in love with me..." He broke off and went to the sofa. "Can we sit down for this?"

I followed and sat down next to him. He reached out for my hand. I let him take it but scooted an inch or two away.

"When you fell in love with me, I couldn't believe my good fortune. I didn't think I deserved it. Anyway..." He let out a deep sigh and then a self-deprecating laugh. "Anyway, I see now I tried to destroy what we had and succeeded. When you finally challenged me about the infidelities, I..." He paused and looked away. "I still can't believe I struck you. I feel bad about that."

"You beat me up, not once, but on two separate occasions, Nick." My voice was harsh and unyielding. "Men are often contrite about brutality after the fact. It's an old story."

He nodded and in a barely audible voice said, "I know, I know. But I've been taking anger management classes, and if this means anything to you, I've never struck another woman since. Not even Kelli, and sometimes it almost seemed like she was asking for it."

His last comment shocked me. Another symptom of this illness is men often think women are "asking for it." "Promise me you'll continue with your anger management classes, Nick. There isn't any woman I know who wants to get knocked around. That's a fallacy."

He dropped my hand and pulled his own onto his lap, almost defensively. But his eyes never left mine.

"I don't expect you to forgive me, and I'm not even asking you to. On a lesser note, I'm sorry about hitting on you in Flint's kitchen too. You were right; it was insulting and stupid. But what I really wanted to say to you is…" He paused and leaned into me. "You're the best thing that ever happened to me. I screwed it up royally, but it doesn't take away what we had together. I want you to know I know that."

He looked away for a moment, then his eyes came back and met mine again. For an instant, I saw remnants of the boy I fell in love with. He was in there somewhere, covered in lots of garbage.

I nodded, not sure of what to say. I didn't want to encourage him into thinking we might share something again if that's where he was going with this. But I also didn't want to blow him off either. If this was some sort of twelve-step program to better mental health, I didn't want to quash it.

"I understand, Nick," I said, patting the hand resting in his lap. "And we all make mistakes. The past is the past. Let's just put this behind us, shall we?"

He stared at me for a moment, let out a laugh, and shook his head. "Spoken like the best of therapists."

I rose, straightened my skirt, and looked down at him. "Nick, it's been four years. As Tío says, 'Learn from your mistakes and move on.' Or as he would say, *muévete*. You and I, we've moved on."

I saw his face lost in memory. "That's so like Tío. I think of him often, and Richard, and even Lila. I was sorry when your father died. I lost your family, too, when I lost you."

He looked back at me, expecting me to say something, maybe like they missed him too. They didn't, but even if they did, I wasn't going there.

"Nick, I'm with someone, and you're with... well, you're not with someone at the moment, but you really loved Kelli, didn't you?"

"I did, yes," he said slowly.

"See? You'll find someone else, I guarantee, especially when you get all buffed up again." We both laughed, and the mood lightened momentarily, but Nick became serious again. Sometimes when you gotta be heavy, you gotta be heavy.

"I would have liked to try again with Kelli, if only... but she's gone now and..." He made another dramatic pause. "Life goes on."

Gee, I wish I'd said that. But it fit right in with the ridiculous kind of conversation we were having. I didn't reply but turned away and picked up my bag. Without looking at him, I said, "While we're on the subject of my family, I would appreciate it if you didn't use Richard's name again if you go into hiding. Or anyone else's in the family."

"I wasn't thinking straight. I promise to never do that again, especially now I'm on my way to becoming a PI. That's not going to bother you, is it?" His voice had an anxious quality to it as if my answer was important to him. "I'll be based here in Las Vegas. I don't see myself ever leaving and going back to the Bay Area."

"Just do right by Flint. He's a good man. Besides, you mess with him, he might squash you like a bug."

"Don't worry." He gave me a little-kid grin, then sobered. "This is a second chance. I'm not going to blow it."

He rose and walked toward me. Opening the door of the small room, I stepped into the corridor. I turned back and extended my hand.

"Goodbye, Nick. Maybe I'll see you around; maybe I won't. Either way, have a good life."

He took my hand with a smile, glancing down at it, and then up into my face. "The same to you, Lee. Thanks for saving my ass. Maybe I can do the same for you sometime. It's such a lovely one."

* * * *

Richard answered on the fifth ring as I walked to the rental car in the parking lot of the hospital. A sudden desert wind came up from nowhere and blew the matching neck scarf from my three-piece tailored outfit into my face and over my eyes, transforming the colors of the blah parking lot into vivid hues of turquoise, teal, and purple. I pushed the recalcitrant scarf back down on my neck and answered my phone.

"Hi, Richard, you got the info I need?" I said, pressing the fob to unlock the car door. I thought fleetingly of how I would never take one of these things for granted again. I slid into the car on smooth, mock-leather car seats while listening to Richard's chastising voice drone on.

"I got it, Lee, but I don't like it. Not any of it. This is dangerous. You shouldn't be going there by yourself. Actually, this is insanity."

"Since when did insanity ever stop me?" I let out a giggle, which floated through the silent air and popped like a soap bubble. Seeing levity was the wrong tactic, I cleared my throat and became serious. "This is the only way, Richard. Gurn is back in Washington, and Flint is laid up. Time is of the essence." I inwardly groaned. Why didn't I add, *It's always darkest before the dawn* while I was at it?

"What's the matter with you?" he said, his voice incredulous. "Are you on something? Whatever it is, don't give me any. And what makes you think she's alive? And in Rio de Janeiro? It doesn't make any sense."

"She's alive. And why not Rio de Janeiro? Where would you go if you had fifty million dollars?"

"Well, it sure wouldn't be there. Maybe Paris," he added with a grumble.

"Richard, what was the ringtone on the phone the police found in the back seat of her car?"

The question brought him up short. "Should I know that?"

"It was in the police report. They are very thorough, the Vegas police. She also sang it the day she showed up to my place and took the cats, but nobody would know that but me."

I started the rental car, a red Ford Fiesta, and hummed a few bars of "The Girl from Ipanema" as I backed out of the parking space. I heard Richard's heavy breathing, then movement, and the steady click of his computer mouse. I could picture him, sitting at his desk, ripping through papers, and clicking madly, looking for the answer, which he would eventually find, our Richard. No doubt about it.

"I just gave it to you. 'The Girl from Ipanema,' Richard, so stop your search. I'm heading for the airport now. You got me the ticket?" I stuck the Bluetooth in my ear, transferred the call over to it, and pulled out into traffic.

"You have a flight to LA in about two hours. Air Rio leaves from LAX tonight at eight p.m. and gets you into Rio at seven a.m., just like you asked. We don't even know for sure it's her. The manifest said an eleven-year-old girl traveling with her father."

"It's her, Richard."

"Lila's going to have a cow if DI has to pay for a first-class ticket to Rio de Janeiro for nothing. Fifty-four hundred dollars!"

"It's Kelli."

"All the more reason to go with backup. Or hand it over to the Brazilian police. They're capable of handling this."

"I've got to do this myself, Richard. I'm the one she snookered. I'm bringing her back."

"Ah, gee, you and your macho tendencies, Lee," Richard whined, quite unlike him. "They get you in trouble each and every time."

"I've got an idea. Let's do a compromise. Remember the two men who came to see Dad about ten years ago for help on starting their own agency in Rio?"

"Wait a minute, let me think."

"Gustavo and Heitor Janardo. One had a beard, like Fidel Castro," I said, hoping to trigger his memory. "The other played with a yoyo."

"Sure," he drawled as the recollection came back to him. "The younger one, Heitor, gave me one of his yoyos and taught me how to do around the world with it. I thought they were out of the business."

"They are, but they're working as bodyguards for one of the wealthier hotel owners in Rio. I'll call them, and see if they can help me. Remember, this is not just for me. It's for Stephen. I know what she's capable of better than anyone. I don't want her to get away again."

"All right," he relented, emitting a long, drawn-out sigh. "If you call the Janardo brothers for backup, I'm with you."

I heard some papers rustle in the background again, a sound like a "thunk," and then a few more clicks of the computer mouse. "Here's what I've got. I don't think she could be at one of the major hotels on Ipanema. I've done some checking, and believe me, it wasn't easy."

"You always say that."

"Because it's always true. But, anyway, I've managed to trace every female under forty years old who arrived about a week ago back to their city of departure. None of them were from Las Vegas."

"Thank you."

"Yeah, there's two twelve-hour days, right there."

"I don't think she'd stay at a major hotel, anyway," I said. "She might get noticed."

"Now you tell me."

"Check out small hostelries, ones that are directly on the beach."

"Now you tell me."

"You're the best brother a girl could have." I ended the sentence by smacking kisses into the phone.

"Oh, please. Spare me." He let out a large, dramatic sigh followed by heavy resignation. "When do you want them?"

"I'll call you in the morning for the info. Mum's the word, Richard."

"What does that mean?"

"What do you think it means?"

There was a quick intake of breath, signaling Richard's current status. We had moved from resignation to alarm.

"You haven't told Mom or Tío where you're going?"

"Not yet."

"What about Gurn? Does he know?"

"No, this is just between you and me."

"Where does everyone think you are?"

"Gurn thinks I'm returning home from a day visit to Flint for some R and R while he's gone. That's why I offered to take Baba again for him. It's nice he still trusts me with her."

"Excuse me?" Strangled laughter ensued here. I waited until he quieted down.

"And Mom and Tío think I've gone off with Gurn to DC. See? That's how I got Tío to take care of Baba, Tugger, and Lady Gee."

"So they don't know you might not be back in time for Stephen's funeral, which is the day after tomorrow? If you're not here, Mom will kill you."

"I'll try my best to be there."

"You don't think this is going to explode in your face?"

"Absolutely. Big-time explosion. But it should be over by then. This is something I have to do, and by myself, Brother mine."

"Man, when you go wiggy, you don't mess around, sister mine."

Chapter Twenty

In Pursuit of the Missing

The flight to Rio was just as I'd hoped, soothing and peaceful. I rarely fly first class, and usually only at Lila's insistence. In this case, I knew I had to get a good night's sleep for the day ahead of me. In first class, the backs of cushy, leather seats went nearly all the way down to form a bed, narrow but doable. A fluffy pillow, soft blanket, eyeshade, comfy slippers, and a strong martini — bruise that sucker, and don't spare the olives — and I was out like a light.

I awoke to a soaring bird's take on Rio de Janeiro, a major, tropical city basking on the edge of a continent. The aerial view of the enormous statue of Cristo Redentor, or Christ the Redeemer, perched atop the Corcovado Mountain, is truly breathtaking. Throw in world-famous Sugar Loaf Mountain directly opposite, and you know why this view is one of the seven natural wonders of the world.

While the plane taxied to the gate, I turned on my phone. Five messages awaited me: one from Richard, another from Gurn, and three from Lila, not a good sign.

I listened to Mom's edicts first to get them out of the way. All began with, "Liana, this is your mother speaking," and segued into variations of the "get-your-butt-home-and-now" theme. I assumed my big-mouth brother spilled the beans. Boy, was I going to let him have it.

To keep it clear, Lila Hamilton-Alvarez does not use words like butt; it's me giving an overview. My mother doesn't even use the word derrière, unless she is speaking to the seamstress about the refitting of one of her designer gowns. She contends you have no secrets from your doctor or your seamstress. But at no other time do ladies discuss body parts.

I deleted her messages because my butt wasn't going anywhere until I did what I came to do. I tend to discuss body parts.

I moved on to Gurn's message. This darling, sweet man called to let me know a dozen red roses would be awaiting me on the doorstep when I arrived home from Vegas. That was the day before, of course, and I could only hope Tío had found them and put them in water.

Then I phoned my turncoat brother and let him have it as soon as he answered. When he could get a word in edgewise, he threw it back at me.

"Listen, you ninny. I didn't say a word. I didn't have to. Flowers arrived yesterday morning from Gurn, saying how much he missed you. Tío figured out right away you were up to no good. You know, he's not a stupid man."

"I never said he was," I interjected, feeling I was losing ground by the second.

Richard pressed his self-righteous point, the stinker. "If you weren't home or in DC, Tío knew you were off getting into trouble. He called Lila; Lila called me, and I never promised I would lie for you."

"No, of course not."

"We don't do that."

"No we don't," I conceded and was contrite. "What's done is done. Let's move on, Richard."

He made a noise like a pelican swallowing a fish too big for its gullet. "Where did that come from? Is that some third-rate mantra from a feel-good school of the seventies?"

"It worked so well on Nick, I thought I'd give it a try on you."

"Well, save it, and get your arse back home."

Richard isn't from Mom's school of thought on the indelicacies of body parts either. His tone of voice sobered after his declaration, less smirk, more sincerity.

"Lee, listen to me. This is serious now. I found out some information late last night, and it changes things. That's why I called."

"Like what?"

"Like the man listed on the manifest as the girl's father. He's dead. Rio police found him floating in an estuary not three miles from the beach the day before yesterday, shot in the back of the head, execution style. Probably an untraceable World War II gun, they're thinking, like a German Mauser. There's a ton of them for sale on the black market where you are. Sis, if this is Kelli, and she did this, you are out of your league. Did you at least call the two brothers yet?"

"I just got off the plane. Give me a minute."

"Just remember, you can't go it alone. If you can't reach them, come home. Or wait for backup. We can send two men to help you. Ed and Pete are available."

"Not happening."

"Lee," he whined, not liking my answer.

"Richard," I whined in return, doing a fair imitation of him. "Stop worrying. It'll be fine. Changing the subject, how'd you do on nearby hostelries?" By now I was off the plane and walking through the terminal, heading for customs.

There was silence for about ten seconds. Richard was the first to give in with a loud expulsion of air causing me to pull the phone away from my ear.

"Okay, for the moment, I'll drop it." I heard the clicking sounds of his mouse, probably as he was bringing up information on his computer.

"There are seventeen of them scattered around. Six don't have computer check-in, if you can believe it. You'll have to check those out yourself. But of the eleven I could rule out, A–there is no single woman registered by herself, B–no younger woman with an older man, or C–no female child with a father. So Kelli's not at one of those as far as I can tell."

"Good going. Of the six left for me to do, are there any, shall we say, of the high-priced spread?"

"What?"

"Elegant, expensive, have the niceties of life?"

"Wait a minute." More clicks.

"That's one noisy mouse you've got there," I remarked.

"I've got you on speakerphone. It picks up everything. Ah, here they are. There are three: La Posada del Mar, Casa de Linda, Hosteria de Bougainvillea. The del Mar and the Linda are both on the border, right over the canal, in Leblon, but most people still think of it as Ipanema."

"All three are on the beach, right?"

"On Avenida Vieria Souto, which is across the street from the beach," he corrected. "Nothing's allowed on the beach. I thought you knew that."

Richard is a stickler for the facts. Whereas I find facts often get in the way of what I'm trying to do.

"Right, right," I said, brushing his words off. "Addresses, please."

Richard delivered, and I scribbled them on a notepad to put into the GPS on my phone. "I'll get back to you soon," I said, almost hanging up.

"You'll get back to me in an hour," he shouted so loud, a passing woman with a baby stroller turned and stared at me. "Or I'm calling the local police and sending them out to find you. You check in every hour on the hour, or all bets are off. Maybe I'll come down and drag you back myself."

"Okay, Tuffy Toes. I get the message."

My reply was light and fluffy, but I knew Richard meant it. I'd have to remember to call him and punched an alert into my phone to beep me every hour. Brothers are such a pain.

Speaking of pains, I'd had to pay an exorbitant amount of money to a San Francisco professional service to get a fast visa for me, allowing me into Brazil. Not sure why, but a passport is not enough. Life is filled with these sorts of things.

While waiting in line at customs, I made a few phone calls. As promised, the first was to the Janardo brothers. There was a long message in Portuguese on their answering machine, something about being out on their client's yacht for the next few weeks. That was all I could make out. Maybe they were guarding him against jellyfish or sharks. Too bad, but it wasn't going to stop me. I'd just keep this little tidbit of info from Richard until I got back home.

The next call was to Gurn, and his voice mail picked up, praise be. I left a quick, cheery message about my change in plans and thanked him for the flowers. I didn't mention I hoped he would be tied up in meetings for several more hours before he listened to it. Maybe everything would all be over by the time he got my message.

And maybe the result of my going "wiggy," as Richard said, was I would be spending some solitary time down here, licking my wounds because I had been cut loose again by a fab guy who couldn't stand what I did for a living and how I did it.

Determined not to stay any longer in the mental valley of death, I looked up the three remaining hostelries on Richard's list on my phone, plus captured a picture of Kelli I'd managed to find, blurry but better than nothing.

Customs went fast enough. By nine thirty, I was standing in the sun at the rental car lot. Waiting for my car, I felt a brain-piercing hit of direct sun on the top of my head. Stupid me, I forgot my sunhat. Way to go, Lee.

The seasons are reversed south of the equator, and weather-wise, it was late spring, pushing into a hot-and-humid tropical summer. I pulled off my jacket and using its scarf, tied my hair back into a ponytail. Beads of perspiration on my forehead and upper lip had already begun to form. It was going to be a hot one.

Deliberately renting a yucky, nondescript beige car, I tossed my small carry-on bag into the massive trunk. Throw in a shower, and I could have rented the trunk out as a hotel room.

Once inside the car, and with the air-conditioning blasting, I set the smartphone on GPS, loaded in the addresses, slapped it on the dashboard, and started the sixteen-mile drive to my destination.

Heading into their summer vacation season, Rio's roads were packed. I looked around and understood why. True, it was warm and humid, but the locale gorgeous, laid back, and fun, especially where I was going.

I had only been to Ipanema once as a kid, but I remembered it vividly. The main drag, Avenida Vieria Souto, attracted the hot, beautiful, and half-naked, swarming the street and sidewalks in their thongs and tans. As a non-Portuguese speaker, Spanish proved very useful during our visit, as it would now. If you speak slowly enough, the cariocas, or locals, understand well enough for everyone to get by.

All three of the hostelries Richard gave me were facing the beach, tucked away at the end of charming cobblestone streets. I looked forward to browsing the cafés, shops, and boutiques jammed alongside each other, colorful and unique. All in all, if you have to be somewhere, Ipanema is not a bad place to be. I found myself enjoying the ride, even singing that stupid tune I couldn't get out of my head.

Speaking of heads, after I parked the car on a side street, I dashed into a small store and bought a wide-brim, floppy hat for traipsing around town. My plan was to walk to all three small hotels, starting in alphabetical order, the Casa de Linda.

The Casa de Linda proved to be a bust, although it cost me two hundred *reals*, or the equivalent of about eighty US dollars. The greedy hotel clerk, an old bag named Alonzia, decided to bilk me for as much as she could before admitting the only female guests they had were three middle-aged women from New Jersey. My new hat and I stood out on the sidewalk in disgust while I formed a better plan. My direct-and-honest approach had not worked. Not only was it money for nothing, Alonzia wasted about twenty-five minutes of my time.

At the end of one the cobblestone streets, and behind thick stone walls, the Hosteria de Bougainvillea sat in regal repose. Once through its massive flamingo-pink wooden gate, I found myself inside a garden of lush, bird-filled palm trees. Covering the ground was a profusion of coleus plants, luxuriating in the perfect combination of soil, sun, and shade. Large, glossy leaves bobbed in the light breeze in patterns and shades of red, maroon, yellow, gold, green, dark brown, and black. Clinging to the outside walls of the hotel, purple bougainvilleas cascaded from roof to ground, exquisite in color and abundance. A narrow pathway of earth-tone-tinted tiles cut through all this glory, leading me under an intricately carved limestone arch and into an indoor-outdoor lobby. Distinguishable from the rest of the garden only by its slate floor and forty-foot-high domed ceiling, it was open to the world on two of its four sides.

Off to the right, one of the two walls was of chiseled stone. Burbling water tumbled down from its crest, passing over fern-dotted rocks, and trickled into a small pool filled with golden koi fish, each roughly the size of a small child. On the opposing wall, orchids of every variety imaginable clung to chunks of moss-covered rocks. In hues of purples, pinks, yellows, and white, these flowers looked happier than a plant has a right to be dangling from such a precarious position.

Overhead, the glass-domed ceiling, inset with swirlings of small, cobalt-colored mosaic tiles, sparkled dark against the lighter blue of the sky. Dappled rays of sun played through the transparent sections of the dome and onto the terracotta-and-cream hues of the airy and sumptuous lobby. Weaving throughout this marvelous room were several sitting areas, with comfortable-looking, cushioned teak and bamboo chairs and sofas. Matching tables proudly displayed sculptures, works of art, and the occasional exotic plant, obviously visiting from the garden.

But before me was the pièce de résistance. I beheld an open, massive passageway leading to the beach, from which long, gossamer-thin white sheers danced in the day's breeze.

The azure waters of the Atlantic seductively beckoned from behind, soft waves caressing a white-linen beach.

The whole effect seemed to invite you in to park yourself and never leave. I, personally, could have spent my life in it. This amazing room was pretty much deserted, though, with only two older, prim-looking women sitting and reading books.

Discreetly tucked away in one corner of the stone wall was the registration desk. A young man of about twenty, dressed in white from head to toe, gave me a warm, beckoning smile. I sashayed over, glad I'd broken down and bought the pricy, floppy-brimmed hat. I maneuvered a flop over one side of my face and giggled as I approached him.

"Hi," I said, in my best Valley-girl voice, trying to sound younger than my thirty-four years. "What a cool place! This is sooooo me." His face wore a quizzical look, but he nodded, encouraging me to go on. "Do you speak English, dude?" I took a chance the younger generation was still using the word "dude," or he would think I was stuck in a time warp.

"Of course, miss." His answer was smooth and polished, with only a hint of a Portuguese accent, the smile never slipping. "How may I help you?"

"Well, I see some, like, older ladies sitting in your lobby, not that there's anything wrong with being old, right? But not for me for a long, long time, if my plastic surgeon has anything to say about it." I draped myself on the counter and batted my eyes at him, although upon reflection, how he could have seen them under my low, floppy brim, I'll never know.

"Yes?" He grew pensive, not sure if he was talking to a potential hotel guest, a nutcase, or maybe both.

"So I was wondering—dude—before I check in and all, are there any younger girls here I can hang with and have some laughs, you know, in their mid-twenties or so? I don't want to be in a place that's not happening, you know?"

"Ah!" His smile returned in full force. We both had glossed over the mid-twenties bit, him probably thinking I'd either had a very tough life or forgotten about ten years somewhere along the line.

"We have two younger women here," he replied smoothly. "One who is what they call a snowbird from Canada and is with us four months out of the year."

"And the other?"

"She is from Florida, I believe." He smiled at me, spreading his upturned hands out and shrugging his shoulders. "Naturally, I cannot say anything more. We respect our guests' privacy."

"Naturally. She's been here four months too?"

"No, about a week." He smiled. "But she is the quiet type and does not go out much, only to take the tan in the garden next to the beach." I could see him struggle with the loss of a potential sale. "I am sorry, but we are not too happening at the Bougainvillea. It is more like the bed and breakfast, not the hotel of full service. We are quiet here. Possibly it is not—"

"Would it be all right if I looked around? Just to see if it's what I want."

His manner became starched and withdrawn. "I would be delighted to send one of the staff with you to show you a room. There are twelve of them, all facing the ocean, six upstairs, six down. The only rooms available are on the second floor — there are two — and the price is eight hundred and fifty US dollars a night." His voice had a slight challenge in it when he recited the price.

"Well, I just love it," I said, sweeping the lobby with my eyes. For the moment, I was telling the truth. And I love a challenge.

"Oh, what the hey, I'll take a room for the night." I reached inside my handbag, removing my wallet. "Cash is all right, isn't it? I left my credit cards in my luggage outside."

"I will still need to see your passport, *señorita*."

"Oh, right." I hauled out the fake passport I carried for such emergencies, in the name *Mildred Pierce*. It's the title of one of my favorite black-and-white movies from the '40s starring Joan Crawford before her wire-hanger days.

Business out of the way, I strutted down the understated but magnificent corridor, with plants on either side dripping from hanging pots, and surrounded by enough artwork to fill a gallery.

A young man, even younger than the desk clerk — so now we're talking twelve years old — marched before me wearing a bellboy's uniform of burgundy and tan trimmed with gold and topped off with a matching, gold-braided hat. I felt like I was in an old Phillip Morris commercial from the 1950s, *Your Show of Shows*.

He opened the door for me, with a preposterously big smile on his face and stepped aside. The cross ventilation from the opened door caused a breeze to rustle my own set of gossamer curtains which led out to a stone- and cobalt-blue-tiled terrace. On one side of the terrace sat my own hot tub and bar. Ahead was a phenomenal view of the ocean. A wall of glass doors, now open, could otherwise slide into pockets at either side during a hurricane or inclement weather. I crossed over and stroked the teak framing and glanced at the unobstructed view of the Atlantic. All rightie, I could live here.

I turned back and concentrated on the interior. The suite was opulently furnished in a tropical, teak, stone, and bamboo sort of way, calming but cheerful at the same time. Different sizes and shapes of mirrors lined walls that didn't have Brazilian art clinging to it. Cushioned furniture in rust, wine, and black, with matching throw pillows and lamps, had been coordinated to live together as only an interior designer can coordinate.

In one corner, near the dining area, a live macaw sat in a large cage, silent, nonmoving, and staring. It wasn't until he flapped his wings that I knew he was real.

A hanging sign, written in several languages, said "Do not feed or tease." Environmentalists would have a field day about an establishment putting a bird into a room with strangers. I planned on saying something about it myself upon my departure.

I dismissed the costumed kid with a ten-dollar tip, hoping it would spread like wildfire about the big tipper, who had just come to town. It might prove useful later on.

The adjacent bedroom had a king-size bed festooned with feather pillows and comforter. I threw myself down on the soft bed, sending carefully arranged pillows flying.

I felt a wave of depression come on. Richard was probably right. I had gone wiggy. And then there was Lila. Man, the thought of my mother's reaction to what I'd done sent me down so low, I had to take a mental elevator to get there.

Mom was going to have a cow — six, probably — when she saw all the time and money I was throwing around in my search for the elusive Kelli. Everybody else, including the police, thought Kelli was dead, a victim of Spaulding's vendetta.

But not me, no matter what anyone said. I shook my head in disbelief at my own behavior. I suspected what I was doing was almost certifiable. Or was it? The feeling, the intuition about her being here was so strong, I couldn't help myself. Scenes had played over and over again in my mind of the short time I'd spent with Kelli,: every nuance, every gesture, every possible hidden meaning. And there was the "Girl From Ipanema" song I couldn't get out of my head.

From what little I'd learned about her, she sent out partial truths mixed with lies, especially if she wanted something. Reviewing it all, I came to believe I knew her better than most other people. And what she wanted, in my opinion, was a change of identity, fifty million dollars, and Ipanema.

Somewhere along the line, I might have to stake my reputation on this belief. Oh, wait a minute. I'd just done that.

Realizing the pickle I'd gotten myself into, I let out a deep, soul-shuddering sigh. Maybe, once again, she'd duped me and didn't even have to be around to do it.

Despairing, I rolled over on my back, spread eagle, and stared up at the twenty-foot-high teak ceiling. Tears rolled down the sides of my face and into my ears. I'd alarmed my brother, disappointed my mother—again—worried my uncle, and probably made my boyfriend mad as hell. In short, I was going to get it from all sides. And for what? Even if she were alive, she could go anywhere fifty million dollars could take her. I had to face it. Kelli, at the tender age of twenty-two, was way too wily for me.

After about fifteen minutes of feeling sorry for myself, boredom took over. I was lying on a soggy pillow; my eyes burned; my ears were wet, and I was starving. Expelling a whumph sound, I fought off the surrounding feather-stuffed bedding, got up, and checked my watch. Eleven thirty a.m. Nearly lunchtime. But first, a barre. That's what was the matter with me. I was no longer centered: spiritually, mentally, or physically.

With a somewhat lighter heart, I left the hotel to collect my small valise from the trunk of the car. Returning to the room, I yanked out my dance clothes with a determined air. I would center myself if it killed me. I threw the leotard on, abandoning the tights in the warm weather, all the while noting again the stunning view of the ocean in the distance and the tops of the palm trees in the gardens below.

I may be doggy doo tomorrow when I return home, but today I was in a plush hostelry on one of the most beautiful beaches in the world. Deal with it, Lee. So I dealt.

I tied the belt around my waist and stepped out barefoot onto the terrace. The stone flooring felt cool and welcoming to my hot feet. Detouring for a split second to the minibar next to the hot tub, I snatched a small bag of peanuts from the top shelf and ripped it open.

Munching happily and feeling better, I padded over to the railing of the balcony and gave myself over to the panoramic feast before me.

Then wondering about the landscaping of the gardens below, I glanced downward. My reaction was so sharp, my startled movement so violent, peanuts went flying in every direction from the small, plastic bag.

For there she was, lying on her side, sunning herself on a chaise lounge.

Kelli.

Chapter Twenty-One

An MIA Sighting

I dropped to the floor as flat as possible. Then I craned my neck up and over the lower rung of the railing, straining my eyeballs to get a view of the prone figure below. I was panting, just like a gerbil I met once whose wheel was her obsession. Kelli was my obsession, so I guess it was only fitting I'd pant the same way.

Just then, my phone started beeping its reminder. I had missed the first hour of the scheduled call to Richard, and there's nothing like being yelled at by an irate, self-righteous baby brother to make you feel like an idiot. I wasn't going to let it happen again.

I crab crawled backward across the terrace to the beeping phone inside the living room. Just as I reached for it, it rang.

Dang, I thought, *Richard is becoming annoyingly like Mom, Frank, and Tío. What's with everybody in the family, anyway? Checking up on me every three minutes. You'd think I didn't have the sense God gave a lemon.*

I looked at the incoming number. *Lila! I might have known.*

"She's here," I blurted out, not even saying hello. "She's right below me in the garden asleep on a chaise lounge in the sun!" I tried to contain my excitement and the volume. It was tough.

There was a slight pause as my mother digested this information. "You mean, Kelli, of course."

"Well, duh! Not Amelia Earhart!" I was giddy in my victory. It was short lived.

"There is no need to be sarcastic, Liana. It is not appreciated."

"Sorry, Mom, but I mean... really, I... sorry."

"Never mind, dear. You're sure it's her?"

I dropped down again and did my crab crawl across the terrace and back to the railing, speaking in a hoarse whisper the entire way. "Absolutely, even though she's got a major tan, and her hair is a different color. I know one of your friends changes her hair color the way I change handbags—"

Mom clucked in disapproval. "Marsha is never satisfied, poor thing."

"Personality overview aside, all I know is, whatever Marsha's color of the week is, it always looks pretty natural."

"A good colorist is the key."

We'd beaten that one to death, so I went on. "Kelli has hers dyed a dark brown, but the cut and curls are the same. And her skin tone is much darker—"

"Probably one of those self-tanning lotions."

"That's my thinking." I strained my neck up again and looked down, taking everything in with more care. Kelli was still lying on the chaise lounge, on her side, arm stretched out under her head, exactly in the same position she'd been on my couch a short time ago.

"There's no doubt about it, Lila. It's her. Or is it, 'it's she'? I can never remember."

"Liana, do nothing and call the police. Watch her from a distance but do nothing. Understand?"

The beauty of phones is, if you don't like what someone is saying, you can pretend you can't hear them, the reception went suddenly and inexorably kaplooey. It's one of the supposed downsides to a modern convenience I embrace wholeheartedly.

"What's that, Lila? You're going in and out now. I can only hear every other word. Hello? Mom? Hello?"

And so a sputtering and exasperated mother found herself disconnected from a headstrong daughter. Wasn't the first time.

Before I did anything, I backed up from the railing again. Out of Kelli's probable sight line, I sat on my haunches and thought things over. One thing for sure, my chaffed knees and hands were going to need soothing lotion after this back-and-forth routine on the stone floor. Maybe a total body massage. Yummy.

I crawled forward again and looked down at Kelli, who was in such a sound sleep, she wasn't even stirring. I set the phone on vibrate, tucked it into the belt of my wraparound leotard, and stood up. I took a chance and went inside for my sandals. Knotting a pareo around my waist to make the ensemble look more beachy and presentable, I threw on the floppy hat before running back out to the railing. I held part of the brim over my face, just in case, and peeked down. Kelli was still in the same position as before. Maybe she'd had a busy, long night spending all that money. Maybe she had a hangover. All good for me.

I tore out the door, loped down the stairs, and through the side passageway leading guests to the street and the beach beyond. A perk for the ground-floor rooms was their own private garden. Comprised of sand-loving tropical trees, bushes, and flora, this well-tended garden had access to the sea while providing a certain amount of privacy from passersby. From the sidewalk, what you saw was a wall of greenery, with a small, centered wooden gate leading to each garden.

Behind the gate, small wrought-iron tables, chairs, and lounges were placed both in and out of the sun, for the guests' preference. Each of the six gardens was separated from the others by the same green, bushy things, which created the illusion of privacy but in reality, provided handy-dandy viewing if you leaned in and parted them a little. I love stuff like that. A quick but stealthy zip around the street side of each garden showed me no one else was using theirs except for Kelli.

While the beach across the street was crowded, hardly anyone was using the sidewalk. It was lunchtime, and the sun was climbing to its hottest of the day, maybe the reason there was no one else around. Or maybe it was my lucky day. I have so few of those; it was hard to tell.

Returning to my original spot, I peered through the tall, green, bushy thing, making sure Kelli was still lying on the chaise. Freeing myself from the lacy tendrils, I followed the sandy path back to the street. Then I hung a left. The sand was silent beneath my sandals as I entered Kelli's garden and crept closer to my sleeping prey.

Kelli was wearing a neon-pink bikini, modest by today's standards. Her deep-golden tan — manufactured, surely — set off the brightness of the fabric even more. She still lay on her side, eyes closed, fingers reaching out soft and delicate from the outstretched arm beneath her head. The cushioned, white-and-tan lounge chair was lowered to lie flat and looked about as comfortable as any bed I've seen.

A pair of hot-pink, high-heeled leather sandals rested on one side of the lounge. On the other side and flat on the ground, lay a large cloth-and-leather beach bag in gorgeous shades of hot pink, orange, and yellow, so high end it screamed, *You have no idea how much I cost, so go ahead and try to buy me. I double-dog dare ya.* A matching headband encircled a hot-pink panama straw hat on the ground nearby, hot-pink sunglasses thrown carelessly on part of its brim. We were into pink, I gathered.

Flickering sunlight from the breeze-stirred palm fronds created moving patterns of light and shade on her sleeping body. Between the cool, light wind from the ocean and the sounds of the surf, I think the savage breast could have been soothed in just about anybody. Anybody except me. I was still hopping mad. Take my cats, indeed.

"Hello, Kelli," I said, tossing the ruby-and-silver ring onto the ground near her. It landed with a clunk. "I brought you your ring."

My voice, even though I'd tried to keep it soft in this peaceful paradise, sounded like an announcement coming from an overhead speaker at a carnival.

She didn't move. At first, I wasn't even sure she'd heard me. I saw a slight quivering of a muscle in her outstretched arm and then a fast movement toward the beach bag lying nearby.

But I was faster. One step forward, and my foot stomped on the clasp of the bag. Kelli froze, hand midair. I bent over, keeping an eye on the still woman, and picked up the bag.

"Looking for your sunscreen? I'll get it for you."

I opened the bag, noting its heaviness. Inside was an old World War II German Mauser. Just like the one Richard mentioned reading about online.

Pushing the well-oiled gun aside with a bit of Kleenex, I rooted around and found a small bottle of sunscreen. After I pulled it out, I threaded the large-handled bag over my arm, resting it firmly on my shoulder. I tossed the bottle on the ground where the bag had been.

"There you go."

Kelli sat up slowly, reluctantly, almost like a little girl being caught playing hooky at the movies instead of being in school. She didn't look up, just kept her head down, her body hunched over, arms interlocked, hands clasped together and placed on her closed knees.

"How did you find me?" Her voice sounded thin and small, almost contrite.

"You do a lovely version of 'The Girl From Ipanema.'"

My voice, in contrast, had a triumphant edge to it I couldn't keep out. *Vindication,* I was thinking. *Maybe I am as smart as a fifth grader. Maybe I'm almost as smart as you, Kelli.*

"I'm not going back," she said. This time her voice had no contrition, only conviction.

"Oh yes you are. You're going back, and I'm taking you."

She looked up at me for the first time, her blue eyes vivid against the dark hair and deep tan.

"Fifty million dollars is a lot of money. I'll split it with you. You can do a lot of things with twenty-five million dollars." She studied me with frank openness.

"No thanks. I see what happens to your business partners. I'll pass."

She looked down at her bare feet and wiggled her toes. A small smile passed her lips.

"I thought you'd say that. I don't know why you hate me so much."

"Kelli, if there was an Olympic medal for standing, sitting, or leaping gall, you'd win the gold."

As outraged as I was feeling, I tried to keep my voice level and calm. I further resisted the urge to bite her on the knee but wished Tugger was there to do it for me.

"They were all against me." She sighed after a moment. "All those men. I had to do what I did." The expression on her face had an innocence a nun couldn't duplicate.

"You're one piece of work, aren't you? But spare me the blameless routine. I know it was you who shot your husband even though you tried to hang it on Spaulding. And I mean your legal husband, Eddie, and not Nick. Although how Nick managed to stay alive around you, I'll never know. Who's this new guy? The dead man who was pretending to be your father? You've got them crawling out of the—"

"He wasn't pretending to be my father," she interrupted. "He was."

My eyebrows shot up into my hairline.

She noticed my reaction and snickered. "Don't look so shocked. Not every man who sires a kid deserves a Father of the Year award. My scumbag of a father didn't, for sure."

"You're sitting there trying to defend murdering your own father?"

She didn't answer but stared at me coolly for about half a minute. I thought she was going to bolt, and I prepared myself to tackle her to the ground if necessary. By God, I found her, and I wasn't letting her get away.

Instead, the only movement she did was to grab each breast with a hand, or as much as her small hands could hold. "You see these?"

"They're hard to miss in neon hot pink."

"I've had them since I was eleven years old. Eleven. That was the summer my loving father made a deal with his boss at the used car lot. A weekend with me in exchange for a promotion and a little extra cash. So dear, old Dad took the deal and never looked back."

She gave out a chortle, then turned away, but not before I saw a hardness come over her features I've only seen on actresses vying for a Golden Globe award. It left as quickly as it came but remained in her eyes as she faced me again.

"Now you really looked shocked. His boss did things to me I still have nightmares over." Her voice changed from anger to bitterness. "And he kept doing them for two years—every time his wife was out of town—until I was thirteen and had the sense to threaten to go to child endangerment." She released her breasts from her grasp and lay back down again, still angry, still bitter.

"My father tried a few times after to do deals with other men, but by then I knew better, not like when I was a little kid." She shook her head in disgust. "That's the kind of lowlife my father was, pimping his own eleven-year-old daughter." She let out a high-pitched cackle, which led into a small sob. "And that's why I often consider these things more of a curse than a blessing." She glanced down at her chest.

"W-where w-was your mother?" I stammered, hardly able to get the words out.

"She took off when I was three. I don't know where she is. Who cares? I don't need anybody."

"How did your father get you involved in this Spaulding scam? It was his idea, right?"

Another cackle, less high pitched but just as off kilter. "Oh, please. He wasn't smart enough. I've spent my life surrounded by stupid men trying to control me, use me." She leaned forward, a wicked smile crossing her face.

"It was all my idea. I brought dear old Dad in on it when I knew I'd probably need to get out of the country in a hurry. The police wouldn't be looking for a father and child. I got the fake passports maybe six or seven months ago. I waited until things were right to use them."

We had a plethora of fake passports going on around here, my Mildred Pierce being only one of them. I felt a flash of resentment. *How dare she? With me, it was different. After all, I was a PI. I had a legitimate reason for... wait a minute... never mind.*

"What do you mean, when 'things were right?'"

She grinned like the Cheshire cat. "You ever play games? I love games. I play them on the computer all the time. Like dominoes. Ever play dominoes?"

"Dominoes? What's dominoes got to do with anything?"

She studied me for a moment, then looked away with a laugh. "Jesus, you really are stupid, just like the rest of them. I thought you were smarter. The night you followed me back to Vegas, you acted like you were. I saw you were right behind us. First, I'd seen Nick in the rearview mirror, with that big guy. That's why I had Eddie leave the car in the parking lot of the Fantasy Lady. I wanted you to have time to get the cats and take Lady Gaga back with you. I couldn't bring her here with me. After you were done, I sent Eddie back out to the car to drive home. You followed him, and I followed you. When you left, I snuck in the back way and took care of business."

"You figured a few additional suspects in Eddie's death couldn't hurt."

"It was easy." She looked at me and said pointedly, "You were easy."

For a moment, I was completely at a loss. Then things clicked together so fast and so furiously, I'm surprised the noise in my head didn't scatter the birds in the trees.

"You set all of us up. Eddie, Nick, Spaulding, me, even your father."

"Now you're getting it." She leaned forward, licking her lips in anticipation of the new game she and I were playing.

"You meet and marry Nick, even though you're already married to Eddie, to get close to his client, Lou Spaulding."

"Exactly."

"Somehow you get hold of Spaulding's books. Then what? Real hubby, Eddie, who's in on this from the beginning, pilfers money from the mob accounts, digitally copied the books on the microchip—not just for the fifty mil but as blackmail."

Kelli looked at me with a disappointed air. She let out a noise that sounded like the buzzer for a wrong answer on a quiz show. She lay down again.

"Incorrect answer. Eddie didn't even know how to read a ledger let alone drain money from it. He was a computer geek. You're just like all the rest. You don't think I'm smart enough to embezzle money. Nobody does. Stupid little blonde bimbo with big tits. Well, I took accounting in night school for a year and a half. It was simple."

"All right, so it was simple." My mind started racing again. Let's face it; I love a good game.

"Let's do this methodically," I said. "You get involved with Spaulding, siphon off money from his bank accounts, taking digital pictures of the entries of the second set of accounting books for extra measure. Eddie steals a microchip and downloads the images onto it, not just as potential blackmail on Spaulding but... so... you could pin the theft of the money on Nick!" The last words were said in a rush. "That's why you put the chip on Nick's dog tags, so Spaulding would go looking for him and not come after you. Nick was a decoy. By the time Spaulding could figure it out, you'd be long gone."

She looked pleased and sat up again. "You're getting better."

"But Nick got away; nobody could find him, and you decided to come to me for help."

Her face clouded over. "That was a mistake."

"You needed me to flush Nick out. Either Spaulding was getting suspicious, or you were simply running out of time. When I refused to help you, you took Tugger and Baba. Another mistake."

"I used them to make you find Nick, so I could tell Lou where he was. And just so you know, I'd never have hurt the cats. But it got you to Vegas, searching for Nick. That's what I wanted."

"And your plan was back in action." She nodded. I looked down at her, totally involved in the game now. "How did Eddie get involved?"

She sat up taller and nodded. "When I was sixteen, I thought he was my ticket out of the horrible life I lived. You know, when we were dating he only kissed me once. I thought I was safe. So I forced my father to sign the papers, and Eddie and I got married. Then it started all over again, the demands, the touching, always grabbing me."

Her body began to writhe in revulsion as she thought of it. "All those *things* he wanted me to do, just because I'd said 'I do.' It was disgusting. But eventually I found it easy to get Eddie under control. He wound up doing anything I told him to and never asking any questions, especially if I did put out now and then. But what I wanted was freedom, and money equals freedom."

"Spaulding and the syndicate's money? Chancy stuff," I remarked.

"Not if I did it right. Last year, Lou Spaulding came into the casino, throwing money around like it was water. He was an important, rich man, part owner of his own casino. I knew he liked the ladies and spent lots of money on them, because one of the women, a pit boss, got a three-bedroom condo out of the deal, and she'd only been with him eight months. Right after he dumped her, he hit on me, but I was a lowly blackjack dealer, so I only got a night in the sack.

"Just one night got me a bottle of perfume and a thousand dollars in chips. But he'd left his books sitting out on his desk, just like that. He probably thought I was so stupid I didn't know what they were. He dismissed me and handed me a hundred for a cab home the next morning, but it came to me. The pit boss, she'd been married to the hotel owner's cousin. He liked them married. Nobody knew I was married; I'd kept it a secret. I was going to tell him, but it occurred to me. It couldn't be as Eddie's wife. It had to be a *somebody's* wife. If he thought I was coming at him like somebody's wife... well... he'd probably pay more attention and for longer. Men like a challenge."

"And you thought Nick was somebody?"

"Nick had a successful real estate business, and I saw him and Lou having lunch a couple of times, talking, laughing, just like friends, equals. I didn't know Lou saw Nick as a small-time asshole until later. When Nick looked at me the same way Spaulding did, I knew I could have him." Her voice tapered off. "It didn't even take much effort."

"So you married Nick even though you were already married to Eddie, and after a respectable amount of time, had a thing with Spaulding for, what, two or three months?"

"He loved screwing around with his real-estate agent's wife, just like I knew he would. It made him feel so macho. What a jerk. Being his girlfriend made me somebody, but I was going for more than that. All I had to do was hold his attention long enough to get at those books. I found out where he hid them in the second week and started making transfers and withdrawals while he was recuperating from our sex life."

"You're kidding."

"I'd put half a sleeping pill in his drink right before we screwed. Having sex took a lot out of him, anyway. You know, he's fifty-eight. He would be out for at least an hour each time. Then, after I had everything in place, I told him Nick was onto us, had managed to get a microchip with copies of his accounting books on it, and was hell-bent on revenge. Lou knocked me around a little at first but got very protective after that." She threw her head back and laughed. "Poor, stupid Nick. He didn't have a clue."

"Your plan was Spaulding would kill Nick for the evidence on the chip. If Spaulding didn't go to jail for murder, maybe you'd make sure he did for embezzlement. Were there two data chips? One for Spaulding to find, and a second one ready to send to the FBI, as added insurance?"

"You're getting good," she praised.

"Why kill Eddie?"

"I wasn't taking him with me even though I'd told him I was, and I couldn't leave him to talk. Men seem to do that a lot." She looked at me with cool detachment. "My father thought getting rid of Eddie was a good idea too."

"He knew about this?" I tried not to sound as incredulous as I was feeling. "All of it?"

"From the beginning. As long as he got his share, he didn't care what I did to anybody else." She threw her head back and laughed. "But he didn't think I would do the same thing to him. Another asshole."

She stared straight ahead for a moment, lost in what seemed to be a deep emotion. Then she burst into tears and leaned forward, almost tummy tucking into herself.

"Oh God, listen to me," she wailed. "What kind of person have I become? I must be crazy, mental." She cried into her hands with deep, gulping sobs.

I leaned forward to comfort her, one consoling hand on her shoulder. It wasn't planned. I didn't think about it. It was instinctive.

I didn't see the knife but felt the sharp sting of it as it grazed my chest in its upward quest for my throat.

Chapter Twenty-Two

An Iago Kind of Villainy

I grabbed her hand just as the blade reached my throat, pushing down as hard as she pushed up. Kelli was stronger than I'd thought. Our arms shook almost as one from the exertion and strain. With her other hand, she grabbed my hair and tried to pull my head forward into the knife. Maybe only a second or two went by, but it seemed like an eternity to me.

My karate teacher will probably never forgive me, but instead of doing one of the exquisite moves I'd been learning for the past five years in his classes, I chose the killer volleyball method from my old college days. I swung my free arm back, the exposed part of the palm where the thumb meets the wrist aimed right for Kelli's face. Then I hauled off and slugged her in the mouth as if she was the ball and I was driving that sucker down into the center of the opponents' court for a winning score. Kelli flew backward over the lounge, with me snatching the knife from her hand as she fell.

Even though my serving hand hurt like hell, I looked down at my burning torso and let out a string of expletives a sailor would have blanched at. From the middle of my chest halfway up my neck, a thin ribbon of red began to show. It stained my ripped leotard even in places not cut by the knife. I studied her weapon of choice, a small, two-and-a-half-inch gutting knife, with a hook on the end. It could have done some serious damage rather than one helluva scratch. This was, indeed, my lucky day.

I hurried around to the other side of the lounge where Kelli lay spread-eagled and moaning. She would revive soon, so I gave her a thorough body search to make sure there weren't any other hidden surprises. Now I understood her need for the more modest bikini. I found and removed the leather sheath for the gutting knife, tucked into the front of the bikini, near her belly. Nothing else. After the search, I pulled the scarf from my ponytail and tied her hands behind her back so tightly, I'm sure I cut off circulation. I wasn't taking any more chances with this one.

* * * *

Twelve hours later, I sat on a plane heading back to the States, too exhausted to sleep, my mind going over what happened again and again, like a film loop stuck in a projector. Looking back on it, the day's luck had held for me. In fact, the next time I crab about any lack of said luck, someone take a CD with "The Girl From Ipanema" on it and smack me over the head.

The officer in charge, Capítan Almaral, speaking fluent English was only a small part of my good fortune. Mainly, he had worked on a drug-running case in conjunction with Dad years ago. In fact, it had been the reason for our trip to Ipanema when I was a kid. Dad had smoothed out some drug-bust improprieties on the California end and went to South America to help wrap everything up, combining it with a family vacation — i.e., the capítan was very familiar with Discretionary Inquiries and the Alvarez family.

Plus, the day Kelli shot her father, an eyewitness had turned in a report of a person answering the description of the new-and-improved Kelli leaving the scene. The Brazilian police had been searching for the suspect for two days. For me, all good luck. Not so good for Kelli. The capítan thanked me generously for doing much of his work for him.

He pushed through papers that should have taken days, had me sign off on my part of everything, and got me on the first plane home. Albeit with a two-hour layover in Atlanta, Georgia, but let's not get petty. I would land in Palo Alto the following day in time for Stephen's funeral. That's all I cared about.

As I stared out the window into black nothingness, I had a long chat with myself about the idea of bringing Kelli back with me and my ensuing, but ridiculous, guilt at not doing so. My ego was at war with my conscience, both putting in an appearance at thirty-six-thousand feet. You can never get away from yourself.

Ego: *Lighten up. You only said you would take Kelli back with you in the excitement of finding your prey.*

Conscience: *Yeah, but you said it. And once it's out there, you need to be true to your word.*

Oh, stop it. You were talking through your hat as Raymond Chandler would say. Who are you kidding? Reality check: Even if you had managed to start the journey back with her, she'd either wait for the first opportunity to cosh you over the head or do something to create a major confusion. Then she'd make a run for it. Just two of the possible thousand things she could pull.

Maybe you're right, but you have a way of being wrong too.

Shut up, Toots. There was no way you could trust Kelli unless she was so heavily sedated, she couldn't move under her own steam. I suspect that wouldn't go over so well with the airlines.

If you'd tried to take her out of the country, where she's wanted for the crime of murder, it would be a felony. Get caught by the Brazilian authorities, and you could wind up in jail yourself. That's all you need. Besides, thanks to you and DI, relations between Brazil and the United States couldn't be better. Okay, maybe only Ipanema and Palo Alto, but still. You have been heralded as nothing short of a hero, a heady and rare experience for you. Even Lila seemed impressed when the capitán spoke to her over the phone, conveying his gratitude.

I sat back in the leather seat, making peace with the events and my unexpected role in them. I am usually the sous-chef of DI, in that I gather, slice, prep, and put the culprits on a plate, so to speak, and hand them over to Lila. Then my mother throws a parsley sprig on them, and presents them to the world at large, collecting all the applause. This time, instead of being behind the scenes, I had apprehended the suspect in an internationally cooperative way. All in all, I had done a good job. I became smug in the assessment of my actions.

Then I revisited the look on Kelli's face right before they took her away because Latina Catholic guilt and I are old friends. Scared and miserable, she'd cast me a fleeting look of hope right before they hauled her off as if somehow I might save or rescue her. Probably at that juncture, going back with me was preferable to spending her life in a South American hoosegow.

"Promise me you'll take care of Lady Gaga," were the last words she'd uttered.

I would have thought she'd curse at me, spit at me, scream that I'd caused her downfall. Instead, she wanted a promise I'd take care of her beloved goldfish.

I felt my eyes fill up at the memory. Even if only a small fraction of what her father did to her was true, she'd been abused horribly as a child. It didn't justify what she'd done by a long shot, but it did explain a part of it. Uh-oh. My conscience was back in full force. My ego rebounded, coming front and center.

Whoa! Hold the phone, kiddo. Before you get carried away and hire her a defense attorney, time for strong Note to Self: You're lucky to be alive. Some people, like her husband and father, were not so fortunate. Save your sympathies for starving widows, orphans, and people in Third World countries.

Kelli is one dangerous woman. Don't let her sob story fool you. And don't let her concern for Lady Gaga get to you either. It's Lady Gee now, anyway. She's yours and has been ever since you took her from the back of the station wagon the day Kelli catnapped Tugger and Baba. Remember?

And putting the fin swimmer aside, Kelli would probably try to kill you as soon as look at you. Wait a minute. She did.

I touched the line of sixteen Band-Aids running halfway down my throat and onto the top half of my chest as if to prove my point. Sometimes I can be tough to win over.

A whispering voice brought me out of my reverie. I turned toward the sound and saw the flight attendant, a blonde woman about my age, leaning in with a smile.

"Excuse me, miss. You're Lee Alvarez, right?"

I nodded, looking around at the rest of the first-class passengers, most of whom were fast asleep. Mom had insisted I fly back first class, and the capítan had managed to get me the last seat.

It being around 1:30 a.m., the lights had been dimmed to accommodate the late hour. Even still, I couldn't help but notice the woman's healthy, clean, and well-scrubbed good looks, in sharp contrast to my own.

The tic had returned to my right eye, and I had steamer trunks loitering under each eye in place of the usual bags. I'd lost the floppy hat somewhere along the line, and my hairbrush had also gone AWOL. Renegade tufts of hair broke through the confines of a rubber band I'd snitched from the capítan's desktop earlier in the day, when I still had the energy to try and do something with my mop. I didn't know what happened to my treasured scarf once it was removed from Kelli's wrists, but gone it was. I was still in the throes of grief over its loss.

I wore no makeup as it had hopefully been packed in my overnighter by police officers while I was being interrogated, in an effort to help me to make the plane. Fingers crossed that my makeup kit was indeed residing with the rest of my stuff in the belly of the plane. If not, I was out several hundred bucks, not to mention my favorite color lipstick, Raspberry Poof. No longer being manufactured, it could not be bought for love or money. My lips and I were enamored of that lipstick.

Speaking of lips, when I wasn't thinking about my swollen and achy volleyball hand, I felt like I was getting a cold sore on my upper flapper. Either that or I had bit my lip when no one, including me, was paying attention. Maybe around the time someone had been trying to cut my throat.

To sum it up, I looked and felt like a bucket of horse manure. It had been a hot day with no shower, so maybe I smelled like one too.

I studied the flight attendant or, rather, what was in her hand. A small metal tray rested directly under my nose on which sat a frosty cold martini, brandished with two huge olives. My eyes crossed as I looked down.

"The captain sent me over with this," she murmured, "at the request of Gurn Hanson."

I blinked several times, staring at her, slow on the uptake.

She smiled again, and I know her orthodontist is proud. She had a sparkling and glorious set of choppers, unlike me. Only moments earlier, I'd found a stray piece of spinach loitering on my front tooth, thanks to the airline's tasty dinner. But did they provide you with dental floss at the end of the meal? No. I had to dig the green stuff out with a toothpick I'd found at the bottom of my handbag.

"T-the pilot of the plane sent this?" I finally stammered, trying to concentrate on the icy liquid and not recalcitrant pieces of spinach.

"Yes, that's right," she continued to whisper, smile never fading. She nodded her head reassuringly as if I were a backward three-year-old, not taking the lollypop as my reward at the end of a visit to the dentist office. Whoa. Do I have teeth on the mind or what? Moving on.

"The captain told me to bring you this," she said again, but this time emphasizing each word. "Captain Silvers said he and Mr. Hanson served together in the navy reserves. They're old friends."

I silently took the drink, still trying to grasp what was going on.

Meanwhile, she undid the food tray on the back of the seat in front of me and set down a napkin. A small silver bowl of mixed honey-covered nuts miraculously appeared from I don't know where. Her third hand, maybe?

"Mr. Hanson contacted Captain Silvers, asked him to do a favor and bring you a martini. He said you probably needed it." She let out a soft laugh. "I think so," she said, more to herself than to me.

I started to laugh, too, and took a sip of the fortifying nectar.

"Oh, and I nearly forgot." She reached into a pocket of her crisp blue uniform. "Here's a note from Mr. Hanson via the captain. I don't know who this Mr. Hanson is, but the captain's never done anything like this before." She thrust the folded note into my other hand, winked, and drifted away as silently as she had come.

I set the martini down on the food tray and opened the note with stiff fingers. It read, *Gurn said for you to have this drink on him, and he would be waiting at SFO when you landed. I saw you come onto the plane. He's a lucky guy. Tell him I said so.* Scrawled right below the hastily written note was the name, *Ron Silvers.*

He thinks Gurn's a lucky man? Maybe I didn't look as bad as I thought. Wondering, I squinted at my reflection in the side of the shiny silver bowl.

OMG, I thought. *As if. Well, there's no accounting for taste.*

Then I giggled, wondering how many rules these two silly men had broken to get me this drink, not to mention the note. I chomped on one of the honey-coated nuts, sipped my drink, and for the first time since I started this mess in Ipanema, felt a bit more relaxed and optimistic.

Chapter Twenty-Three

A Winding Down

"That's the last of them," I said, after I'd practically slammed the front door shut on the backsides of the funeral attendees, a couple I'd never met before, who ate more than some frat boys I've known. True, Tío had made some amazing food for the gathering after the short but intense funeral, but still. "I thought they'd never leave."

"Liana, there's no need to be rude," my mother chastised me, heading back to the family room. I followed, while she warmed up to the subject. "In a situation as sad as this, people need time to mourn with friends."

"Six hours? I think they met Stephen once at a Bar Mitzvah. And they ate all the samba corn fritters…"

I stopped speaking as Mom stopped, turned around slowly, and glared at me. I almost bumped into her but pulled myself up short.

"Not that I begrudge anyone a fritter," I finished lamely.

"*Mija,*" said Tío, coming over to me, carrying a small white porcelain tray. "I have made more. *Aquí tenes.*" He thrust the tray at me, laden with hot, golden corn fritters, fresh from the oven. I grabbed one. I still hadn't made up for nearly being starved to death the day before. These days, airplane food, even in first class, just doesn't cut it.

"If people *wanted* to stay and remember Stephen," Lila sniffed, "then it was only *right* we let them do so and extend the hospitality of our family. Jennifer was *deeply* grateful for our taking charge of these arrangements."

I remained unswayed. "Mom, the funeral was over at one thirty. We came back here supposedly for a small gathering of friends and family. Even Jenn and the kids left at five. It is now seven thirty p.m. We're lucky the food held out as long as they did."

The kitchen door swung open. Richard and Gurn walked out, chortling quietly together as if they had just shared a private joke. They sobered instantly, when they realized they were among others and at the solemnity of the occasion.

"I guess we should start clearing up," Lila said, ever the mother. She let out a deep sigh and picked up two glasses and some soiled napkins from the coffee table.

"Here, Mrs. Alvarez," Gurn said. "You sit down and rest for a minute. I'll do that." I watched the man I love empty Mom's hands while guiding her to the sofa. After everything all of us have been through together, him practically saving her life a few months back, he still addressed my mother by her surname. That's a Southern gentleman for you. Of course, Mom still lets him, but that's a California snob for you.

"Why don't we all park ourselves for a few minutes?" I said. "We haven't had a chance to talk, what with all those people milling around, and my feet are killing me."

"We don't 'park' ourselves, Liana. We are not a car," Lila chastised again quietly. I watched Richard, Tío, and Gurn struggle to keep smiles from their faces. Mom's gentle chidings have become something of a family tradition, especially when directed at me.

"However," she continued in a much warmer tone, glancing over at me with approval, "I think it is a good idea to sit for a moment, converse among ourselves, and reflect upon the day."

I reflected if anyone wanted to check out a living, breathing character straight out of one of Jane Austen's novels, just come on over to my house and meet my mother.

"Yowser," I said, flinging myself into one of the overstuffed leather chairs. I removed the brand-new four-inch dark gray stilettos, which would never see my insteps again, comfort being mandatory for any pair of shoes worn by me. The soon-to-be banished heels had been purchased to go with the rest of my outfit, a battleship gray vintage designer suit I'd found in a consignment shop a few months previously. I would keep the suit. I usually hate dreary colors, but when I saw this beauty for a fraction of its worth, I couldn't pass it up. I'd never worn it before — like the shoes — and hoped to never have to wear it again for such a somber occasion. Maybe at a happier time, I could spiff it up with a bright blue dickey, instead of the current black one, and throw on a few of my turquoise baubles.

I watched as the rest of my family and Gurn positioned themselves on the sofa and in the matching chairs arranged around the large coffee table. I was glad we were done with the funeral and the gathering, not that the aftermath of Stephen's loss was spent, but we could all take a breather and maybe try to get back to normal, whatever that was.

I turned to Richard. We'd both been so busy playing junior hosts to the fifty-odd people who showed up, we hadn't had any time for chitchat since I'd retuned from Ipanema.

I opened my mouth to ask about the whereabouts of his wife and my sister-in-law, the much-adored Vicki, when he said, "You did a good job in Brazil, Sis. How you managed to pull it out of the fire, I don't know, but good job." He picked up one of the warm fritters from the tray Tío had set down on the table, held it up in a salute, and took a huge bite. Everyone else muttered in agreement, nodding their heads in unison.

I tried not to preen. I was feeling pretty smug, not to mention awfully lucky.

There's the luck thing again, I thought. *At any time we cross a street, we can find a million dollars, get hit by a car, or get to the other side with nothing happening, where we go about our business. The X factor.*

I looked over at Lila for confirmation on my terrific-ness, but she wasn't listening. She looked tired, more tired than I'd seen her in a long time. There was something on her mind, too, something weighing as heavily as the day's happenings.

"Mom, you look exhausted. Why don't you head upstairs? Don't worry about the mess. We'll clean up here."

I could see she was considering it. Mom stood and stretched in a languorous, chanteuse sort of way, very unlike her.

"Maybe I will. But first, I want to inform the family of something, now we're gathered together." She sat down again, studying her pale-pink enameled nails, as if taking time to find the right words. "Tomorrow morning Jennifer and I are looking at houses around here. I want to show her a three-bedroom two blocks away I've found at an excellent price, with good schools and a mother-in-law unit in the back, perfect for her mother. In fact, the house is perfect for them. It was a rare find. There will be no other."

I studied my mother for a moment, a woman who looked like the cat that swallowed the canary, albeit wearing pearls.

"You've already bought it for her, haven't you?"

I've never seen Lila Hamilton-Alvarez so taken aback.

"W-well, I..." she stuttered and then froze. Even with trust funds floating around like balloons at a parade in our family, buying a house in a place like Palo Alto was noteworthy.

"Well, I..." she said again.

Then she drew herself up into a stiff sitting position and spoke as belligerently as a fourteen-year-old boy caught with a *Playboy* magazine.

"Yes, I did, as a gift from Roberto and me. The truth is Stephen didn't leave Jennifer as well provided for as I'd hoped what with the economic problems the country has been having lately. He had lost quite a bit on his investments. I'm sure he'd planned on making those losses up..." Mom stopped talking abruptly and pressed quivering lips together.

"It's a wonderful gift, Mom," I said, leaning in. "I'm sure it will make all the difference to her and the boys, especially now."

Mom gave me a grateful look. "I hadn't known until recently there were two mortgages on their home in Arizona, almost for more than its current value. Even if she could manage to sell it, she'll make no money. In fact, it might be better if she simply walked away." She paused for a moment and added in an almost inaudible tone, "I think your father would have liked my doing this."

"Yes, he would have, Mom," said Richard with certainty. "Dad always believed that we need to take care of our own."

Mom let out a deep breath and smiled, obviously feeling loads lighter.

"I'm glad the family understands. I was somewhat concerned you might see this as me being foolish or intrusive in Jennifer's life. It's not that way at all. The house is in her name to do with as she sees fit in the future. But for now, she will have a home and be near us. Even her mother thinks it's a good idea."

"And she's one tough sale," I commented.

"Indeed," Mom said, agreeing with me, something she rarely does.

"*Eres muy generosa, hermana,*" Tío said. "But I do not know you to be less."

"Thank you, Mateo. It feels right." Mom turned to me, changing the subject. "Liana, did I hear Frank tell you a short while ago nearly every partner in the Fantasy Lady had been indicted on charges of illegal gambling and match fixing? He left before I could ask him."

"Well, it might be more complicated than we'd like," I said. We were back at talking about business. The tenor of the room changed, becoming less fragile and emotional.

"Putting aside most of the owners of the Fantasy Lady reside outside the United States, the crimes themselves took place in different countries. This could take years to sort out."

"But the syndicate is no longer operational," Gurn said, jumping in. "Spaulding is locked up without bail, having been charged with the attempted murders of Flint and Lee. Then, thanks to the evidence Richard got from the casino and coupled with what the FBI got off the microchip, most of the partners tied to Spaulding have been indicted for aiding and abetting, no matter where they reside." Gurn glanced in my direction. "After what Spaulding tried to do to Lee, though, I've made it my personal business to see he and his syndicate go down. In fact, I fly to Washington day after tomorrow to sit in on a meeting of an expert panel on the process of international crime convictions. Representatives from several countries affected—Peru and England come to me off the top of my head—will also be there. Working together, I believe justice will be served."

"And is there justice for our Stephen?" asked Tío quietly. "And for all the poor ones whose lives are gone?"

"No, of course not," Gurn answered, looking into his almost empty coffee cup and studying its contents. "No one can ever make up for that. All we can do is to punish the guilty to the fullest extent of the law and try to give the surviving loved ones a little peace."

There was a moment of silence, heavy and oppressive. I can't speak for anyone else, but it felt like someone had dropped a fifty-pound weight on my chest. Richard's voice filled the void.

"It's one of the reasons Vicki and I decided to name the baby Stephen, if it's a boy, or Stephanie, if it's a girl. Maybe a little more familial peace."

I gaped at him, springing to life only when his words registered. A baby!

"Richard," I screamed. "Richard! You sly dog, you! Is that why Vicki keeps disappearing all the time?"

I lunged from the chair and threw myself at my baby brother, grabbing him around the neck in a bear hug. He stood up pretending to fight me off but holding me just as tightly as I was holding him. He giggled, and I giggled, and suddenly everyone in the room was giggling.

"It's her morning sickness, but it comes all hours of the day. It should be over soon. She's nearly ten weeks." He giggled again and then sobered. "Not that it's funny. I shouldn't be laughing at her morning sickness. She's so tired of saltine crackers."

"Ten weeks! How long have you known?"

"About two weeks now. We were slow on the uptake. We thought she had the flu," he said, his voice filled with joy and laughter, no matter how hard he tried to be serious.

I broke free, searching the other, happy faces gathered around. No one else seemed surprised.

"You all knew? The rest of the family knew?" They nodded, even Mom grinned from ear to ear. Most unlike her.

"Some days, it was the only thing keeping me going. I wanted to tell you, Liana," she offered. "But your brother insisted it should come from him."

"*Un bebé*," said Tío. Tio came over and clapped his nephew on the shoulder, words of congratulations and love uttered in Spanish. Simultaneously, Richard and I reached out for him. Tío went on, "*Dios*, he closes one door but opens another."

We heard a sharp intake of breath and, locked in our three-way embrace, looked over at Mom, still sitting in the same position as before.

"Every time I think about it, Roberto," she said as if Dad were in the room, "our first grandchild…" And then my mother, Lila Hamilton-Alvarez, burst into tears, burying her face in her hands. "I'm sorry," she said through tapered fingers. "All these highs and lows have been difficult. Forgive me."

Well, that did it for me. I ran over to her, threw myself down by her side, and started boo-hooing on her shoulder.

Richard joined in, laughing as much as crying. Tío offered up prayers of thanks, which would have done the pope proud, his watery eyes shining with happiness.

I heard Gurn's voice amid the lamentations. "Well, Lord love a duck; does everybody in your family cry at such good news? Must be the Latin way." He set the dirty cup down on the coffee table and looked at us, one after the other. "When Rich told me, I smiled and clapped him on the back. I think I even bought him a cigar."

"What do you mean, when he told you?" I shot Richard a questioning look, then turned back to Gurn. "How long have you known?"

Gurn, realizing he might have put his foot in it, waffled. "Oh, not long. How long would you say, Rich?" He threw the question back at my brother.

"Maybe a week," Richard answered, head held high.

"A week?" I said indignantly as only an older sister can say. I glared at my brother.

"Listen here, Sister mine, I tried to tell you. You never let me."

"Well, I had a few things on my mind, like solving Stephen's murder and getting the cats back. Trips to Vegas, and Ipanema, and getting shot at, and knifed—"

"I'm not saying you didn't," he interrupted, "but I tried to tell you," he repeated, "at least four times." He held up four fingers for emphasis.

"Don't you worry about it, Richard," Mom said, dabbing at her eyes with a silk hanky she always carries on her. "Your timing is just fine. Liana, stop this nonsense right now. Until today, other things have taken precedence over sharing this news within the family." She blew her nose delicately. "Honestly, you and your hot-blooded temper. Why do you have to take after your father in *every* way?"

"You're right, Mom. I'm sorry. Sorry, Richard." I leaned over and kissed him on the forehead. "Sister yours apologizes."

"And what's this about you being knifed?" Mom said suddenly, her voice raised and demanding.

I watched as all eyes turned on me except for Gurn's, who had seen the fine exhibit of Band-Aids on my chest earlier, when he helped me put antiseptic on the wound... among other things.

"Knifed?" My voice had a high-pitched, strangled quality to it. Gurn looked me dead in the eye as if to say, "Get out of this one if you can, Toots." I gave it a try.

"Did I say knifed? Ha ha. I meant scratched. I got a scratch. By a little, tiny, small, insignificant sort of... thing... sort of like a nail clipper. It's just a scratch. Nothing. It's nothing. Forget I mentioned it." I turned to Gurn, who was biting his lower lip to conceal the smile.

"Gurn, why don't we start taking stuff back to the kitchen?" I babbled, jumping up and grabbing a stack of dirty dishes before anybody could say anything more. "The rest of the family, stay put. Relax," I ordered. "We've got this."

Gurn picked up glasses and soiled napkins from the table. I ran over to him and started pushing him through the door. Once in the kitchen, I dumped the dishes on the white marble countertop, where they landed with a clatter.

"Whoa! That was close."

He didn't reply but grabbed me in an embrace and started laughing.

"What's so funny?" I demanded.

"Here you are, on your high horse because Richard didn't tell you about the baby first thing, and you didn't tell them what Kelli did to you in Ipanema."

"Well, I don't want to scare them. And they need never know. Fortunately, it's cooler weather, so until the world's longest scratch heals, I'm wearing turtlenecks." I looked at him with a sheepish grin. "Do you think I'm a bad person for not telling them?"

He pulled me close, nose to nose. "Yes, just awful," he whispered.

We kissed, and my toes curled. All right, maybe not literally, but they sure felt like they lifted off the tiles a little.

I let out a small sound somewhere in between a gasp and a sob, then leaned against his chest, glad for the support. "It's been a horrific last ten days. I can't remember being this exhausted."

"As my mother would say, you're 'bone weary.'" He kissed me on the forehead. "I think what we need is a small getaway for a day or two. The four of us."

"The four of us?" I repeated.

"You, me, Tugger, and Baba. I know a charming bed and breakfast near Hearst Castle where they take pets."

I leaned my head against his chest again and nodded into it. *If only I could shrink-wrap my heart, protect it a little. But it's too late for me.*

Aloud I said, "Maybe after a rest, I won't feel so guilty about keeping what Kelli tried to do to me from my family. It's the first time I've ever done that. Usually, I burp, and the Alvarez clan knows about it."

"There's an enchanting image."

We both laughed. He went on.

"Most people have a secret or two they keep even from those they're closest to, Lee. Sometimes for their own good. Like when you didn't tell me about Spaulding attacking you, until after the race."

I raised my head and stared directly into his eyes not saying a word.

"I know what you're thinking," he said. "You're thinking postponing saying something is different than never putting it out there at all. Too many secrets can separate a couple, keep them from being as close as they should be, as they'd like to be."

I moved away and over to the sink.

"I thought you'd say something like that." Gurn turned toward the dishwasher.

"Smart, aren't I?"

"Help me load the dishwasher, will you?"

"Sure, as long as I don't have to handle any knives. I'm a little leery of them these days."

"You hand me everything but the knives. I'll get them later. How's that?"

He swiveled, faced me, and gave me the Gurn grin. I threw it right back at him. We stood there for a moment basking in each other's grins.

"Man, I do love you, Liana Margaret Alvarez. You are worth just about anything to me."

"Enough to tell me who you really are and what you really do?"

"Probably." He turned away again and opened the door of the dishwasher. "Rinse the stack of dishes and hand them over."

We both worked for a time, not saying a word, not looking at one another, but there was something sure and easy about it. I felt oddly content, even happy.

"Lee." Gurn's voice broke through my thoughts and dreams. My back was still toward him, but I held my breath. "I want you to come to North Carolina with me and meet my parents. I told them about us. It's time you met."

I stopped what I was doing and turned around to face him.

"It's a long plane ride," he continued. "There's a lot of time for me to tell you… some things."

I swallowed hard, almost unable to reply. Finally, I said, "I would love that."

~~

Read on for the first chapter of
Book Four of the
Alvarez Family Murder Mysteries

DEAD... If Only!

DEAD....*If Only*

Book Four

In

The Alvarez Family

Murder Mystery Series

Heather Haven

Chapter One
Can It Get Any Dirtier?

According to song and legend, for the past few centuries hot sulfuric mud is sucked out of caverns loitering beneath the hills of Calistoga. For the privilege of parking your backside in the stuff, big bucks are sucked out of your bank account. Only in California do you pay through the nose for something most kids can run outside and jump into after a rainy day.

I did find a twig or two earlier, but was reassured by the spa attendant, Rainbow, the trees and all their inhabitants died long ago. I tried to embrace the thought as my new phone rang out with Beethoven's Fifth.

At eight-oh-five in the morning I should have been suspicious. I should have known disaster can find you wherever you go, but I was a reluctant PI on much needed vacation. I guess you could say my sixth-sense was on vacation, as well.

My name is Lee Alvarez and I'm the in-house P.I. for Discretionary Inquiries, the family owned Silicon Valley detective agency. I was tired and in need of a little R and R, having recently wrapped up a case, a big one, involving the entire Alvarez clan, gawd help me.

There are probably worse things than working hip-to-hip with CEO and mother, Lila Hamilton-Alvarez, she who can shoot the tattoo off a fly at fifty paces in her size six stilettos, but I can't think of them. She's still your mother and there's something unnatural about it.

Throw in a techie geek of a brother, Richard Alvarez, he who fobs off the latest gewgaw on me while I'm busy taking down felons, and you have my life as of late. That's the downside of a successfully run family business, the family. The upside eluded me for the moment.

But glory hallelujah, everyone was out of my hair for an entire week, thanks to my brother's wife, Vicki. Said sister-in-law was opening a new branch of her hat shop, The Obsessive Chapeau, in New Orleans's French Quarter. Lila, Richard, and my Uncle Mateo, better known as Tío, went to help out. For one week. *Laissez le bon ton roulette*. Yup, let the good times roll.

They'd have been rolling a lot better if I'd known whether or not the mud I was laying in had been washed and hermetically sealed. I have a thing about creepy crawlies.

Regardless, when the Boston Philharmonic Orchestra plays its heart out, it's apt to get your attention. Especially when the blaring phone in question is out of reach and you're in a vat full of mud pretending to enjoy it.

The song ended but the melody lingered on, reverberating around the large white-tiled spa room. Meanwhile, I wondered who called. Not many people know my private number, just family and close friends. Still, there was the occasional carpet cleaning service drumming up business or wrong number. Was that it or was it something important? Let's face it, there's nothing more awful than an unanswered phone, even a smart one that makes you feel stupid.

"Sweetheart, I told you not to bring your phone into the mudroom." The voice of Gurn Hanson, the love of my life, wafted over the steam rising from our side-by-side tubs. He spoke in a slow, lazy voice and didn't even open his eyes; he was that relaxed. Mine were bulging out of my head.

We'd reached the point in our relationship where we could throw out the occasional 'I told you so' remark, in between proclamations of love. I hope we never neglect the proclamations.

I'd been in a disastrous early marriage, where not only were the 'I told you so's sans any declaration, but my ex- threw in the occasional punch for good measure. Thanks to a good helping of self-esteem and a black belt in Karate, I'd filed for divorce several years back.

So here I was, thirty-four years old, five foot eight inches of me, four pounds over the allotted one-hundred and thirty-five, curly dark hair in a knot atop my head, sprawled out in a revolting tub of mud, and telling myself to relax. After all, I was on a long awaited vacation, eating and drinking my way through Napa Valley, and sharing the experience with a honey of a man.

"Relax, sweetheart, relax," Gurn crooned then opened green-gray eyes and looked over at me. "Is it the phone you're worried about or leaving Tugger and Baba alone in the room?"

"No, I'm sure the cats are fine. They're noshing on kippers and catnip. I'm the one chin deep in disgusting muck. Who's sorry she's not a cat?" I muttered the last bit and wasn't sure Gurn heard me. It was just as well. I tend to complain.

The two aforementioned felines were my Tugger and Gurn's cat, Baba Ganoush, named after the eggplant dish. The fact our two cats were with us had nothing to do with the wine or mud, because I've never met a cat into that sort of thing. It was more the Alvarez clan, as previously mentioned, was off in New Orleans and I trusted no one besides Tío to take care of the little darlings. So we threw the cats into their carriers, climbed aboard Gurn's Cessna, and flew here to spend a glorious week living the high life, putting aside the current visit to a mudslide.

My phone sprang to life again. The Boston Philharmonic Orchestra and Beethoven's Fifth bounced off the walls once more. I tried not to think about it. Eventually, the phone stopped ringing, but Beethoven's 'ba ba ba bum' continued to bong around the room and in my head. I gotta change that ring one of these days.

"I think you should have left it in the room, but I probably shouldn't say that." Gurn gave me another wide grin.

I had to think for a moment of what he was talking about. Oh, yes. Phone. Mud. Yuk.

He exhaled a long, relaxed breath and closed his eyes, looking quite yummy, even covered with black gunk.

"It's your phone, sweetheart. You take it wherever you want."

"Thank you, but you're right. I am kind of indisposed and shouldn't have brought it with me." *Relax, relax, relax. Nope. Forget it.*

Too late I remembered that even as I kid, I was never the mud-cavorting type, preferring to stay clean and dry, playing with my Legos on the patio. My brother, however, sought every opportunity to be in mud. Gurn seemed to be enjoying his own foray. Maybe this was a guy thing?

I took a deep breath and choked on the sulfuric smell rising on clouds of steam. Buried under steaming dirt, I reflected on how a pig at a luau must feel. All I needed was an apple in my mouth. Then I thought about the posted warnings overhead: do not put your feet down on the bottom of the tub. I wasn't exactly sure why you couldn't, but it became my raison d'être. Among other things, that's French for 'What the hell did I get myself into?'

A large bubble found its way to the surface and exploded into the air. I tried not to scream. Rainbow, a flower child of the '60s, was quite firm in her introductory statement that any bubbles appearing were only trapped sulfuric gas. I chose to believe her.

Rainbow had passed what we define as "older" decades before, and was now racing toward eighty like a thoroughbred coming down the homestretch. Dressed in a tie-dyed, free-flowing robe, slathered in patchouli oil, and weighed down by dozens of love beads, her look was finished off by two silvery-white braids hanging down to her knees.

Barely audible New Age music piped through the sound system completed our trip to the Age of Aquarius, geriatric style. The phone rang out for the third time with Ludwig's finest.

"You know, Lee, you could move over to the side, get out, shower off, find out who's calling, and then jump into the hot tub. I'll join you there in about ten minutes."

Gurn opened his eyes and looked over, his wondrous lopsided smile enchanting me down to my muddy toes. "I suspect you're not enjoying this part of spa day."

I didn't need to be told twice. With about as much grace as a beached walrus, I rolled over to the side of the tub and splashed down on the white tiles, flinging dark glop everywhere. As I stood dripping onto the once spotless floor, I realized what a bitch it must be to keep the room clean. Note to self: never use white tile on floors. Too unforgiving.

The BP Orchestra went silent.

I leaned over to see who called and a chunk of mud fell from my neck onto the phone, obscuring the ID number. I gave up and padded toward the shower area. I'd like to say I rinsed off fast and easy, but I found mud in crevices of my body I didn't even know were creviced.

The phone beeped with sounds similar to Morse code on helium.

"What the hell is that?" I shouted from behind the curtain, hoping Gurn could hear me.

"That's your messaging notification. Someone's texted you."

"What do you mean, texted me? I don't have texting."

"You must have. Otherwise, it wouldn't be beeping."

"Fer crying out loud, you need a degree in computer science to figure out these phones."

I continued to grumble and grouse, but finally turned off the water and snatched a towel. Wrapping it around me, I made a dash for the phone, which stopped beeping as I reached for it.

Gurn chortled. "Somebody's persistent. I'm glad I left mine in the room."

I chose not to answer but picked up the phone, wiped off the mud with a corner of the towel, and looked at the incoming call list. "The number's blocked. It must be Richard."

"What makes you think that?"

Gurn no longer sounded like he was being fed Prozac intravenously, but alert and back with the living.

"He's one of the few people I know who has the guts to have a blocked number and not be an insurance salesman."

"So maybe it's Met Life."

"No, it's Richard." My sixth sense returned, albeit if only on two cylinders. "And where's this texting business?"

"I'll get out and show you." He made a move for the side.

"You don't have to do that, just tell me."

"It's better if I show you."

We heard a soft knocking and without waiting for a reply, Rainbow opened the door. She wafted inside, love beads clicking in rhythm with the braids swinging from side to side. How did she keep those braids out of the mud, I wondered? Tie them in a bow around her neck?

"Love, peace, and harmony, friends," her small voice wavered. "It's only Rainbow telling you it's time for grooving in the hot tub." She saw me on my phone and got a little prickly. "Oh, no, no, no. No cell phones in the place of tranquility." She straightened up as much as possible, waggled a finger at me and came forward, assuming the attitude of an elderly drill sergeant.

Gurn tried to cut her off at the pass. "Rainbow, why don't we let Lee do her thing and we'll do ours?" Without thinking, he tossed two muddy legs over the side of the tub and with the nimbleness of an acrobat threw himself into a standing position.

Rainbow gasped and turned away. We'd been told several times rules state that men's private parts must remain beneath the mud whenever female attendants are in the room.

"Sorry, Rainbow," Gurn said, as mud sloughed off him. "You'd better leave and come back in ten."

Our octogenarian ran out of the room like a vestal virgin pursued by a legion of Roman soldiers.

"You know, that could be considered elder abuse." I raised an eyebrow at Gurn.

Gurn ignored me and went back to the phone. "What makes you think it's Rich calling? I thought everybody was in New Orleans." He pulled excess mud from his arms and hands as he spoke, flinging it down to the floor. A not so clean hand was extended in my direction, with the goal of taking the phone from me. "Here, let me see it."

I turned away from him, deep in thought. "Okay, maybe it isn't Richard. He knows I don't text. My thumbs don't work that way."

"Only one way to find out. Give me the phone, Lee. I'll see." Gurn reached out a persistent hand again. "Come on, blue eyes."

"No, you've still got mud all over yourself. This thing cost over four hundred bucks, even with the trade-in of my old phone. Go wipe your hands on one of those towels over there." I pointed to several towels neatly folded at the side of the tub. "I can find the text thingamajiggy. After all, it's my phone." I pushed buttons and managed to turn on the flashlight.

With a shake of his head and a laugh, Gurn ran a quick hand down the front of my towel and made a grab for the phone. He was playful about it. I was not. Reluctant to let go of any power I had over the phone, be it zip, we went into a mini tug of war. Hands grappling one over the other, the phone escaped our grasp in an upward motion like a slippery bar of soap. Following a neat arc, it landed with a 'kerplop' in the middle of the tub.

"Now look what you did!" I stared in horror at the phone floating belly up in mud.

"What I did? Never mind."

Gurn reached over and lifted the phone out, snatched the towel off my body, and wiped off the mud.

"Is it dead?" My voice trembled at the thought.

"No, of course not." He continued to wipe the back of the phone with care, while he inspected it. "When the mud dries completely, we'll scrape it off. It didn't get inside, because you've got the protective case on it. See? Nothing's hurt."

He handed the relatively clean phone back to me and kissed me on the nose. I rethought my position. I was being too possessive and grumpy about one of my shortcomings. Technical stuff and I do not get along. And if Gurn knows more about Smartphones, who was I not to let him help me out?

The phone in my hand started its Morse code thing again.

"Sorry I was so snarky before. You want to show me texting? At least I know where the flashlight is now. You never know when that will come in handy."

He took the phone with a grin, swiped at something, and handed it back to me. "There you go. Just touch on the messaging icon."

I followed instructions and began to read the short missive. When I finished, I sank down to the side of the tub. It took me a second or two before I could utter anything, and then it was only a single word.

"Gurn."

He turned to face me, the one word stopping him from wiping his face on his towel. He carried it with him and sat beside me.

"What's wrong?"

"It *is* from Richard." Together we read the short but disturbing message in silence.

Fly to NOLA General Hospital ASAP. Terrible danger. Think Vicki will be arrested for murder.

I looked at Gurn. His face registered all the shock, confusion, and fear I was feeling. My voice shook when I spoke.

"If this is a sample of texting, I don't like it one bit."

~

Books by Heather Haven

The Alvarez Family Murder Mysteries
Murder is a Family Business, Book 1
A Wedding to Die For, Book 2
Death Runs in the Family, Book 3
DEAD... If Only, Book 4
The CEO Came DOA, Book 5
The Culinary Art of Murder, Book 6
Casting Call for a Corpse, Book 7

Love Can Be Murder Novelettes
Honeymoons Can Be Murder, Book 1
Marriage Can Be Murder, Book 2

The Persephone Cole Vintage Mysteries
The Dagger Before Me, Book 1
Iced Diamonds, Book 2
The Chocolate Kiss-Off, Book 3

The Snow Lake Romantic Suspense Novels
Christmas Trifle, Book 1

Docu-fiction/Noir Mystery Stand Alone
Murder under the Big Top

Collection of Short Stories
Corliss and Other Award-Winning Stories

Multi-Author Boxed Sets
Sleuthing Women: 10 First-in-Series Mysteries
Sleuthing Women II: 10 Mystery Novellas

About Heather Haven

After studying drama at the University of Miami in Miami, Florida, Heather went to Manhattan to pursue a career. There she wrote short stories, novels, comedy acts, television treatments, ad copy, commercials, and two one-act plays, produced at several places, such as Playwrights Horizon. Once she even ghostwrote a book on how to run an employment agency. She was unemployed at the time.

One of her first paying jobs was writing a love story for a book published by Bantam called *Moments of Love*. She had a deadline of one week but promptly came down with the flu. Heather wrote "The Sands of Time" with a raging temperature, and delivered some pretty hot stuff because of it. Her stint at New York City's No Soap Radio - where she wrote comedic ad copy – help develop her longtime love affair with comedy.

She has won many awards for the humorous Alvarez Family Murder Mysteries. The Persephone Cole Vintage Mysteries and *Corliss and Other Award Winning Stories* have garnered several, as well.

However, her proudest achievement is winning the Independent Publisher Book Awards (IPPY) 2014 Silver Medal for her stand-alone noir mystery, ***Murder under the Big Top***. As the real-life daughter of Ringling Brothers and Barnum and Bailey circus folk, she was inspired by stories told throughout her childhood by her mother, a trapeze artist and performer. The book cover even has a picture of her mother sitting atop an elephant trained by her father. Heather brings the daily existence of the Big Top to life during World War II, embellished by her own murderous imagination.

Connect with Heather at the following sites:

Website: www.heatherhavenstories.com
Heather's Blog:
http://heatherhavenstories.com/blog/
https://www.facebook.com/HeatherHavenStories
https://www.twitter.com/Twitter@HeatherHaven

Sign up for Heather's newsletter at:
http://heatherhavenstories.com/subscribe-via-email/

Email: heather@heatherhavenstories.com.

She'd love to hear from you. Thanks so much!

The Wives of Bath Press

The Wife of Bath was a woman of a certain age, with opinions, who was on a journey. Publisher Heather Haven is a modern day Wife of Bath.

www.heatherhavenstories.com

Made in the USA
Monee, IL
16 November 2021

82275761R00164